THE HOME AT GREYLOCK

The
Home
at
Greylock

BY

ELIZABETH PRENTISS

AUTHOR OF "STEPPING HEAVENWARD," AND "AUNT JANE'S HERO."

CURIOSMITH

MINNEAPOLIS

Published by Curiosmith.
Minneapolis, Minnesota.
Internet: curiosmith.com.

Previously published by ANSON D. F. RANDOLPH & CO. in 1876.

Scripture verses are from *The Holy Bible*, King James Version.

Definitions are from *Webster's Revised Unabridged Dictionary*, 1828 and 1913.

French translations are from Google Translate.

All footnotes were added by the publisher.

Supplementary content, book layout, and cover design:
Copyright © 2014 Charles J. Doe

ISBN 9781941281031

CONTENTS

CHAPTER 1

Mrs. Grey had been the happy mother of seven children; they all lived to grow up and marry, and to rise up and call her blessed, with the exception of her youngest daughter, Maud. People said it was a wise and kind thing on the part of Providence, that Maud was not one of the marrying sort. Her mother needed one child to help her down the declivity of life, and it was delightful to see them together. Some who were not acquainted with them, and who only knew them by sight, at church, contrived to see, out of the backs of their heads, that these twain could not live without each other. Maud shared in this opinion to the extent of firmly believing that she could not survive her mother. She was a good, dutiful, devoted child, whose sunny temper made her life like a song in the maternal ear.

"How good God is to me," was Mrs. Grey's frequent thought, "in giving and in sparing to me this darling child! How strange and how sad it would be to live alone in this large house! And Maud fits in to every crack and crevice there is in me as very few girls could. And she is so thoroughly and genially happy that it is not selfish in me to rejoice that she does not care to fly out of the nest!"

They were always together; and in their walks, and talks, and readings, in their visits to the sick and the poor, in their good-fellowship and innocent sallies of humor, they were more like two

sisters than mother and daughter. So they went on their way, rejoicing, till Maud had reached her nineteenth year, and then a stealthy
step crossed the threshold, and an inexorable hand seized upon this
young life and crushed it out.

But is this the way to put it? Is this the truth, the whole truth,
and nothing but the truth, uttered in the fear of God and the love
of Christ? No! a thousand times, no! The event had its sad, its tear-
ful, its sorrowful side; every stricken mother-heart knows that to its
core; but it had another side. The life of a young, blooming, mortal
frame was brought, humanly speaking, to an untimely end; but the
life of an immortal soul went to expand in a congenial atmosphere,
where it was far more at home than it had ever been on earth, where
all the problems that had ever baffled it, and all the trials that had
ever wearied it, had their full explanation; with none to molest, to
misunderstand, or to grieve it; beyond temptation, suffering, and
sin; in a word, to be "forever with the Lord."

Is it, then, a lot to be desired to die young? Certainly not. We
are to desire to die young, or live to a useless old age that cumbers
the ground on which it totters, according to the Divine will, not
according to our own short-sightedness; and this is what Mrs. Grey
thought and felt when the strong, bright light of Maud's presence
faded away from her vision, and she could see her no longer, save
by the eye of faith. Perhaps some few misunderstood the patient,
unselfish way in which this bereavement was met, and thought the
brave heart that endured such a sorrow with no clamor, was made
of steel. But those who really knew this bereaved mother, knew
the whole story. The life-long habit of Gospel love to the neighbor, and of faith in God as One who could not by any possibility
make a mistake, came to her rescue. It was right because He did it.
And what if she was sorely wounded, was she the only one lying
mangled on the battle-field? With characteristic energy she sum-
moned her absent children home; with her own hands she threw
open the rooms they were to occupy; and when, during the next
days, they came from all directions, in twos, and threes, and fours,

to gather around and comfort her, they found cheerful fires blazing, the sweet sunlight streaming in at the windows, and a smile upon her loving face. Not one of her children was surprised; they all knew what mother was. But some of the grandchildren were puzzled; why didn't grandmamma cry more? Why was she so taken up with all their little interests? Why, she even remembered that Julius was fond of oranges, and that Fergus liked cream-cakes! But they had been educated into such faith in her that they did not trouble their young heads with this problem; she was their dear, bright, loving grandmamma, and that was enough.

In a few weeks the little crowd she had called about her disappeared, and she was left alone, quite against their judgment. They all had pleasant homes to offer her, and it seemed to them that the large house they had once peopled would be fearfully lonely now. But she maintained that, with her health and strength, it was better that she should have a home and cares of her own, and a rallying point where they could meet on festal days, as heretofore. So she gradually fell back into the old routine, entering into every one's cares, and interests, and joys, and sorrows, exactly as if she had been created for their special use and comfort, going hither and thither on all sorts of busy commissions, and appearing very much as usual, only a trifle sweeter and gentler. One of her first deeds of kindness was gathering all Maud's clothing together, and sending it to her young friends or needy maidens; and so far from weeping over this task, she took delight in it, realizing how much pleasure she was about to give, or how much service to render. She even smiled at her own mistake, when she saw a very tall young girl try to adapt herself to one of Maud's petite dresses, and rectified it at once. But when it came to her child's favorite books and pictures—the things her heart and soul had reveled in—it was very different; she could not part with them. They had been separated very little, so that she had not a single letter from her to treasure up; but she found in the pocket of the last dress she wore a copy of an evidently favorite hymn, together with a few texts of Scripture. She gave away pearls, and diamonds, and lace that had been Maud's; but no king was rich enough to buy that half-worn scrap of paper.

Maud had many schemes of benevolence which it was now a sacred pleasure to carry out; and although when she now went forth on her errands of mercy, she appeared to go alone rather than with her loving child's companionship, she was not alone, and not unhappy; nay more, she was happy. For when, without a frown, she gave her darling into the Master's hand, He came and more than filled her place, giving the peace that passes all understanding. Now this consciousness of the presence of Christ in the soul is the one thing whose loss the Christian believer, who has once enjoyed it, cannot do without. Husband and wife, home, children, friends, reputation, may all go, and the heart still have a song to sing; but let Him go, or even seem to go, and all the beatitudes on earth are broken fountains that can hold no water. One may find distraction in congenial employment, and comfort and joy in home and friends; but real, abiding *happiness*, in its full sense, can only be found in Him for whom the soul was created.

Maud's room, with its lovely adjoining boudoir, was left for a long time unchanged. Her mother fed the canary and tended the plants she had loved, exactly as if the child had gone on a short journey and was soon to return. One or two books lay open, just as she had left them; and the whole air of the apartments was kept just what it had been, neat and orderly to precision, refined and tasteful to perfection. Mrs. Grey thought she should always keep these two rooms sacred to the memory of the bright, happy maiden who had made them what they were with her own hands; no other head should touch the pillow on which that fair one had once rested; no other eye should linger on the objects of beauty gathered there—the dainty furniture, the pictures and vines on the walls, the quaint hanging-baskets and brackets, and woodland and sea-shore trophies. She could almost hear the tap of the little hammer with which Maud used to go about nailing up this, that, and the other pretty thing she had picked up, or bought, or invented, and her gay song the while. But as time passed, there began to steal over her a vague sentiment, which later became thought; she must keep the rest of the house for the children and grandchildren; but was it right to shut up those beautiful rooms for one who would never return to them? Could not some other young girl come and nestle there, and enjoy what Maud no longer needed? When she first consulted friends on the subject, they all protested against it. Such experiments always proved failures, they said. It would have to be an extraordinary girl to fill Maud's place, etc., etc.

"But I never thought of filling Maud's place," she argued. "I was only thinking of the happiness it may be in my power to give."

"I should think that among all your grandchildren, one, at least, might be spared," some one suggested.

"But even if I were willing to break into a family circle in that way, and I am not, this would not meet my plan. My grandchildren all have happy homes, and need nothing better. But if I should light upon some friendless girl, think how she would enjoy my dear Maud's forsaken nest!"

"But you might find her uncongenial, even disagreeable."

A sweet, happy smile lighted up Mrs. Grey's face, as she replied:

"I should be doing her good, and trying to make her happy. And after all I have gone through, sustained by the Divine hand, ought I to doubt that if He sends me an uncongenial girl, He will give me grace with which to bear with her?"

Some said this was faith, and all right. Others said that if people went and thrust their heads into a bear's mouth they must expect them to be bitten off, faith or no faith. Now some years before, Mrs. Grey was feeling her way through the dark hall of a tenement-house in the city of New York, when her steps were arrested by the sound of a girl's voice, crying so bitterly that sympathetic tears rushed from her own eyes.

"Oh! mother, mother, mother, *don't!*" groaned the voice in an agony. "Oh! mother, mother!"

"Some brutal mother beating the poor child unmercifully," she thought, and knocked imperatively at the nearest door.

The sound instantly ceased, but as no other response was made, she opened the door and advanced, with a firm step, into the room. But she started back, shocked at her intrusion, when she found herself face to face with the weeping girl, who was at the bedside of an unconscious woman, reclining on a bed which had been drawn near an open window.

If the agony of the girl had been impressive, the control she was now exercising was not less so. She stood quietly, even coldly, confronting her unexpected visitant, who shrank back embarrassed, hardly venturing to utter a word. But the tender sympathy in her face did more than words could have done.

"Madam, do you know anything about sickness?" demanded the girl.

"Yes, my poor child, a great deal. Do not, I beg of you, treat me as a stranger; but tell me what it was you were entreating your mother not to do. She does not look to me in a condition to do anything. She appears to have fainted."

"I thought she was going to die; that was what I was begging her not to do. Oh! if I knew she had only fainted!"

"Has she been long ill?" asked Mrs. Grey, while she laid aside her cloak and proceeded to examine the prostrate form.

"Not to my knowledge, Madam. She was working, as usual, until twelve o'clock last night; but this morning she did not get up. I spoke to her, but she seemed confused, and kept growing paler and paler till I was frightened, and dragged the bed up to the window to see if the air would revive her. We had a doctor for her a month ago, and he said bad air was like to kill us both."

While the girl was talking, Mrs. Grey had taken from a basket of hospital supplies such restoratives and such refreshments as she thought best, and in a short time had the pleasure of seeing her patient aroused sufficiently to take the nourishment provided for her.

She had now time to take an astonished glance at the room in which she sat. It was not only kept with nicety and care, but there were signs of refinement. A palette with its brushes hung upon the wall; unfinished bits of color were pinned here and there; two or three plants grew thriftily on a shelf by a window, and the seats of several old chairs showed that undeveloped, but artistic taste had had to do with seats covered with woolen patchwork, beautifully put together.

By degrees Mrs. Grey gained the woman's story; it was commonplace enough, but was not narrated in a commonplace way, for not only was her tale adorned by a pretty foreign accent, but by sound common sense and good feeling.

She had married, young, a poor artist, who found her in her Swiss home, and was too eager to secure her to perfect himself in his profession. Neither of their families approved of the match, and they had made a foolish, runaway affair of it, coming to this country full of hope, but without a friend in it.

"My mother hadn't any mother, or brothers, or sisters; and her father wasn't her own father, and wasn't good to her."

Mrs. Grey looked the girl full in the face and smiled. "You think that makes a difference?" she said.

"I do, Madam. My mother never did anything wrong in her life."

What a firm young head was set on those young shoulders! It is not easy to describe, in words, the impression made by both mother and daughter.

"And how did you get on?" Mrs. Grey inquired, turning once more to Mrs. Haydon.

"Well, Madam, we got the punishment our self-will deserved. We knew no one in this country. My husband worked hard, but had no friend to encourage him. He sold pictures enough to keep us alive and, at times, comfortable. But we lived from hand to mouth, and if we had sickness, things went very hard with us. Then he began to get disgusted with his work. He would begin a picture that looked beautiful to me, but would throw it aside unfinished. And it ended just as such stories always end. He died, and I was left alone with my little ones to support myself as best I could."

"You must have married *very* young?"

"Madam, we were a boy and a girl, nothing more. The laws of my country compel education. I was at school when this folly took place, and when I was left a widow, my position was a very embarrassing one. I was not capable of teaching because I had left school so young; and yet I had come of a good family and been used to certain comforts. For a time I supported myself by embroidery, but this life of confinement and deprivation of sleep—for I had to work till midnight—injured my health; and a physician, whom I consulted a few weeks ago, told me that, what with over-work, poor food, want of exercise, and living in a sphere so different from that in which I was born, I should soon break down completely."

"What do you propose to do, then? Apply to your own or your husband's family?"

"Madam, they return my letters unread. No! I have made up my mind, and Margaret will make up hers when she sees that there is but one way of saving her mother's life. It is a poor life, not worth saving in itself; but it is everything to her. We have supported ourselves with needlework up to the present time, and the work I finished last night will bring in enough to give me a few days' rest, and we shall then go out to service."

"To *service!*" cried Margaret. "My mother go out to service!"

"Yes, my child. The bad air and the midnight work are killing me. The doctor says so. If we can get a situation in a gentleman's family, and get good air and good food, we yet may be well and happy."

"And your other children?"

"They are all, Madam, safe with the Good Shepherd."

"I admire and respect your resolution, and wish more of my country-women were of your mind. Thousands might lead useful, happy lives in our homes, who now lead aimless and comfortless ones. Servitude is no disgrace. I have formed friendships with women in my kitchen that I expect to last a lifetime. Still, I wish I could find some more suitable position for you. You would look for that of seamstress, I suppose?"

"The doctor says I must use my needle no longer."

"Ah, I have it! One of my daughters wants a nursery governess. That would be the very thing. You would take your meals with the children, drive out with them, get excellent compensation, and be as happy as the day is long. And to have a woman in her nursery who fears God, would be most delightful to her."

Mrs. Haydon looked down, and was silent.

"You think you could not have Margaret with you, perhaps?" asked Mrs. Grey, surprised. "But I could manage that, I think."

"Madam, have you a young daughter?" Mrs. Haydon somewhat abruptly asked, in the pretty foreign accent that made everything she said pleasing.

"Yes, and a very beloved one."

"Well, Madam, the position you so kindly propose would be everything I could ask for myself, but no lady would allow a girl of Margaret's age to associate, on equal terms, with her own children, nor live in her house in idleness. This would bring her into contact with other servants, who might be such persons as I should be willing to have her associate with, and might not; probably not. But if I undertake general housework, I have my kitchen all to myself, shall be free from the mental strain of not knowing today how we are to live tomorrow, can look after Margaret, and keep her out of harm's way. You see, Madam, that my child's welfare ought to be my only thought. If she were older, and steadier, and had fixed religious principle, it would be different. But as it is, I will submit to anything rather than be separated from her."

"But general housework is very hard; and you look so delicate. And you would get very low wages."

"I am stronger than I look. Housework will come hard at first, after so many years of sitting all day and half the night at needlework; but I gain strength very fast by using what I have, and Margaret is very handy, and will save me a great many steps."

"Still, you do not look like a woman born for a general housemaid."

"And I don't look like a woman born to be a lady," was the reply, with a faint smile. "You see, Madam, that it is my own fault that I am in this difficult position. A girl who makes a runaway match deserves to suffer for it. But it would grieve me sorely to drag my poor child down with me, and therefore I mean to educate her as well as I can, and try to prepare her for some useful position in the world."

"But are you sure of getting situations together?" asked Mrs. Grey.

"Yes, Madam—quite sure. God has humbled my pride, which has long held out against this method of support, and made me willing to live in any honest way He suggests. And He will not forsake me now. He knows that my Margaret is not at an age to face the world without her mother's restraint and her mother's love."

"But," said Mrs. Grey, "you talk like an educated woman, and Margaret's language is not such as one expects to find in a house like this."

"What education we have will make us all the better servants," was the reply.

"I *hate* to have you call yourself a servant!" Margaret broke forth, impetuously.

"If it is a disgrace, it is one I deserve," was the reply. "I have brought my trials on to myself."

CHAPTER 2

Mrs. Grey went home thoroughly interested in her new charge, and tried to concoct some plan for keeping the two together in a sphere better fitted to their evident refinement. She could think of nothing; therefore she tried the next best thing, namely, to find a family capable of appreciating their good fortune in obtaining such services. In this quest she was successful. Mrs. Haydon and Margaret found a home in a small, Christian family; they had a neat room to themselves, and were treated not only with kindness, but consideration. Mrs. Haydon was respectful, quiet, made a system of her work, found time to read, to attend to Margaret's lessons, and the ladies of the family confided to Mrs. Grey that they should feel as if heaven had come down to earth but for the girl. They did not know what to make of her, and did not like her. Mrs. Grey thought she did understand her; she had not forgotten the anguish of the child when she fancied her mother dying, nor the sudden act of self-control occasioned by her presence. She knew she had heart and soul, and that innate desire rather to hide than to display them, only found in a refined nature.

And now, as she sat meditating by her lonely fireside, she came to the conclusion that if it could be managed, Margaret Haydon would be her choice. Yet a score of difficulties arose at once. It would never answer for the mother to be at service and the daughter living in ease and luxury; in fact, they ought not to be separated in any way. So thinking, she renounced Margaret, and looked about her for some other young person, seeking, as a matter of course, and constantly, Divine direction. Still, Margaret filled her thoughts to such a degree that she was persuaded that, for some reason, hers was the lot to be cast in with her own. A visit from Mrs. Haydon, and some mysterious hints dropped by her, so far settled the question, that she resolved to lay the case before her, and take counsel with her. It was some time before they met again, but when they did so, she opened the subject as delicately and kindly as she could. Mrs. Haydon listened to the whole story in silence, and at its conclusion said, quietly:

"You will see, dear Madam, the hand of God in it all. You say that on the 18TH day of January you began to think of my Margaret, and of offering her a home. On that day, after many a sleepless night, I asked leave of my mistress to see a physician; she not only permitted it, but sent for the family doctor. He told me I had six months to live, and no more. Now, here was my poor child to be deprived of her mother, not well-educated enough to teach, too well-educated to be happy among a crowd of ill-bred servants, and I knew not what would become of her. There was only one thing I could do, and that was to leave her with my God. He knew I had no wicked ambition for her, though I did want her so bred, that if her father's family ever fell in with her, they need have no occasion to be ashamed of her. And then I knew that if her natural tastes could be at all gratified, it would keep her from a fondness for dress, and visiting and idling, and other follies to which young women are prone. Now, all my prayers for her are answered. Before you knew of her coming need, your heart was made to yearn over her; and now I can die in perfect peace, for you will be a mother to my child, and teach her all I could have taught her, and far, far more."

"And where do you propose to die?" asked Mrs. Grey.

Two remarkable women had got together, and were talking in

this quiet, passionless way of so solemn an event as death. How was this? It arose from the fact that commotion, and hue and cry, and clamor belong only to undisciplined characters. Who ever heard of the General of an army becoming panic-stricken and demoralized? He leaves that to the common soldier.

Both Mrs. Grey and Mrs. Haydon had passed through too many and too deep waters to regard death as anything more than a little rill, over which one passed at a single footstep.

"I shall have to go to a hospital," said Mrs. Haydon.

"And have Margaret nurse you?"

"That is not allowed. And if it is not asking too much, since you so kindly propose to care for my child, might she come to you directly?"

"While you go off, alone, to die in a hospital? No; oh, no. Were you to go at once?"

"Yes, at once. I have toiled on till I can toil no more."

"Is it possible that you are so ill, yet show it so little?"

"It's the quiet mind, the doctor says, that keeps me up. He said that if I had worried, it would have hastened my death. Thank God, I have learned to cast all my care on Him, and He has cared for me."

There was silence for some minutes. What might be mistaken for dogged submission, Mrs. Grey recognized as the kind of faith that travels across and moves mountains. She was decisive in all her ways, always knew her own mind, and now came to a very rapid conclusion.

"Does Margaret know?"

"No, Madam. Would you be willing to break it to her?"

"Yes; and I will see that your last days are made as comfortable as possible. Leave everything to me. On the day you are to leave your employer's, send Margaret to me. I will tell her what is before her. Poor child! her distress will be dreadful."

"Would it be right for us to have no farewell?"

"No, no, indeed, you shall have a farewell. Leave everything to me."

Mrs. Haydon took leave, and Mrs. Grey rang; her factotum[1] immediately appeared.

"Mary, we are going to have some visitors; that is, I want *the* room prepared for a sick person and a young lady. And Mary—their appearance, when they arrive, is to be a matter between you and me; no one else is to know what sort of clothes they wear. When asked questions in the kitchen, just say they are friends of mine."

Mary, discretion itself, withdrew, and in a few days Margaret unsuspectingly made her appearance. Mrs. Grey had a most trying task before her, and expected some such burst of anguish as that of four years ago. But Margaret had passed through much discipline during those four years. To see her mother a kitchen housemaid; to feel herself the yoke of servitude, had been hard, very hard. She did not shed a tear when the truth was told her, and only said, setting her teeth together, "I always have said that if the Lord loved my mother half as well as she loved Him, He'd take her out of a kitchen and find a more suitable place for her."

"He loves her, as He does all His children, so much more than any of us love Him, that we have no arithmetical terms with which to describe it. And if a manger and a carpenter's shop were suitable places for Him, what spot is too humble for us?"

"*You* would not like to lie in a manger, or work in a carpenter's shop, or drudge in a kitchen."

"No, dear, I do not pretend that I should; but I hope I should act, under the same circumstances, as your mother has done. I think she did the best she could for you. And now she has toiled in an uncongenial sphere long enough, and her Master has by His providence told her so."

"But what will become of her? Sick people need homes. We have laid by some money, but you know mother's wages were very small because she had an incumbrance. Yes, that's all I am in this world, an *incumbrance!*"

"It will not be so in the next world. But here is the question, as

1 Factotum—a servant employed to do all kinds of work.

to where your mother is to spend her last months. She has decided to go to a hospital."

"Poor mother! But I will not let them neglect her. I will take care of her day and night."

"My dear, you will not be allowed to do that. An occasional visit is all that is permitted."

"An occasional visit to my sick mother!" cried Margaret; "I should like to see them undertake to separate us! I would tear them to pieces first!"

Mrs. Grey remained silent, and Margaret ran furiously on till the silence struck and checked her.

"We will get your mother safely into a hospital, or what is as good as a hospital, without tearing anyone to pieces. A room is all ready for her, and there you shall take care of her."

"Oh, Mrs. Grey, it is impossible. We haven't nearly enough to justify our taking a room."

"How would this plan suit you, then? Suppose your mother enters a hospital where I know she will be kindly treated, and I give you a home with me? You would be here exactly as if you were my own child, could be well educated, and surrounded by all the refinements of life. Look around you. This beautiful room, with its luxuries, would be yours; you would have books, pictures, everything you wanted."

Margaret looked as she was bidden, and at one glance took in all the charms of the spot. Then rising scornfully to her feet, she burst into tears, jerking out the words in jets of indignation:

"That I should live to be bribed to forsake my dying mother! Now I *am* degraded!"

Mrs. Grey's experiment was a success. For that it was only an experiment the sagacious reader has at once divined.

"Ah! I knew I was not mistaken in you!" she cried; "I knew you would prove as true as steel!"

She rose and caught both the hands of the excited girl in her own, then said in tones that elicited instant obedience:

"Follow me."

They entered now a large, airy room, which contained two dainty, white beds; an open wood-fire burned on the hearth, near which a cat sat, purring.

"Here is your mother's hospital," said Mrs. Grey, "and you are matron, doctor, nurse, daughter, everything she can need. On these shelves," she added, opening a door, "are the hospital supplies; with this spirit-lamp you can make tea, warm liquids, and do a score of things. Here is a shade from the gas at night; this is a tray for food, when your patient takes to bed; this little nursery refrigerator will keep you supplied with ice day and night, and preserve milk and the like twelve hours and more. This candle will be of service when you have to move about at night, and these dressing-gowns can be washed at your pleasure. You see I am an old soldier in this sort of battle-field, and keep my armor always at hand."

All this, spoken in a cheerful, business-like manner, gave Margaret time to recover herself; without a word of thanks on the one hand, or of demur on the other, she accepted the situation, took off her outer garments and hung them up, and turning to Mrs. Grey, asked, as if all that was befalling her was an everyday occurrence:

"When is my mother coming?"

"I am going for her now. She thinks she is merely to call here to bid you farewell, and then go and languish her life away among strangers."

And then, as Margaret was going to speak, she said:

"I wouldn't talk about it just now, if I were you." So saying, she drove off in her carriage, and in a few hours mother and daughter were alone together in the sweet, fresh room which was now their home. They sat down before the fire, and looked in each other's face as they only look who know that death may part, but never separate them.

"Do you know where you are, mother?" Margaret asked at length.

"Yes," was the surprised answer, "I am in Mrs. Grey's house, on my way to the hospital."

"No, you are *in* the hospital now, on the way to heaven!"

Then they laughed and cried, and said it was a dream. So they sat, hand in hand, in the long twilight; then Margaret made tea, and cut bread and toasted it, and from the adjoining store-room brought out such delicacies as invalids sometimes will fancy when better food grows insipid, and then helped her mother into one of the soft beds, shaded the gas, and sat thinking, thinking, thinking, till the soft breathing of the sleeper admonished her that she, too, ought to be asleep.

It was not till late next morning that Mrs. Grey came to inquire after her guests, and when she did so, she was in such brilliant spirits, and acted so exactly as if this were a real hospital, miles away, that there was no use in trying to prove that it was not. They had never seen her otherwise than very much in earnest; now she came out in a new character. She told stories; she read amusing extracts from a book she had with her; said she believed she would take lunch with them in case Margaret could stew some oysters on that wonderful little lamp, and made them feel so thoroughly at home that Margaret became quite gay, ran around laying the table in a way that would have put brisk Mary to the blush, and soon had a cosy little lunch prepared, which they all enjoyed.

"If such times could only last!" Margaret thought. "But good times never do." And then she asked leave to exhibit Maud's rooms to her mother, and not an object of beauty escaped their notice, while Mrs. Grey enjoyed their appreciation of her darling's taste.

So time slipped by; Mrs. Grey invariably keeping up Mrs. Haydon's and Margaret's spirits; making the best of everything; suggesting employments for hours when the invalid was free from pain; change of food; change of position; change of furniture; change of pictures when the eye wearied of them, and never out of patience or out of heart. At times the two women fell into sweet and grave talk that Margaret, sitting silently at her work, could not understand.

Their *doctrines* puzzled her beyond measure. She said to herself now and again:

"*I* don't think so! *I* don't believe that!" And then would try to reconcile their happy, cheerful lives, their patience, their submission, with her own theories, failed to do it, but carped and caviled within herself, and watched for flaws in them as cats watch for mice, all ready to spring out upon them and rout or devour them.

"It's so queer," she thought, "to hear two people, who have been born and brought up in different countries and in entirely different ways, talk together as if they'd always belonged to one family. They're just like Freemasons—they know each other by the touch. I can't understand it. And now mother has got me off her hands, I verily believe its the nicest thing in the world to die. But I don't believe she's going to die. People that are going to die are solemn, and mother isn't in the least solemn. She is just exactly what she was before that horrid doctor said she could only live six months. Now I know that, what with freedom from over-work, and nice, tempting food, and living with such a dear, good, funny quaint old lady, she'll see too well what is good for her, to die. To die! Ugh! I hope *I* shall live a hundred years! It will take fully that to make up for the time I've lost."

It is easy to believe what one wants to believe, and Margaret found it agreeable to delude herself into the fondest hopes. Her love for her mother, though rarely exhibited, was her ruling passion; it was the only master to whom she would ever submit, yet more than once she became its slave.

Mrs. Haydon's disease, however, was making progress, as she knew perfectly well; and from time to time she tried to give Margaret the parting counsels a Christian mother would naturally wish to give. But Margaret never would allow any allusion to be made to an event she was resolved should not take place, and so the precious time passed on. Mrs. Haydon conferred with Mrs. Grey on the subject, who advised her to put in writing some of the things she longed to say. But the poor woman did not hold the pen of a ready writer, and was, besides, in constant pain; so day after day passed and nothing was done. Then came a sudden change for the worse, and after that a gradual loss of strength, till at last, to her perfect horror, Margaret had to admit that the case was hopeless. The first warm days of June proved exhaustive of what little vitality was left in the worn frame, and the end came rapidly. Mrs. Grey lived through hard times with the passionate girl, whose grief was like a tempest that threatened to sweep her away. In vain she reminded her of the ecstasy of joy in which her mother had entered into rest; in vain spoke of the peaceable fruits of grievous sorrow; in vain took her from place to place. The unsubdued will could not, would not rest.

At the close of the summer, on their return from many wanderings, Margaret was installed in Maud's rooms, and Mrs. Grey introduced her to her friends as her adopted daughter. They had lived under one roof together nearly a year now, but though Margaret's faults were obvious—she taking no pains to conceal them—Mrs. Grey had never wavered in her attachment to and interest in her, and was sure that the Divine hand had brought them together. As to Margaret, she loved Mrs. Grey as she did the few she loved at all, intensely, and by degrees began to regard her with somewhat of the enthusiasm she had felt for her mother. Still she spent a great deal of time by herself, reading the letters of her father and mother in the days of their youthful love. She hardly remembered him, but these letters moved her wonderfully; they were such as she should write if she were in love; and for the first time in her life the thought came to her what it would be to become the object of such devotion.

Theirs had been a real romance, and she had never read of one in any book that touched her as these revelations did. There was not much in her mother's handwriting that was original, but what there was, was tender and girlish. One letter, written during the early part of their marriage, and during a temporary separation, contained the only allusion to herself, and she read it with mingled emotions:

"Nous chantons deux, je lui répète,
Nous chantons d'amour;
Deux dans notre nid d' alouette,
Trois peut-être un jour."[1]

She was recalled from the past to the present by a tap at the door, and reluctantly opening it about an inch, saw Mrs. Grey, who said, "I am sorry to interrupt you, dear; but Mrs. Cameron and Agnes are here, and Mrs. Cameron wants a little confidential talk with me, which would be rather a bore to a young girl; so, if you will entertain her half an hour or so, I shall be very much obliged to you."

"I am not looking fit to go down," said Margaret.

"So I see, poor child!" replied Mrs. Grey. "But Agnes would not mind coming up; indeed she would like to do so, for she has spent many happy hours here in dear little Maud's day."

Margaret rose and went, in a lifeless way, to bathe her tear-swollen eyes, and in a few moments a bright, smiling girl made her appearance.

"Oh! this lovely room!" she cried. "How glad I am to see it once more. You naughty child! why haven't you been to see me? Well, I never saw so many pretty things together in any one room in my life. I am sure you must be the happiest girl living. If you couldn't be happy in such a room as this, you couldn't be happy anywhere!"

"Well, then, let me tell you that it takes more than a beautiful room to make one happy. All this room is good for for me is to be wretched in!"

"Now, Margaret, I did think you would get over moping when you settled down here and found yourself openly adopted by Mrs. Grey. Why, my mother says you ought to be overwhelmed with gratitude."

"I know I ought. But I never do what I ought!"

---

1 We sing both, I repeat it, We sing of love; Two in our nest of lark, Three maybe one day.

"Then you ought to be ashamed of yourself. Dear me! if I had such a boudoir as this, and such a bedroom, and a bureau all to myself, I should be as happy as the day is long. As it is, my sister Jane and I have one room together. She takes the two upper bureau drawers, and I have to put up with the two lower ones. Then she contrives to use nearly all the nails in the closet, and nearly all the shelves; and she is forever getting my towels, and mislaying her hair-brush and using mine; besides, I dote on having things tidy and in order, and she keeps all her things helter-skelter. Well, if you won't be happy, you won't; so there it is! Goodbye. Come and see me, do."

"*Is* it won't?" Margaret asked herself, as the door closed upon the good-humored chatterbox. "If I thought it was—"

She had made the acquaintance of Agnes Cameron during the summer; a shallow friendship had sprung up between them, which would never amount to anything more; now a heedless word from a thoughtless girl had done what all Mrs. Grey's wise counsels had failed to do.

Margaret went to the glass and looked at herself. She had no vanity, and had never cared what people thought of her. She stood, straightening up now, and studied her own face for the first time.

"What a will you have got, Margaret Haydon!" she said; "and what is the use of it, if you sit crying and wailing like a child? *I am ashamed of you!*"

She folded the letters she had been brooding over all the morning, tied them together with a bit of white ribbon, and locked them up in a drawer. Then she climbed upon a chair and threw the key as far and as high as she could; it alighted behind a box, and there it lay for a year, untouched. Then she walked downstairs and into the library, and gave Mrs. Grey a good, wholesome, sound kiss.

"Now, aunty," she said, "I hope you've had the worst of me."

Mrs. Grey looked up, and smiled, How many times she had prayed for this day!

CHAPTER 3

Margaret never knew what caused this sudden change, but it was simply this. If it was a passion with her to love, it was also a passion to avoid unpleasant sights. And the picture drawn by Agnes Cameron revolted her. To have somebody share her room who kept everything in disorder would be something intolerable. All her life long she had been used to the beauty of perfectly-kept rooms; on the mother's part this was mere feminine nicety, such as any woman might possess. In Margaret it was the artistic element inherited from her father; she must have order reign where she dwelt, not because it is meet and right to be orderly, but because it hurt her eye to see confusion. At this stage of her history, she would have been surprised to be told this; perhaps have stoutly denied it. But a realizing sense of what a hardship it would be to her to have such a roommate as Jane Cameron had come over her now, and, with it, confusion of face that she had behaved in so ungrateful a way. It was not in her to ask any one's pardon, out and out, but the kiss and the little speech from her were equivalent to going down on her knees, had she been somebody else.

Mrs. Grey seized this gentler mood at once.

"I have been thinking," she said, without comment or ado, "what is to be done about your education. You are too old to go to school, and perhaps I could manage to teach you myself. But in order for that, I shall have to find out how far your mother took you."

"She took me as far as she could, and then let me go on by myself. Now, about algebra, for instance. She knew nothing about it, but there was a number of old school-books in the house where we lived, and I was allowed the use of them."

"And you studied algebra?"

"Yes, I studied it just as I should take a dose of medicine—swallowed it down, and then helped my self to a lump of sugar, to take the taste out."

"A metaphorical lump, I suppose?"

"Yes, I made patchwork."

"What an extraordinary idea! However, I think I understand it. Your needle represented a brush, and those bits of bright-colored flannels, paint. We must look into that. Now, what else did you study?"

"Mother *made* me study English grammar. She said she owed it to my father's family to have me understand his language."

"*English* grammar? How is that?"

"Why, as a general rule, mother talked to me in French, but she was very particular to have me keep up what English I had learned from my father. She had a few French books, and taught me to read to him, and until his death I had plenty of time for it."

"I did not know your father was an Englishman."

"But he was. He was travelling through Europe on foot, stopping to sketch when anything took his fancy, and one day he saw my mother standing near a *châlet*, with a child in her arms, and fell in love with her. The child belonged to a neighbor who often lodged artists for weeks at a time, and he contrived to spend a whole summer there."

But our readers need not hear the whole story of Margaret's fragmentary education. She was now between seventeen and eighteen, and had managed to pick up a wonderful amount of information;

but culture she had none. This she soon began to feel, but as the companion of a woman cultivated to the last degree, and with her own brilliant powers, she glided, without difficulty, into regions most girls in her position would have had to reach through laborious toil. And as to art, Mrs. Grey had only to provide her with materials, and give her opportunity to experiment, and the next thing she knew, grace and beauty dropped like magic from the tiny point of her pencil. But so many other gifts developed themselves, that there was no danger of one-sidedness.

So she dashed on, eager, breathless, like one running a race; entering into everything with zest and enjoyment, and undertaking work enough to exhaust a less dauntless nature. And then another cloud began to arise. Christmas was coming, and with it twelve human beings to criticise, misunderstand, dislike her.

Twelve human beings for her to criticise, be jealous of, and, as like as not, hate. At least that was the way she chose to put it, but this is Mrs. Grey's version:

"They'll all come, this year; my darling boys and girls, and their little folks. Will they find it somewhat awkward, before they get acquainted with Margaret? It will be trying for her, poor child, to see a mother and children together."

However, she had tact—the kind of tact that comes from Christian instincts. She talked to Margaret about the home-comers, exactly as if they were her brothers and sisters, got her interested, asked her to manage a Christmas-tree, and consulted her about everything.

"Do the children have a tree every year?" asked Margaret.

"Oh, yes—every year."

"Then I should like to get up something different; I don't know what, but I can think out a plan."

The next morning she came down as radiant as the sun.

"I have a plan," she announced, "and now I must have a carpenter."

The carpenter was forthcoming, the plan shown him; he had

little folks of his own, and entered into the fun of the thing, glee-fully. Christmas Eve arrived, and the house was full. As lively greet-ings were exchanged, Margaret began to shrink into herself, and to wish she could hide in some cranny till all was over. Is this natural? Is this picture true to life? It is. *Reality* never tries to shine, to display its plumage or clap its wings. It is Unreality that comes strutting forward, crying, "Go to, and admire my gifts!"

. The Christmas breakfast was a failure. In vain Mrs. Grey tried to persuade herself that her children had taken Margaret into their hearts, and loved her like a sister; in vain they reproached them-selves for not being able to do it; in vain Margaret tried to appear at her ease with all those eyes upon her; a cold silence fell upon every sally made by some bold adventurer, and all were thankful when the meal was over.

"And now," said Mrs. Grey, "you older boys must come imme-diately to help Margaret through with her Christmas surprise, what-ever it may be: for what it is I know no more than the rest of you."

Two or three stout fellows volunteered, and were led off by Margaret, who unfolded her plan to them, and was at once placed on a pedestal as an object of admiration.

"It's just capital!" they all agreed, and in a few minutes the ice between them melted, and they were laughing, working, joking together, like fellows well-met. The entertainment was to come directly after the children's dinner, as many of them were too young to bear excitement at night, and while Margaret and her allies were pushing on their preparations, the mother and her children sat together in one of those family councils in which the more there are the merrier. One does not often see so many happy faces together, for while no one forgot how Maud used to enjoy those festivities, they would not allow themselves to spoil the day by sad retrospec-tions. After a time most of the party went to church; then came the bountiful lunch Mrs. Grey was so fond of getting up, and the children's dinner, followed by the expectant procession headed by Margaret silent and shy. Instantly a great hue and cry arose, as they came into view of a real house at the end of the large parlors, rooms rarely used now, from whose tall red chimney Santa Claus was emerging, with his arms full of snowballs, with which he began pelting the crowd with might and main.

Margaret's house appeared to be covered with snow, as was the ground on which it stood; and she had contrived to produce the effect of moonlight, the illusion being perfect. Some of the very little children fell back in affright at the weird scene, the strange figure of Santa Claus and the shower of snow-balls. But that was all set right when they found that the balls were made of cotton, not snow, and each contained a gift. Such a scrambling as followed this disclosure!

Little Sam Grey was knocked off his legs, and lay prostrate on his back, holding a large snow-ball in each hand, and a well-aimed blow at delicate, blue-eyed Mabel Heath, sent her spinning over the fleecy floor, to her great amazement, and that of the "baby" she held in her arms.

The whole scene was as picturesque as possible; and Margaret was in her element now, and forgot to be either proud or shy, as she moved about among the children, enjoying their enjoyment. She did not know she was fond of girls and boys and babies, for she had never come in contact with them, though she had heard plenty of screaming and quarreling among those who lived in the house with her in times past. But here were sweet, well-bred, daintily-dressed little mortals, the very ideal of babyhood and childhood; and with the quick instinct of their age they speedily elected her as the beloved of their hearts. And as the road to a mother's heart lies through that of her children, before the day closed Margaret had won, without trying to do it, the admiration and the love of the six young mothers whose coming she had so dreaded. They, too, were relieved. They had not known exactly how they were to take this new inmate of the family, and had some misgivings, which they frankly confessed the next morning as they gathered around the library-fire to have a family confab. Margaret had established herself in what used to be the day-nursery, and which was still used as such when the grandchildren came home, and could have been seen with a baby on her lap, a little darling, blue-eyed Mabel standing behind her on the chair she occupied, with her arms around her neck, and two or three others clustered at her knee.

"Well, girls," said Mrs. Grey, "what do you think of my Margaret?"

"Oh, mamma!" cried Belle Heath, "it is *such* a relief to find her what she is! Cyril and I were afraid some designing creature had taken you in. You know you are so easily taken in."

"I know no such thing," said Mrs. Grey, greatly amused. "I know of no one so hard to impose on as I am."

"'O wad some power the giftie gie us,'"[1] quoted Frank Grey, who had just entered the room, after a late breakfast, and was bending his six-feet frame to kiss his mother.

"I wish it *wad,*" said his sister Laura, "for then you would be up in season for breakfast. It isn't nice to come down after everything has grown as cold as a stone. Does Lily let you do so at home?"

"Lily set me the example," he said, laughing. "Besides, mamma grows indulgent in her declining years."

"Perhaps I am a little indulgent," said Mrs. Grey. "Parents who are severe with their children when they are young, are apt to relax as they grow older."

A shout of laughter followed this remark. Mrs. Grey looked around, surprised.

"Now, what have I said that should make you so merry?" she asked, innocently.

"That little word 'severe' lies at the bottom of the joke," said Frank. "The idea of our beautiful lady-mother insinuating that she was ever hard upon her offspring!"

"At all events, if I could live my life over again, I would deal very differently with my children from what I did—especially with you two older ones."

---

1 Translated: "And would some Power the small gift give us;" a quote from *To a Louse* by Robert Burns.

"O, we were more depraved than those that came after," said Belle. "And if you hadn't taken us in hand, in a summary way, I do not know what would have become of us. Papa never would do anything but spoil us, he was so indulgent."

"It's not a man's business to manage his children," said Cyril Heath. "It's the mother's."

"I don't agree with you," said Frank Grey. "It's the man's."

"Of *course* it is," said his wife.

"Well, why?" pursued Cyril.

"He is supposed to have more weight of character than she."

"And suppose he hasn't?"

"I can't suppose any such thing. Men are born to rule, and do rule; women are born to yield, and do yield."

"They are born to rule in their own sphere, it is true," interposed Mrs. Grey, who, as the reader ought to know, had written a book on the subject of education. "But home is not their sphere. It is woman's kingdom, and there she should reign."

"But I always took the ground that a modest woman would doubt her own judgment in regard to the children, and defer to the father," objected Frank's wife. She was a little, delicate creature, who admired her husband above all things, though she could pretend to be ashamed of him now and then.

"A man ought to be master in his own house," said one.

"That applies to the kitchen as well as to the nursery," said another. "A woman who makes her husband manage the children will make him manage the servants."

"Well, some do."

"The more shame to them."

"It's rather hard upon a man when he comes home at night, hoping for a smile from his wife, and a romp with his boys, to see an anxious wrinkle on her brow, and hear her say:

"'O, John, I am so thankful you have come! There's Tom won't take his powders, and I can do nothing with him! And Sue has stolen and eaten four slices of cake. Four slices! Just think of it!

And Hetty struck her nurse twice, and nurse says she'll leave.'"

Everybody laughed, and everybody had something to say.

"Why, of course such a woman as that has no force of character," said Cyril Heath. "Really sensible women do not behave in that way."

"And really good ones do not have children who are disobedient, who steal cake, and strike their nurses," said Mrs. Grey.

At this there was a great clamor, some denying, some affirming the point.

"I think, mother, you forget some of our childish misdeeds," said Frank. "I know a very good mother who had some very wayward children."

"Being wayward is one thing; being low, and vulgar, and rude is another," she replied. "I suppose all spirited children like to have their own way, and will get it if they can; but it is inconsistent with my idea of a Christian home that its inmates should be wanting in refinement, have the habit of giving way to passionate temper, to duplicity, to dishonesty, to meanness—"

"We all know you can't stand meanness," interrupted Frank. "But go on, please. We young fathers and mothers are ready for any number of hints."

"But children are born totally depraved," said one of the daughters-in-law. "We have to take them as they come."

"That depends; my dear, if you and that boy of mine there are living self-controlled lives, are at peace with God and at peace with each other, your children will enter the world at great advantage. They will be different, at their very birth, from the children of undisciplined parents, who pamper their bodies, indulge in unholy passions, and reproduce offspring like unto themselves. You may depend upon it that your duty to your child begins before it sees the light. But lunch is ready, so I'll stop preaching in order to feed you."

Lunch was a lively meal, because so many children were there. Margaret came in with her face fairly shining. A score of little feet came pattering in with her. Their quaint ways of eating their dinner amused her so that her own plate remained untouched. She watched, with great amusement, the tiny, infantine hands that held spoons they had not skill to manage; how they picked up their food with their fingers, placed it in the spoons, and then manfully and laboriously conveyed it to their mouths. But not one who could wield a spoon would allow itself to be fed.

"After we get through with lunch," Mrs. Grey said to her, "I want the children to see some of your pictures."

"Do you suppose they would care for them, auntie?" asked Margaret, in some surprise. "I should think they would enjoy 'Old Mother Hubbard' more."

Consternation, then laughter.

"Mother means us," explained Frank. "To her we are as much boys and girls as ever."

"Oh! But I have done nothing fit to show," said Margaret. "And I don't see how any one who can look at these lovely little children, can even want to look at anything else. Just see these tiny, dimpled hands!"

The young mother who had most interest in the dimpled hands, left her seat, and came to Margaret's side of the table on hearing this, and said:

"Before I came home I wondered what I should call you. But I know now. I shall call you Mag., and you must call me Oney."

"Well, Oney, I will," said Margaret, and then both laughed a gleeful, girlish laugh of good-fellowship.

"If you were a boy, you would be a wag," said Laura.

"And if you were a horse, you would be a nag," retorted Margaret; upon which the girl-mother took her into her confidence; told her how she felt the first time baby cried, after the nurse left; how many dresses she made for it, and how many things mother knit; and how she nearly died with laughing when it began to walk. She also communicated that she kept four servants, was fond of housekeeping, and "oh, what do you think of mamma? Isn't she splendid?

So straight and tall, such white, wavy hair, such bright eyes, and *so* full of talent!"

Margaret would call her Oney, and listen to her; but whether she should ever confide in her she wasn't sure; still, she was very nice, and her baby's hands were so pretty!

CHAPTER 4

The next day most of the sons departed, various duties calling them back. The Rev. Cyril Heath, and Belle, his wife, stayed several weeks, as he could take his vacation more conveniently in the winter than in the summer. Among them all they persuaded two of the sisters to remain likewise, and to Margaret's delight, most of her special pets belonged to these three families.

"I don't like to say it even to you, mamma," said Belle Heath, "but it is a relief to have Frank's children gone. They are so wide-awake, so independent, and so spoiled."

"Their mother tries to do well by them," said Mrs. Grey. "And they are very fond of her. And Frank seems contented enough."

"He may seem so, but I am sure he isn't. Is there nothing can be done to tone Lily up? Couldn't you talk to her, and make her see that she will ruin those children?"

"My dear Belle, no, indeed. Young wives abhor having their mothers-in-law interfere with them."

"But just listen to this. Yesterday Frank, Jr., came rushing in like a mad creature, and rushed up to my poor little Mabel, seized her by the leg, and floored her. Mabel hit her head against a chair, and began to cry.

"'Why, Frank,' said his mother, 'what spirits you have. But it is rude to treat your little cousin in that way. Go and tell her you are sorry.'

"'I won't,' said Frank.

"'Very well, then you shall not dine with me today.' Thereupon he set ·up one of his dreadful shrieks, when Lily said, 'Don't cry; on the whole it won't do to forbid you dining with me, because it would annoy grandma. Ask Aunt Belle if that isn't the case.'

"She looked at me, and I said, 'Lily, dear, don't break your word; for the child's sake, I beg you not.'

"'Oh,' she said, 'I spoke impulsively; it will just spoil my lunch if Franky is in disgrace. Belle, I wish you didn't make so much of every trifle.' I said I could not think it a trifle to break one's word."

"I hope Franky did not hear this discussion," interposed Mrs. Grey.

"Not he; the moment Lily let him off as to the matter of dinner he was at his ease, and rushed off into some other piece of mischief. I said a good deal to Lily, and at last, she called Frank and said to him, 'Your aunt thinks you ought to be punished for your naughty ways; now, if I let you off about the dinner, I shall have to think of some other way of dealing with you. Perhaps I shall use papa's little rod.'

"'Ho, papa's little rod! *You* can't hurt me with it.'

"'Yes, I can, and I shall, too; and now, go away, and play.'

"This morning I reminded her of her threat to the child, and asked her if she had carried it out.

"'Why, no,' she said, 'I couldn't punish a child today for what it did yesterday. He is good and pleasant now, and I couldn't go and pick a quarrel with him.'

"'Oh, *never* pick a quarrel with him,' I said, 'but keep your word, Lily.'

"She yawned, and called Franky, who came running up.

"'Here, you young rogue,' she began, 'come and feel the rod I promised you yesterday;' so then they got into a regular frolic together, and he finally wrenched it out of her hand and threw it into the fire."

"Yes," said Mrs. Grey, "that's Lily to the life. But she might be a hundred, yes, a thousand times worse. I had rather see her inefficient and amiable than ever so energetic, but ill-tempered."

"Of course. But the children won't respect her."

"But they'll love her."

Belle sighed. "Frank was always my favorite brother," she said, "and when he became engaged to Lily, I thought him such a lucky fellow; she was so pretty and so sweet, and seemed so fond of him. But those children. She can do nothing with them."

"Well, Frank makes them obey him."

"But he is able to be with them so little. And you must own, mamma, that it is the mother who moulds the child."

"No, not where both parents live to be joint educators of their children. You do not remember much about your father; but Lily reminds me more of him than any of you do. Nothing would have tempted him to punish you; he would contrive to forget his threats, or laugh them off, and I always thought that as you grew up, you would love him better than you did me, he was so gentle with you."

"Yet, it is the law-giver who is invariably loved the best. Frank's children love him far better than they do their mother."

"Yes; but that is chiefly owing to his loving them so intensely."

"Poor Lily. She is never intense in anything. But she is a dear little thing, and they may all get on together, somehow."

"I think, my dear, it will not be 'somehow.' I think there will be cause and effect. Frank can do more by his pure and thoroughly religious life, than Lily can undo. As the children grow older they will feel his influence everywhere. It certainly is a fact at in many a home where the mother is amiable, well-disposed, but weak, the father comes to the rescue, becomes the ruling spirit of the house, and his boys and girls turn out good and true men and women."

Belle smiled. "You will never say die," she declared. "I wish I was as sure of my mother-in-law's Lily is of hers. And now I want to talk to you about my own little men and women."

"No wonder. They are charming."

But at this moment several others entered the room, some with babies, some with needlework; they all sat around the library table, by the open fire, making as pleasant a picture as one need desire to see. There was a little desultory conversation; one wanted to learn a particular stitch in knitting, and another taught her. Belle came and looked on, and learned it in half the time.

"Now, Belle," said Laura, "I wish you would teach me the secret of your children's excellent manners. They are as full of spirit as mine, but they are not rude, and mine are. They slam doors, and slide down the banisters, and interrupt me when I am talking."

Here there was a general outcry.

"I never *would* allow my children to interrupt," said one.

"They all do it, except Belle's children."

"Then all children are disagreeable—and very disagreeable."

"Come, Belle, speak up. How have you contrived it all?"

"There has not been much contrivance about it. There were certain things I made up my mind to have, and I've had them. There were certain other things I wanted to have, but have not, thus far, gained. In other words, I do not consider our household life perfect. We every one of us, father, mother, and children, have our faults and foibles."

"I should hope so," said Laura. "You would be fearfully uninteresting if you never said or did anything but what was prim and proper."

"Oh, as to that, we are not prim, as you very well know."

"What, not when you go on straw-rides? Dear me, I have been black-and-blue ever since you and his Reverence inveigled me into going blackberrying in that style. But come, now; what have you done to your children?"

"I don't know," said Belle, trying to think. "Perhaps they were born with good manners. I never fuss over them; they seem to take to things naturally."

"May I say what *I* think about it?" asked Margaret, coming eagerly forward.

"Yes, do, child," said Mrs. Grey, who had been listening in

amused silence to the mixture of fun and earnestness visible in her young folks.

"Mrs. Heath always *does* what she wants the children to do; she never tells them to say 'I thank you,' but always thanks them, down to the youngest, whenever she has a chance; she never orders them about, either, but always gives directions kindly; and she never speaks unkindly to them at any time."

"And never slides down the banisters or slams doors," Belle added, right merrily.

By this time Margaret had shrunk back, rather frightened at having spoken out before so many listeners.

"You are right, Margaret," said Mrs. Grey, not a little pleased at the girl's close observation; "emphatically right. In my observation of life, I have seen plenty of illustrations to prove that you are.

"Listen, while I rehearse:

"'John!'

"'Sir!'

"'Go upstairs and get my slippers.'

"John makes no answer, gets the slippers unwillingly, resumes his book, or whatever work he may be at, and then:

"'John! John Burt!'

"'*Sir!*'

"'What under the sun did you bring these old slipshods for? I wonder if you ever did an errand right in your life? I never saw such a boy. Take them upstairs, and get the other pair. And be quick about it, too. I can't sit here in my stocking-feet all night.'

"Or put it thus:

"'John, my boy?'

"'Yes, papa!'

"'I wish you'd trot upstairs for my slippers?'

"'Yes, papa!'

"'And don't bring the old ones; they're done for; bring the pair Susy worked for me.'

"'Yes, papa, all right.'

"'Ah, *thank* you, old fellow! When I am thirteen and you are fifty, I'll do as much for you. How nice it is to have a pair of young legs at one's service!'

"Now, all this may seem small business, but this boy is being *educated* into refinement, and courtesy, and kindliness, or the reverse."

"Curiously enough," said Belle, "without having any conscious theory on the subject, I have always acted on this principle with my children."

"Are children, then, mere monkeys, imitating all they see done?" asked Laura.

"They are not," was Mrs. Grey's reply. "Some children are so original that they cannot imitate. They think and act for themselves. They are hard to deal with in most cases, each needing a mother all to itself. But they are the exception, not the rule. Most of us owe almost everything to unconscious influence."

But all serious talk was for the time put an end to, by a curious little incident. One of the nurses entered the room, leading by the hand Laura's baby-girl, who had just learned to walk. Another baby, who had not yet attained this art, was creeping about, picking up and putting into its mouth everything it could find; and no sooner did the older child perceive this, than down it went on all-fours, and began to creep too, to the great amusement of all present.

"How perfectly ridiculous!" said Laura, snatching up and kissing her child.

"'She stooped to conquer,'" said Margaret.

And then followed any amount of youthful talk, and nursery tales from the family urchins. Mrs. Grey's extraordinary memory, where everything they ever said and did was stored up, together with some that, amid no little protest and fun, was warmly challenged.

CHAPTER 5

"I have always wondered," Laura proclaimed at the dinner-table that night, "how I came to be such a charming creature. But in the light of this morning's instructions, I perceive that it is through constant imitation of mamma."

Now as Laura was considered in every way unlike her mother, this sally called forth, as it was intended to do, numerous personalities.

"The resemblance is, indeed, astonishing," said Belle. "For instance, you are punctuality itself."

"Of course," said Laura.

"What unblushing effrontery!" cried Belle.

"And I suppose you never lose money; keep your accounts to a T; can keep a secret—"

"Oh, as to that," said Laura, "I am of too generous a disposition to keep anything. You see it is all owing to the nobility of my character that I have the reputation of being such a leaky vessel that you all turn me out of the room, when anything is going on you don't want the whole town to hear. By the by, mamma, you haven't told me what your next book is to be about?"

"It is to be the history of Mrs. Laura Hosmer, *née* Grey," said her mother. "Therein will be set forth all her gifts and graces, her deeds and her misdeeds."

"And a most instructive and entertaining work it will be," cried Laura. "I shall buy up a whole edition to give to my friends, shan't I, baby? Mamma, what a mistake you made in giving me the name you did," she ran gaily on. "All the Lauras one reads about in books are such proper creatures! See Miss Edgworth's stories, for instance. Look at her Lauras. But really, now, what *is* your next book to be?"

Mrs. Grey smiled and shook her head.

"Very well, if you won't tell me, I shan't tell you what mine is to be."

"*Yours!*" cried everybody, amused and incredulous.

"Oh, I don't see anything to laugh at," protested Laura. "Pray why shouldn't I write books as well as mamma?"

"Mamma didn't begin at your age," said Belle. "She began about as soon as she was born; and so would you if you had inherited her gifts."

"That doesn't follow," said Laura. "And I have hit upon a capital subject! Now just listen." And in an animated way she imparted her secret.

"It *is* capital," said Belle. "But it is foolish to proclaim it. Next news some one will get hold of it and cut you out."

"Yes; I think so, too," said Mrs. Grey. "I shouldn't mind cutting you out myself."

"If you did, it would be your first dishonorable action," said Belle.

The children were all brought in now, and had a frolic till bed-time, when they were escorted off by mammas and nurses, and Mrs. Grey and Margaret were left alone.

"Oh, aunty," said Margaret, as the door closed, "I do wish *I* had a baby!"

"I don't see that I can help you to one," was the reply. "But I am glad to see your love for the little folks, and when Belle goes home, I think I can persuade her to leave Mabel with us for a while."

"Oh, she'll never do that. Mabel is such a perfect little darling!"

"I have usually charge of the last robin while a new one is settling into the nest. It keeps me young, and it relieves Belle. In fact, what with one thing and another, there are almost always some of the little ones here."

"I'm so glad! so glad! I shall take the whole care of them."

"And at the same time study, draw, paint, and dabble with a thousand other things?"

"I can study evenings. As to painting—why, aunty, it's nice to paint; but there isn't any picture in the world to be compared to a little live baby!"

"I haven't seen all the pictures in the world," said Mrs. Grey; "but I do not doubt that God makes objects of beauty that man can, at best, only imitate. Margaret, my child, do you know how relieved, how thankful I am, to find this true womanly instinct so strong in you? I have been afraid you might live in the mere gifts of genius you must know you possess, and crowd out the feminine element. But you are safe. A little child shall lead you."

"Why, aunty, I never knew I had any gifts," Margaret whispered.

"There will be plenty of worshippers to tell you so, sooner or later. But I want to impress it upon you, that the greater your gifts the greater your responsibility. Now several paths lie before you. You can devote yourself to art and win a name for yourself, I do not doubt. Or you can choose a literary life, and shine there. And if it were necessary for you to do something for your own support, either of those careers would be honorable. But there is a third vocation in a human sphere open to you. It is to be one of the truest, the best, the most unworldly, most unselfish of women."

"Like you, aunty," said Margaret, her eyes moistening. "I choose your vocation."

They sat silently together after this, until the rest of the family joined them; and after a time Laura asked:

"Where is Hatty? Seems to me it takes her an age to get her kittens to bed."

"Something is going wrong with Kitty," explained Belle. "I

thought Mabel would never get to sleep, it distressed her so to hear Kitty cry."

"But why should Kitty cry?" asked Mrs. Grey, uneasily. "She appeared to be perfectly well when she went up to bed."

"It's something about saying her prayers," said Belle, reluctantly. "Poor Hatty means right, but I think she makes mistakes."

"That child is crying dreadfully," said Laura, going out into the hall, and listening. "Hatty doesn't know how to manage her. Mamma, do go up and see what the matter is."

Mrs. Grey hesitated. She was not fond of meddling with her sons' wives.

Just then, however, a servant appeared with a message to the effect that "Mrs. George" would like to see her, and she flew upstairs, alarmed. She found Hatty flushed and excited, standing over Kitty, aged twenty months, fast asleep on the floor, her breast heaving, the tears shining on her lashes.

"Oh, mother, what shall I do? Kitty wouldn't say her prayers, and I said she shouldn't go to bed till she had, and I slapped her arms over and over again, and she wouldn't yield, but at last dropped to sleep here on the floor. And I've got to leave her here all night, and she'll catch her death of cold. Oh, dear, I wish I'd gone home with Fred. Fred can always conquer her."

"My dear Hatty," said Mrs. Grey, "I am very sorry for you."

There was no reproach in tone or look, but the sincere sorrow of a loving, sympathizing heart, and Hatty, young and inexperienced, burst into tears.

"I never saw such a will," she said, "never."

"She comes honestly by it," was the reply; "and it will be of service by and by. Meantime I would put her into bed, if I were you."

"But that would be breaking my word; and Fred says I must *never* do that. He says there is a special blessing for him who swears to his own hurt. Oh, my little darling, how can I let you lie on that cold floor all night?"

"It is unfortunate to threaten children. But I believe all do it in their youth and inexperience. In this particular case I think you ought to break your word as to its letter. As to its spirit you do not break it; you certainly never meant to treat this dear little lamb cruelly."

"But suppose I put her to bed, and she remembers what passed between us tonight, shan't I lose my hold on her? Won't she expect to disobey me again?"

"I hardly think this baby-memory will recall tonight's scenes in a definite way. If it does we will devise some way in which to preserve its faith in you. Come, shall I put the little thing to bed? I haven't threatened it, you know."

"Oh, dear, I wish Fred was here. Fred is so particular about having Kitty obedient. He says it is indispensable."

"I am glad to hear it, and glad to know that you two are united in your plans for the child. And now, suppose as you are a little confused as to your duty, we kneel down and get counsel from One who knows how to set you right."

A few simple words followed, and as they rose, the young mother threw her arms around Mrs. Grey's neck, and kissed her.

"How I love you!" she said. "Fred said I should if I stayed long enough to know you. I'm glad I stayed."

And here baby woke up, rubbed her eyes, and smiled.

"Me rested now; me say p'ayer now," she said. "Me was bely tired."

"I thought this was how it would end," said Mrs. Grey. "The little creature was all tired out, not naughty. I am afraid you and I should not like to have our arms slapped when we were too tired to pray."

"I hope I never shall threaten my poor little kitten again," said Hatty, as she tucked the child snugly in its crib. "Why, I am almost ill with the pain I have suffered. But now about tomorrow night? Suppose Kitty forms a habit of refusing to say her prayers?"

"Dear Hatty, the children of *believing* parents never form habits of disobedience."

"Oh, are you sure of that? I know a number of truly good and faithful parents whose children have turned out badly in every way."

"Investigate the cases and you will find something wrong in the parents. It may be neglect, it may be over-doing; it may be too much will, it may be too little will; I do not know, and unless I can be of service in the matter, do not want to know the history of individual experiences. But when I see a brook muddy, I like to know who stepped in to trouble it, whether man or beast, especially if I am obliged to drink from it."

Hatty smiled. "I rather think it was I who stepped into this brook," she said; "I thought I was acting for Kitty's best good, but perhaps I was as willful, and as resolved to have my own way, as she was. But before you go I want to ask you if we may pray about little things?"

"How little?"

"Well—for instance, what you did just now?"

"My dear Hatty, it is not a little thing to own our human helplessness, and cast ourselves on Divine strength."

"But when it comes to a conflict between a mother and child, a mere baby like Kitzie, ought the Lord of heaven and earth to be expected to interfere?"

"Let us judge Him out of His own mouth. Recall His language as He moved about on earth among just such beings as we are. He says, distinctly, that He feeds the fowls of the air, sees to the growth of the lily of the field, that no sparrow falls to the ground without His notice and consent, and that He takes such personal interest in each of His children that He knows exactly how many hairs we each have in our heads. Can the tenderest mother say anything like this?"

"It is very puzzling."

"No, my dear, it is very simple. It is just taking God at His word. Now, you sent for me, a mere mortal, fallible woman, to sympathize with and help you out of an emergency. Do I then love you better than your Father does? Am I any more ready to come to your rescue than He is?"

"Do you mean, then, that we are not to seek human counsel, but just go to Him about everything?"

"No; I believe also in taking counsel of flesh and blood. The answer to your prayer for light must come from God, but He often sends those answers through human agency. And so I am very glad you sent for me tonight. I love to be intrusted with His commissions. And now don't you think we ought to go down and join the rest of them?"

As they entered the library, every one took a hasty glance at their faces, and the tranquil expression of each satisfied what anxiety they had felt. The next day was Sunday, and quite a procession set off for church. Margaret came last of all, leading her beloved little Mabel by the hand. The child had never been to church before, and her mother thought taking her there such a doubtful experiment, that when Margaret proposed it, she demurred a little. Finally, she consented to her occupying a seat whence she could be easily removed, if troublesome. Then she made her stand at her knee, took her hands in hers, and said:

"Mabel, darling, we are all going to God's house, because we love Him, and He wants us to come."

"Yes, mamma."

"And it isn't like other houses; people who go there do not go to talk, and laugh, and play; they go to pray to God, and sing to Him, and hear about Him. And it isn't nice for little children to fidget and whisper while that is being done. And if I let you go to His house this morning, I shall expect you to sit still, and not to say a word."

"Yes, mamma. Will Christ be there?"

This child, through her whole life, invariably spoke of God as Christ.

"Yes, dear, He will be there, and will look at my little Mabel, and know if she is quiet. But you will not see Him; no one does that."

And then turning to Margaret, she said:

"Have you ever taken a little child to church?"

"Oh, no! I wasn't born among such luxuries."

"As a general rule, it is anything but a luxury to break these little colts in. They are accustomed to have liberty of action and of speech at home; they do not understand the services at church, they get tired, they nestle, and, if allowed, will whisper, on an average, once in three minutes. Now, if Mabel whispers to you, take no notice whatever; be lost in attention to what is going on. I lay great stress on this. If my children go to church, they shall not distract me or annoy others."

This reminded Margaret of many and many a scene she had witnessed at church, and supposed, as far as she had thought of it at all, a necessary evil. At first, in full remembrance of what her mother had said, Mabel sat very still, but before long she began to grow tired and restless.

"Is it most done?" she whispered.

Margaret appeared to be deaf, and Mabel repeated the question.

Margaret's deafness increased.

"I'm thirsty," said Mabel.

No answer.

"Doesn't Christ keep any water in His house?"

Here Margaret was tempted to smile, and so open the way for a discussion. But she was true to Mrs. Heath's direction, and presently the child, finding it useless to try to gain attention, gave up the attempt. Now, in most cases, it is the mother herself who is to blame when her little one claims and absorbs her chief attention at church. If she replies to its question, she sets it an example of talking during public worship, an act not to be tolerated, unless a case of illness makes it necessary. And as long as she will listen and reply, the child will vent its restlessness and weariness by incessant whispering. Rather than receive no notice at all, it will call forth such expressions as these:

"Julia, if you don't keep still, you sha'n't come to church. Julia, you *must not* get down from your seat. Julia, if you keep up this whispering I can't hear the sermon. You're thirsty? Well, I can't help it. Tired? I told you you would be tired, but you would come. Put down that fan. Don't open my parasol. What a naughty little girl you are!"

On their return from service, Mrs. Heath asked how Mabel had behaved, and Margaret reported things just as they were.

"I learned that scheme of deafness from mamma," said Mrs. Heath. "She never would listen to a word from us at church."

"Fred says she gave him warning one Sunday morning that if he got down from his seat, as he had a trick of doing, she would take him home," said Hatty.

"Yes, Hatty, I remember her doing that, and he never forgot it. Mamma had been an invalid, and unable to attend church, and his nurse used to take Fred, and she let him behave outrageously. It made a sensation, I can tell you, when mamma led him, roaring, down the broad aisle," returned Laura.

After dinner, Mabel was allowed to stretch her limbs by playing with Kitty; then her mother read to her and to the child next in age. Mabel sat with her doll in her arms, but intent on the reading.

"Why, *Belle!*" said Hatty, who was beginning to get over shyness that had kept her silent hitherto in the family gatherings. "Do you let Mabel have her playthings on Sunday?"

"I never made any laws for my children in regard to Sunday, save this: they should not be noisy on that day, and disturb those who wanted quiet. As soon as they ceased to be mere animals, and began to reason and to imitate, they laid aside their toys on Saturday night of their own accord."

"But Mabel has her doll."

"Yes, she has her baby, and you have yours."

Hatty, in fact, played more with Kitty on Sunday than on any other day in the week, except on nurse's afternoon "out"; for, like most mothers, she had charge of her child in order to let the servants attend church. And she would have thought the Lord a very hard Master if He had denied her this privilege. Mabel, on the other hand, had left off playing on Sunday, though she still allowed herself to hold her baby in her loving little arms. Now, is it likely that He who implanted this maternal instinct begrudged this child the caress she gave her doll?

"I don't think the cases are parallel," objected Hatty. "I *must* have Kitzie, and *must* amuse her. My mother locked up all our toys on Saturday night."

"Yes, many mothers do, and pride themselves on it. And so, as children must and will have occupation, they are likely to eat apples, gingerbread, or whatever they can get hold of, to pass away the time. This makes them heavy and ill-natured, and they get to quarrelling."

"But think how strict the old Jewish law was! A man stoned to death for picking up sticks!"

"The world was in its infancy then; and at any rate, He who made the law had His own reasons for it. But we live under a new dispensation, and ours is a Christian, not a Jewish, Sabbath. I have a great dread of making it a disagreeable day to my children."

"But you can't deny," said Laura, joining the group with her baby, "that there is awful laxity in regard to the Sabbath nowadays."

"No, I do not deny it; there always is reaction after pressure. It is to be hoped that things will right themselves in time."

"Well, I wish the Bible had given explicit directions about everything."

"Hasn't it?"

"No, indeed. Here are you and Hatty, both good souls as ever lived, taking contrary views of so apparently plain a thing as to how to keep Sunday. Now, the promise to those who don't do their own ways, nor find their own pleasure, or speak their own words, staggers me as much as any admonition or threat could. Thousands of Christians will tell you this is their ideal of Sunday; but who lives up to it? Goodness! Think of the worldly talk that has gone on today among those who profess to be saints!"

"Now you go too far, Laura," said Belle.

"No, I don't, an atom too far. Didn't I dine, not a month ago, at the Rev. Dr. Enoch Rivers', just after he had preached one of his solemn sermons, and didn't he slip into his luxurious dressing-gown and have his own way in it? And didn't he seek his own pleasure when he sat down to his roast-beef? And didn't he speak his own words exactly as if it was Monday?"

"And if he had preached while eating his dinner, you would call him a prig. And you surely would not ask him to come to the table in gown and bands! And as to the roast beef, what could be more wholesome?"

But by this time signs of discomfort and weariness began to show themselves in the little Heaths, and though their mother saw fit to be blind and deaf to this at church, she would not neglect them elsewhere. So dropping all further discussion, she turned as she always could, into a bright, animated, live mother, and entertained and interested her little flock, till it was time for tea. Sunday to them meant a great deal of mamma; a good many stories, sweet singing, cheerful faces, and invariably some special indulgence, such as having their bread-and-milk in special silver or special china, and eating with special spoons. No hard tasks were given on this day, such as committing to memory chapters from the Bible, hymns, catechism; it was entire rest.

Mr. and Mrs. Heath wanted their children to love God's day, and respect it, but they shrank from making them dread it as one full of needless restriction, hard tasks, toils, and tears. Nor were they willing to *force* them to spiritual exercises too early, or to incur the hazard of religious disgust by long exhortations. Their aim was so to live the week throughout, as they would have their children, in their measures, live. To the casual spectator, they seemed to do very much less for them than other Christian parents did for theirs. But the fact is, they never lost sight of their best interests, but pursued those interests quietly, persistently, without parade or fuss, and with the deepest possible sense, that under God they would lose or gain everything through them.

Happy are the children that are in such a case.

CHAPTER 6

As the next day was stormy, there was no going out for any one, and everybody seemed to have some special business on hand that kept the groups apart until after lunch, when they all got round the library fire, and Mr. Heath volunteered to read aloud to them. This answered very well for a time, but by degrees the ladies of the party fell into an animated discussion which silenced his voice. Of course the subject was a very important one.

"I never heard of such a thing," said Laura; "mamma, Mag does it all on the right side, and *so* beautifully!"

"But it should be done first on the wrong side and then on the right," said Belle.

"Oh, no, all on the wrong side," said Laura.

"Why, no," said Mrs. Grey, "you should pick up the stitches all around, draw the hole partially together, and then fill in—so."

Each was sure she was right, that all the others were wrong, and so they went on, laughing, explaining, exclaiming, and declaiming; the Rev. Mr. Heath looking on amused and puzzled, and wondering on what mighty deed these vivacious creatures were intent.

"How provoking that Cyril cannot act as umpire," said Laura; "but of course he knows nothing about it."

"What is there, pray, that I know nothing about?" he cried.

"Why, how to darn a stocking, to be sure."

"Ah, I have you there," he said, gravely. "Hand me the biggest hole you have."

"As if I *could* hand a hole!"

"Here's one of your own unconscionable hose," said Laura, "with holes as large as oranges. Oh, Cyril, how can you go so? Just suppose you should break your leg sometime, and somebody take off your boot and see such holes!"

"Oh, yes, and suppose when the surgeon comes to set my limb, you refuse to let him approach me lest he should discover my holey habits. There, I defy any of you to mend a hole as quickly as I have just mended this."

The grey stocking was passed from hand to hand and received due disgust from every feminine soul. Mr. Heath had gathered the hole into a hard bunch and tied it with a bit of twine.

"Well, now, I maintain that my way is the only true and proper one," he declared; "it saves time, saves eye-sight, saves yarn, and has the merit of originality."

"Oh, you men!" said Belle. "Mamma, you ought to have seen his clothes when he got home from his last European trip. They were a series of just such bunches, and all his white garments were tied up with black thread, and all the buttons sewed on his coats and pantaloons had been sewed on with white."

While this skirmish was going on, Margaret had finished her work and slipped off to the children. It was Saturday's work, but she had neglected it, and everything else in her absorption in her new delight.

"Where's Mag?" asked Laura, suddenly missing her.

"In the nursery, I'll venture to say," said Mrs. Grey.

"She's a perfect enthusiast about those buntlings," said Mr. Heath.

"So she is about everything," said Mrs. Grey.

"But the last idea, whatever it may be, fills her full, and she can only, by a great struggle with herself, find interest in anything else."

"What an inconvenient character to possess," said Mr. Heath. "It is fortunate for my people that I am not of that sort. Fancy my spending weeks shut up sermonizing, and then forsaking that sort of work, and taking to visiting; and then staying both employments and falling to reading."

"Why, I don't know that it would be so much amiss," said Laura. "You could make up a batch of sermons when the mood was on you, and that care off your mind you could wander round your parish at your own sweet will, and then, as you would have written and talked yourself out, you might, very properly, read yourself up again."

"There's no use in discussing Margaret," said Mrs. Grey. "You can't, any of you, possibly understand her, in this short time."

"But I see no complications or contradictions in her," said Mr. Heath; "and if there are none, why should we not understand her? What I should say of her is this: she is a shy, rather awkward, undeveloped girl, very young in her feelings, and so preferring the society of children to that of grown persons, and will, one of these days, make somebody a nice sort of a wife."

"Oh, you men!" repeated Belle, "you can't see through millstones when they have holes in them."

"If you mean by that, that I can't read a feminine at a glance, of course you are right."

"It provokes me to think Harry has so little discrimination," said Laura, "that he might have married a dozen girls whom he would have adored as much as he does me. Men are so queer. They fall in love today with black eyes, and are sure they shall never think of any other maidens. And then, tomorrow, its all 'blue eyes, of course.' The fact is, marriage is a mere lottery."

"Oh, for shame, Laura," said Belle; "I am sure Harry never could have been happy without you. You were made for each other. However, you were not in earnest; you never are, so what's the use of arguing with you?"

"Well," returned Laura, "it makes me feel so flat when Cyril reads such a girl as Margaret superficially. Why, that girl is a genius."

Mr. Heath smiled incredulously, but further argument was put an end to by the triumphant entrance of all the children, followed by Margaret. She had been teaching them an exercise it is impossible to describe: it was not a dance, nor yet a romp; but they made as pretty and unique an exhibition as it is possible to imagine, delighted themselves, and delighting the spectators. But as they whirled about the room, there flew out of Mabel's pocket a lump of sugar. The child stopped, blushed, and looked anxiously at her mother, who rose instantly, and led the child to her room.

"Who gave my little Mabel the sugar?" she asked, gently.

Mabel burst into tears.

"I didn't eat it, mamma! I wasn't going to eat it! I was going to give it back, I was."

Mrs. Heath could not doubt the child's sincerity; every tone of her voice said that, plainly. But that she had taken it by stealth, under sudden temptation, was equally clear. She remembered that she had herself placed her, standing on a chair, to regulate a shelf in the nursery closet, an amusement in which she was often indulged at home, and that a bowl of sugar was on this shelf. Now, in the case of her elder children, whose consciences were well aroused, Mrs. Heath did not find it necessary to keep them out of temptation of this sort; but she was usually careful to be watchful over the little ones. She blamed herself, now, for not putting the sugar out of reach, and as Mabel had, apparently, repented of her petty theft, and not eaten the coveted lump, she felt puzzled to know what course to pursue.

At last she said, tenderly, but decidedly, "My little Mabel knew it was wrong to take the sugar, but I am glad she meant to put it back. Never take *any*thing without leave. And the next time you want a lump of sugar very, very much, don't go and get it, and grieve mamma, and please Satan, but come straight to me and tell me all about it. Very likely I shall give you the lump, for I would rather give you a whole bowlful than have you take the tiniest bit yourself, because God wants all His little girls to be perfectly honest."

After the children were in bed that night, Mrs. Heath sought her mother's council in the matter.

"Ought I to have punished Mabel?" she asked. "It was a difficult case to manage. I cannot doubt her word. She never has shown the slightest disposition to falsehood."

"I think you were wise in doing nothing but give an earnest warning. But I would keep my eye upon her if I were you. You know the tendency to peculate dainties is so inherent in children that the Germans have invented a word for it, a verb, in fact."

"Yes; and this sort of peculation in a child might run into great criminality in an adult. You can't think what pains I have taken to keep the children free from this evil habit."

"One point is to keep them so busy and so happy, that they will not have time to hanker after forbidden dainties. Another is just what I presume you do: show sympathy with them in their frailties; tell them to come and ask for the luxuries they are in danger of appropriating feloniously, and as far as it is good for them, indulge them."

"Yes, I do that; yet isn't there danger of pampering gluttony?"

"No danger that a sensible woman, like you, will do that. You will easily lead the children to despise gluttony. And want of sympathy with them in their youthful longings after good things, will be sure to engender habits of deceit and dishonesty."

"What power the little creatures have to pain us," said Belle. "Oh, how it *hurt* me when I saw that bit of sugar! How it *hurt!*"

"My dear Belle," replied Mrs. Grey, "I considered you a very conscientious child, but you are a far more conscientious woman. Some might think you take this trespass of little Mabel's too much to heart; but I do not think so. If all young mothers looked at sin as you do, our eyes would not be assailed every time we take up our morning journal with the staring words, 'Embezzlement!' 'Fraud!' 'Burglary!' 'Murder!'"

"But, mamma, though my children have had their little faults and foibles, this is the first *dishonorable* act I have ever met with among them. There were certain things I was determined to have—obedience and uprightness."

"By uprightness you do not mean perfection?"

"No, I mean by it just what you do: freedom from everything mean and petty; a tendency upward, instead of tendency downward."

"And don't you see that this desire has come from God, and that He has responded to it? Don't you know that your children are wonderful children?"

"Perhaps they are, but I am not sure. They have been free from the temptations to which many others are exposed, because I have just lived in my nursery and kept the peace there. And their father enters into all my plans for them, and is not only kind—he is positively, and on principle, *courteous* to them."

"Yes, I see that. And you do not know what a mercy this is. Some men, even good men, as the saying goes, seem to think an imperious, harsh tone to their children, perfectly becoming. I can recall some scenes of discord that it makes me sick to think of. I saw a hand-to-hand fight once, between a father and a boy of fourteen. The latter had got irritable over his Greek; his father, a naturally impatient man, reproved him for it, in a sharp way, and at an unfortunate moment; (it is such a mistake to find fault at an untimely season) and the boy answered back. This called forth a severe reprimand; then came an impertinent reply; then an attempt to box on the boy's ears, which, being nearly as tall and strong as his father, the fellow resisted; then followed a scene which I am afraid is witnessed too often in that spot which ought to be a Paradise, but which ungoverned passion can turn into a hell."

Belle listened in painful silence.

At last she said:

"If my husband were that sort of man; if he so tampered with one of my boys—I should drop dead on the spot. Oh, mamma! do you really think such scenes occur in decent homes?—in homes where children are beloved?"

"Here you come to head-quarters. A happy home is one where first of all God is loved. Secondly, and as a sequence, where father and mother and children love each other."

"But all parents and children love each other," said Laura, who had just joined them.

"Yes, but there is love and love. Family affection is an instinct; even animals have it. But the sort of love to which I refer is of a higher sort. For instance, you are my child, less than two years of age, say. I caress and pet you. I supply all your wants, we get on admirably together, till some day you refuse to obey a direction I have given you. Now I may know, well enough, that I ought to oblige you to obey me, but I am weak and irresolute and selfish; I say to myself, I love my child too well to punish it; but do I speak the truth?"

"No, you deceive yourself," said Belle.

"Well, here is another method. Suppose I suddenly take you by the shoulders and give you a good shaking, or an angry blow?"

"The case is not supposable," said Laura, who could not be serious half an hour at a time.

"Don't, please, make a jest out of everything," said Belle; "I have got mamma agoing and I want to hear her talk."

"Then let me call Hatty if we are to have a treatise on education," said Laura, who rushed off and brought back her young sister-in-law with great zeal.

"Go on, mamma," said Belle. "We are talking about the way to deal with such little folks as yours, Hatty."

"I was saying," Mrs. Grey went on, "that my little child disobeys me; I may refuse to punish it under the delusion that I love it too well, or I may rudely shake or strike it. Both acts would proceed from selfishness and want of self-discipline. A hasty shake or a hasty blow, means anger, and does not mean love. It means something un-Christ-like, and is, therefore, unholy. Now, there is yet a third course before me. I may refuse to act from impulse, and resolve to act from the principle of love to the child, not its mere emotion."

"The *principle of love?*" Hatty repeated, in a low voice to herself.

"Yes, my dear. Love, as a principle, can make God its supreme object, while the emotion is, or appears to be, wanting; and this is true of all our earthly relations. Now I love my child better than I do myself, and I am going to hurt myself for its sake. It *must* learn obedience for its own sake. Therefore, whenever it opposes its will to mine, some penalty shall invariably follow."

"What, for instance?" asked Hatty, eagerly.

"Oh, there can be no one rule. The gentler the punishment the better, if the object desired is gained. We are dealing now with a child under two years of age. The tender little creature will not need the thunder of the law. Put it in a corner; seat it in a chair apart from the rest; it may be safe to shut it up in a closet, but it may not be; it depends on whether it is of a timid or a courageous character. The point is to make it aware that it is under law. With some natures this is easily taught."

"But what of a very willful one?" asked Hatty.

"Such a child will greatly tax parental faith and patience," was the reply. "But it will yield to wise, unselfish, Christian determination; and its strong will, once disciplined, may become one of its most serviceable characteristics."

"Would you use a rod?"

"What, on a little child? No."

"Hatty meant a metaphorical rod, I think," said Belle.

"Yes, I did. I mean should one slap a child's hands?"

"It depends upon the character of the mother, and on that of the child. There is no one rule for all parties. Children ought not to need corporeal punishment after they are two or three years old; and if properly managed, I doubt if they need it at all. But you see, my dear girls, that before a young father and mother are fit to train children they must be disciplined themselves. Pain should be inflicted by them without ill-temper, without hasty impulse, and in tender love. Children should know that love lies at the bottom of all parental law, and is its foundation."

"Doesn't it seem strange," asked Hatty, "that God commits children to such youthful hands? Why, how we blunder our way along! I have always heard that the eldest child had the hardest time in the family—the object of all sorts of experiments and mistakes."

"The eldest child certainly has that disadvantage," said Mrs. Grey; "and it has also the added disadvantage of entering the world with characteristics that children born later may possess but in a mellowed form. On the other hand, the first-born gets most from its parents as its birthright. Belle, here, has had a mother thirty years; but Fred has had one only twenty-two."

"How funny!" said Laura.

"Oh, dear! nothing looks funny to me," said Hatty, with a sigh. "Kitzie is so headstrong, and I am such a young little mother, and know so little how to manage her! And Fred can't endure spoiled children."

"Why, Hatty, you are not spoiling Kitty," Mrs. Grey said, with some surprise.

"Are you sure? Oh, but you don't see me at my worst! I'm on my good behavior when I'm here, trying to make you all love me. But devoted as I am to Kitty, living among you all here has made me see my own faults as I never did before. She often provokes me so that I want to do something awful—something one of my teachers did to me when I was specially naughty."

"What was that, pray?" asked Laura.

"Look daggers at her!" Hatty reluctantly replied.

"If you take lessons from my mother, you'll look milk and honey, not daggers," said Laura. "Dear me! do you know how late it is? Consider yourselves kissed, all around, for I'm off to bed." And singing like a bird, Laura hopped away to her room, hung lightly, for an instant, over her sleeping child, and was soon asleep, not much more than a child herself.

CHAPTER 7

This was the last family council, for the time—as Fred grew "wife and child sick," as he expressed it, and came and bore them away in triumph; and the Heaths, and Laura and her babies, soon followed. Little Mabel alone remained, without a fear on Belle's part that grandmamma would over-feed, or spoil, or neglect her darling—who, for her part, was content to stay with Margaret, between whom and herself there had sprung up a beautiful friendship.

Before Fred bore away his household gods, he sought a private interview with his mother, eager to know what she thought of them; for immediately on his marriage he had taken his wife abroad, and this was the first time she and his child had come under her roof.

"I think you a lucky fellow, young man," she said, good-humoredly. "Hatty is coming into full sympathy with us, and has in her the makings of a very fine woman, as Mrs. Goodwin once said of her Sophie. I suppose you do not expect anything more from me than this?"

"Now, mother, this isn't fair," he remonstrated. "I never pretended that she was equal to you, or to the girls; but she has a great deal of character, and yet is very impressible. I can wind her round my finger like a piece of silk."

"She's much more likely to wind you round hers. She has a will of iron. But I do not object to that."

"Indeed you wouldn't if you could see her bear pain. Oh, you'll love her to distraction when you come to know her as well as I do. Poor little thing, how she did dread running the gauntlet of all you keen-eyed, cultivated women!"

"You ought to have spared her that. You know we never pick flaws in each other. Why, Fred, I expect, in time, to love Hatty just about as I love you. But you know my affections move slowly."

"I know I never saw anyone whose affections move with more rapidity," laughed Fred. "But I suppose a mother never finds a paragon worthy of her son."

"Oh, as to that, I consider Hatty quite your equal, if not your superior. In fact, her greatest fault is one she will outgrow."

"And what is that?"

"Youth. She stepped out of school into a nursery; she has had no liberty, no stopping-place between girlhood and motherhood. I cannot imagine how her mother could permit her to marry so young, poor child."

"Her mother could tell you the reason," said Fred, with a good-humored smile that had in it just the least touch of complacency.

"Well, the thing is done, at any rate. And now, my dear boy, I charge you to make allowance for Hatty, if, amid the wear and tear of domestic life, she falls below the ideal you now make of her. Depend upon it, there are no ideal characters on earth."

"Well, isn't Kitty a perfect beauty?"

"She is very pretty."

"Is that all you have to say? In my eyes, she is the most beautiful child on earth. But as to her behavior, I can't say I have anything to boast of. She is a little fury when she is provoked."

"Strange, isn't it?" said Mrs. Grey.

"But, mother, I have outgrown all that sort of thing. And it is provoking to see one's faults repeated in one's child. But you may depend upon it, we are not going to spoil Kitty. Her mother fights her out on every line of battle."

"But be cautious, Fred. This little human flower must expand elsewhere than on a battle-field. You can't begin too soon to let her see that intense, unselfish love lies at the bottom of all restraint and correction. You and Hatty are both, by nature, law-givers, and I do not doubt you will have a family of obedient children, as you ought to do. But think of the goodness as well as the severity of God, when you discipline your child. Never enter upon a conflict with her without asking Him how to proceed; in this way you will avoid a thousand mistakes."

Fred colored and looked embarrassed. It had not occurred to him that a grown-up man was not quite equal to the task of training a little child; on the contrary, he had rather prided himself on his skill.

"To go back to Hatty," he said, "she is perfectly wild about you."

"Well, then, if you have failed to find me as enthusiastic about your little wife as you hoped to do, I may as well own here that I am not fond of having people 'perfectly wild' about me. It can't last. I am no angel; and it isn't pleasant to be soaked in hot water one day, and left to freeze the next. Just as soon as Hatty will let me get off the throne on which she has placed me, and seat myself on the everyday chair on which I belong, I shall love her and enjoy her love as I can't do now, when I have a mean sort of feeling that she is giving more than she gets, and that I am taking more than I deserve. Now the murder is all out, and we can start a little more fairly and squarely than we did at first."

Fred smiled and took the frank hand his mother offered him in both his.

"I wouldn't own Hatty if she did not admire my mother," he said. "And do you think there is a fair prospect of Kitty's turning out well at last?"

"Yes, my dear boy, if you will lay to heart the counsel of your mother, and part with all pride and self-reliance, and rely on Divine strength alone. Oh, that I had realized this in the early years of my married life, and taken counsel of God at every step!"

"I don't see but we must go home and reconstruct our domestic life," said Fred. "We were young and strong, and of one mind; we were resolved to have an obedient child, at any cost; and of course we have prayed for her; but I am afraid not specifically enough."

"Kitty is not a common child, and I dare say will cost you a great deal. I would make just as few laws for her as possible, and train her to obedience by long patience. Never threaten her, never fight with her, never strike her."

"Never fight with her! Why, mother, she disputes every inch of ground. We *have* to fight with her. And as to whipping her, why, I thought you believed in the rod?"

"In some cases I do, but not in Kitty's. She has such a strong character that you might, sometime, whip her to death."

"She gets fortitude from her mother," said Fred. "What are we to do with her, then?"

"Punish her, invariably, for every act of disobedience, and let the matter rest there."

"What, let her have her own way? Why, mother, I know grandparents generally do grow lax as they advance in years, but I did not expect it of you. Oh, you forget what rebels some of us were."

"No, my son, I do not forget. I look at life differently from what I once did. I know that, mingled with some high principle, I had pride, self-reliance, and self-will in the management of my children, and now I want you all to have the benefit of my experience. You may depend upon it, there are times when a wise parent must make humbling concessions to a proud, excited child, when it is acting its worst self."

"Well, now, suppose I tell Kitty to say 'Please,' and she won't, what am I to do?"

"You might threaten to whip her till she said it, and she become so tired out as to be utterly unable to utter the word. Parents are continually making mistakes of this sort. A child has not always control of its tongue. Doesn't yours sometimes cleave to the roof of your mouth? And there is another thing, Kitzie is shy. What it would cost an ordinary child no effort to do, might be torture to her; you must be careful what you direct her to do, lest you should demand something she cannot perform. I once knew a timid girl of ten years, attempt to slip out of a room full of company unobserved. When her mother called her back to bid the party goodnight she came directly, but blushing painfully, and the words she tried to utter died on her lips. Her mother was a strict disciplinarian, and thought it her duty to say, 'You cannot go to bed till you have obeyed me.' The child stood there a long, long time, weeping bitterly; she was not disobedient in her habits, she was tired, she longed to get out of sight of those astonished eyes; but the words would not come. At last, ready to drop with fatigue, she shrieked them out, and was allowed to creep to bed, with a sense of being the naughtiest girl in the world. Ah, Fred, let no careless word tamper with the delicate, complicated machinery of your child's soul."

"I shall go home a wiser, but a sadder man," said Fred. "I never realized before that the work of training up a child is such an *awful* task."

"It is only awful when undertaken by a fool or a knave. You will find, as other children come to you, that rules that apply to one, fail in regard to another. What I have advised in regard to Kitzie, may not apply in the least to your Fred, Jr., when you get that young man."

Fred Grey was worth all he had cost his mother, for his was a strong, thoughtful character. And all that she had now said to him impressed him, as it did his wife, when he repeated it to her. Poor little baby Kitty never had another battle with her resolute young parents; yet day by day she was learning obedience; day by day they were learning humility and self-control. Their love to each other and to their child grew purer and sweeter, and cooperating together in all their plans for her, her lot bid fair to be a most enviable one.

Mrs. Grey and Margaret had plenty of work on their hands after quiet once more settled down upon them. Letters and cards had accumulated, and must be attended to; there were protégés to look after; there was Mabel to love and to watch and to care for. And, as readers ought to know by intuition, but young Master Accuracy declares they do not, there was Mrs. Grey's new book on the stocks, and which the Christmas festivities had brought to a stand-still.

CHAPTER 8

Although Mrs. Grey had spent a large part of her life in the city of Gotham, that was not, at this time, her home. When they had a house full of boys and girls she and her husband met with so many annoyances in their summer resorts, growing out of such a flock to dispose of, that they at last secured a large house in the vicinity, thereby not only adding greatly to the comfort of the family, but improving their health, since, with a table at her command, Mrs. Grey could provide wholesome food for her family. Mr. Grey's death occurred before any of the children had become settled in life, and the loneliness of her widowhood was cheered by their presence. But when, midway between fifty and sixty, she was left alone with Maud, and ceased to have any special cares, she became everybody's property, and was used by all sorts of people in all sorts of ways. Soon after her work on education appeared, she received numerous letters, asking counsel in special cases to which she had made no allusion there, the following being one:

DEAR MRS. GREY:—

Charlie and I have just finished your last book, and think you must be *perfectly lovely!* I should like *so* much to see you. May I come? And if I may, will you tell me what train to take? I have so many things to say to you. And Charlie says he shall be so glad to have me come under your influence.

Your admiring friend,

MRS. LIBBIE CLARE.

No. —, Fifth Avenue.

Mrs. Grey's keen eye took in the measure of "Mrs. Libbie Clare" at a glance. But if it was keen it was not unkind. Turning to Margaret, who sat near, she said, "Will you answer this, and tell the child she may come out by the 9:10 train any morning this week?"

"Oh, aunty, you are not going to give up a *morning* to a woman who signs herself 'Mrs.'? Can't she come in the afternoon?"

"No, the days are too short."

"But, aunty, you have had no leisure for a long time, and have got intent on your book again."

"Yes, dear, I know, but here is a chance to gratify and perhaps be of use to one of those 'neighbors' we are told to love. Now, self-ishness might urge me to go on with my work, but obedience to Christian duty may and ought to be stronger than self."

Margaret said no more; but she was puzzled. She did not under-stand the readiness shown by Mrs. Grey to be "pulled about," as she termed it. Somehow she felt sure that Mrs. Libbie Clare was not much of a woman, and was coming to exhibit herself rather than to see her aunt.

And she was right. Mrs. Clare was quite young, was very proud of her husband and children, told their whole history, gave her own views of education, and hardly allowed Mrs. Grey to utter a word. Two mortal hours she stayed, and then when she took leave, put up her mouth for a kiss, without taking her hands from her muff, said she had had a delightful visit, and hoped it would soon be returned.

Mrs. Grey went back to her desk feeling decidedly flat, and found that Margaret, according to her wont, had been illustrating her MS. with a ridiculously funny caricature of a young father holding his son and heir most awkwardly in his arms, while there proceeded from its mouth the words, "Oh, how he pinches! how he pinches!"

She laughed, cut it out, and threw it into a drawer, where kindred sketches already reposed. She had just resumed her pen when Mrs. Grosgrain was announced.

"Who is Mrs. Grosgrain?" asked Margaret. "I don't remember ever seeing or hearing of her."

"No, she was in Europe when you came here, and has only just returned. I shall want her to see you, sometime." So saying, Mrs. Grey proceeded to meet her guest, and after some animated conversation together, the latter said:

"I hear you have adopted a young orphan girl, to take the place to you of your darling Maud. Yet, I don't see how you could."

"You have not heard the story quite correctly," replied Mrs. Grey. "It is true that I have adopted a young girl of Maud's age, but not to fill her place. No one can or ought to fill that. But there were so many things left by her that were adapted to gratify the taste of a young person, and that young person a girl, that I longed to see them enjoyed. There was Maud's piano standing idle; her rooms tastefully furnished, left empty; and, to tell the truth, plenty of love in this old heart to give away. That *I* was to gain much, if anything, never crossed my mind. But all has turned out delightfully."

"Is she like Maud, then?"

"Not in the least. She is a girl of very marked character; once I could not have tolerated her faults. But she amuses me and keeps me young; and she is going to become a very fine woman in time."

"And in the meanwhile?"

"Why, I shall have to put up with some decided opinions and habits that are not to my mind. But I did not look for, or expect to find, a faultless character. Margaret has heart and soul; she has enthusiasm; she knows her own mind and decides upon this and that at once, and once for all. She does not care for music, as Maud did; in fact, she hates it."

"*Hates* it!"

Mrs. Grey smiled. "Oh, it is all love or hate with her. She can't be indifferent to anything. I found she had decided, though undeveloped, artistic talent, and she is taking lessons in drawing and painting. I never met a person who could do so many things well."

"Is not her sudden good fortune turning her head?"

"Not at all. She has too much good common sense for that. In any sphere she would have been self-reliant, and perhaps appear, to some persons, conceited. But she is too proud to be conceited."

"Proud, indeed," thought Mrs. Grosgrain, who did not comprehend the vigorous character described. "I should think she had little to be proud of. Poor Mrs. Grey, she ought to have a very different young person about her at her time of life. Some sweet, lovely girl like little Matty Rhodes. Dear Matty! I wish she had such a home as this. What a pity it all happened while I was abroad. I would have spoken a good word for the child if I had known. My sister would have been so thankful to see one of her six girls provided for."

During this soliloquy, Mrs. Grey had gone on talking, but Mrs. Grosgrain had not heard a word, and now took leave.

"Well, girls," she said, on reaching home, "I have seen Mrs. Grey, but she did not exhibit her new acquisition. Still, you must all go and call on her prize."

"I don't intend to go," said Miss Grosgrain. "Mrs. Grey ought not to expect people in society to fall in with her oddities."

"You must either call on this girl or give up Mrs. Grey altogether. She has taken her right into poor Maud's place, and is quite infatuated about her; although, from her description, I should judge her to be a disagreeable creature."

"But to expect *us* to associate with a person picked up out of the streets, as it were; really it is too much."

"You needn't associate with her; merely go and make a short call, just to keep up appearances with Mrs. Grey, you know."

"Why not drop Mrs. Grey, and done with it?"

"Because we can't afford to have her drop us. You seem to forget the struggle we have made to get a position, and to fancy we can maintain it without difficulty."

"We might forget it if you ever gave us a chance, but you are forever reminding us of it. People are too glad to eat our splendid dinners, and to attend our elegant parties, to drop us."

"Mrs. Grey never eats our dinners or comes to our parties. Now, girls, I am determined to keep up the acquaintance. Hers is one of the few old families we have got into; she is rich, she is popular; one meets nice people at her house, and my policy always has been and always will be, 'Hold fast what I give you and catch what you can.'"

"For my part," said Miss Mary, "I am curious to see and to put down this upstart of a girl. I flatter myself that I am gifted in that line."

"Yes, let's go," said Miss Flora, "it will be such fun!"

Accordingly, the next day, the four Misses Grosgrain went in a body to call on Margaret. She had just set her palette in order, to paint some tea-roses before they began to droop, and was anything but pleased at the interruption. The moment she laid eyes upon them she conceived an aversion for them which she found it almost impossible to conceal. They, on their part, had made up their minds that she was of low origin, and intended to make it at once clear that the visit originated in no intention to gratify her.

"Mamma has told us about your singular good fortune," began the eldest young lady, "and desired us to show our respect for Mrs. Grey by calling on you."

Instantly hurt by this intentional sting, Margaret was tempted to reply in like manner. But she controlled herself, and said, stiffly:

"My aunt's friends are welcome, of course."

"Oh, is she your aunt, after all?" cried Miss Flora. "We supposed you were not related to her in any way."

"Nor am I," replied Margaret; and condescended to no explanations.

"It was a curious freak of Mrs. Grey, taking you up so, was it not?" inquired Miss Mary in a most innocent tone. "How surprised you must have been! How strange it must seem to be suddenly introduced to such new scenes! Do excuse our curiosity, we would not do anything ill-bred for the world; but how did you contrive to ingratiate yourself so with her?"

"By no contrivance whatever; I scorn contrivance!"

"Oh, I did not mean to offend you."

"I am not offended."

"Well, touched, then. Not one of us would intentionally say anything ill-bred. Mamma has trained us *so* carefully! We have just returned from Europe, where we spent nearly three years. It is very improving. You ought to coax Mrs. Grey to take you abroad. You have no idea how refining it is to see works of art, and to mix with cultivated people."

"I never coax," was the reply.

"Comme elle est fière!"[1] said one sister to another.

"Et assez jaune!"[2] said the other.

"Proud and yellow," repeated Margaret, "but unfortunately not deaf or dumb."

"Goodness! Who could fancy you understood French! What an unlucky blunder we have made."

"Our respect for Mrs. Grey—"

"Rules of good-breeding—"

"Difficult position—"

cried the sisters in chorus, each warbling a different tune, and each pretty thoroughly mortified and embarrassed. There was nothing left for it but to take leave.

"What a disagreeable scrape that girl has got us into!" said Miss Grosgrain, as soon as they were safe in their carriage.

"Well, it's rather hard, I must say," complained another, "to have to demean one's-self to visit a creature about whose antecedents one knows nothing. Where can she have picked up French, I wonder?"

"Very likely from some fellow-servant, some nursery-governess, where she has lived," cried Miss Mary.

---

1 Comme elle est fière—As she is proud.

2 Et assez jaune—And pretty yellow.

"Now, Mary Grosgrain, you don't mean that she has been any-body's servant?"

"Well, I do not say that, positively, but I know Mrs. Grey picked her up in a tenement-house. Fancy our visiting an inmate of a tenement-house!"

"How tall she is!"

"And how she was dressed! Not a ring or a bracelet, or a bow or a puff. But of course Mrs. Grey has to keep her down."

"I saw a great smooch of paint on her sleeve," said Miss Mary.

"She hasn't a particle of style," said Miss Flora.

"Of course not; how should she? She has not had our advantages."

"I heard that she was a splendid-looking girl," said Miss Grosgrain.

"From whom?"

"Fred Rogers."

"Pooh! Fred Rogers!"

"Mamma, we've had such a time," cried all four, when they reached home. "Such airs as that girl puts on. And somehow con-trived to make us feel flat, though she is a nobody. Mrs. Grey is altogether too Quixotic. It is very annoying to have to humor her whims. What in the world did she want of another daughter, when she has a dozen or so of her own?"

"But they are all married, and live at a distance, and she was getting old, and probably needed a companion to wait upon her, mend her lace, do her clear-starching, draw her checks, do her shop-ping, go to market, and all that sort of thing," said Mrs. Grosgrain. "She has put her right in Maud's room. Of all things how strange! And has given away all Maud's beautiful clothes! Why, if I should lose either of you I should regard your garments as the most sacred things in the world; no mortal should ever touch them. But some people have so little feeling."

"It isn't quite fair to say that Mrs. Grey has little feeling," said Miss Grosgrain, "for when they were screwing down the lid of Maud's coffin she fainted away. She's *queer;* that's the word to describe her—*queer.*"

"Well, yes, that *is* the word," said Mrs. Grosgrain. "When I called the other day, she seemed—well, it's an awful thing to say, and I hope you won't repeat it, girls, but she actually seemed— happy! Why, if one of you should die I should not have another happy moment. I should consecrate my life to grief."

In the privacy of their own room that night, Miss Grosgrain dutifully remarked to Miss Clara:

"Mamma did not 'consecrate her life to grief' after papa's death, but to spending his money."

"Oh, as to that, I think she did all he could have expected," was the reply. "She wore the deepest and the most fashionable mourning she could find; had the deepest possible black edge to her cards, and always put on a mournful expression whenever anyone called."

Miss Grosgrain smiled grimly.

"You are right as to the 'mournful expression'; she did 'put it on' with a vengeance."

CHAPTER 9

Margaret, meanwhile, returned to her work, with burning cheeks.

"It is true," she said to herself, "that people have a right to sneer at me. My mother has been a servant and so have I. But we were not born to it, either of us. Even if Mrs. Grey hadn't taken me up, I shouldn't have spent my life in a kitchen. Nobody ever did who could paint like *that!* And yet, my poor father never got on, and it isn't likely I have more talent than he had. But stop; it was only yesterday aunty was saying that gifts sometimes overleap one generation; it is quite possible that I had a grandfather or grandmother whose abilities have come to me. How horrid it is not to know one's relatives!"

Just here letters were brought in; one for Margaret, several for Mrs. Grey. Margaret seized hers with a thrill of surprise and delight, for this was an era in her life, her first letter! And she has no objection to our reading it:

Dear Margaret:—

I cannot help loving you for your love to my mother and to my little Mabel, and wanted to tell you so when I was at home, but have no faculty for showing what I feel. We are all glad mother has your bright face to look at when she misses ours. And, Margaret, don't let her work too hard. She does not realize how dear Maud's death has worn upon her, but I see it plainly, and it almost vexes me to see how she allows herself to be at everybody's beck and call. And yet, I love her for it, too; it is only living out her religion, as we all must learn to do.

Now, a word about my little pet; and don't laugh at me as a silly mother who makes a fuss about trifles, but please watch the lammie, without seeming to do it, and if you see anything dishonorable dawning in her character, write and tell me so. I know it is generally a thankless task to tell mothers of their children's faults, but I can bear it if it is done kindly, though as bad as anybody if it is done unkindly. Just now this is all I have time to say, except that I am your affectionate sister,

BELLE.

"'Your affectionate sister, Belle!'" Great, bright tears filled Margaret's eyes as they fell upon the words.

"How *could* I let those dreadful Grosgrains hurt me so," she asked herself, "when I have such friends? Oh, Belle, how I do admire and love you! But what is this about my pet? Mabel dishonorable? That little white lamb! I'm sure she isn't!"

She handed the letter to Mrs. Grey, and stood leaning over her as she read it.

"Isn't it just lovely in B.—Mrs. Heath—to write me such a letter, and call herself my sister?"

"It is just like her," said Mrs. Grey, "and it is worth having, because it cost her something. Now it is different with Laura. Laura takes everything easy."

"But what a curious question about Mabel!"

"Oh, that is on account of the bit of sugar the child took from the nursery-closet."

"When?"

"On the day you exhibited the children so prettily."

"And who dares say my innocent little darling is a thief?" cried

Margaret, her color rising. "I gave her sugar in order to coax her to take her part with the other children, for she was shy about it at first. Did her mother fancy she took it herself?"

"She naturally thought so, but as the child had not eaten it, and said she did not mean to do so, she did not punish her."

"It is a thousand pities. But as Mabel knew herself to be innocent, why didn't she declare it? Why did she blush and cry as if she had done something wrong?"

"Because she had done wrong in accepting it. It never would answer for such a young child to eat whatever injudicious persons chose to give it, therefore Belle forbids her little ones receiving dainties save from herself or some other authorized hand. You can't imagine how recklessly many people behave in such matters. I have known a conscientious child to be almost laughed into eating and drinking forbidden luxuries, such as coffee, mince-pie, and rich cake."

"I did not know one had to be so careful with children."

"It is the case, though, and if it seems to you that Belle has made too much of this affair, you must remember that she must adapt herself to the very small world in which Mabel lives, and whose trivial wants are as great to her as the most serious ones will be, by and by."

"I shall write to B.—Mrs. Heath—this very minute," cried Margaret, "but what shall I call her?"

"I think she has settled that. Call her Belle. But, before you begin I want you to see what a lovely little note the mail has brought me!"

And if Margaret reads it, why shouldn't we?

DEAR MRS. GREY:—

I have not the faintest idea that you are pining for a letter from me, but it is a relief to me now and then to say that I love you, and the size of the sheet I write it on is no symbol how much.

I am reading a delightful book to my invalid auntie; in it a lady speaks of a friend as an "Amen to the Bible." *That*, say I, is what Mrs. Grey has been to me.

Again, "Mrs. Jameson was the consoler of her sex in England."
Ah, say I, *Mrs. Grey* is the consoler of her sex in America.

But you will think I have been kissing the blarney stone. But
when people *mean* things, can't they say them?

I stay with auntie all the time, day and night, and am real happy
in a quiet way, for I do feel, in a small degree, I know, but a great
deal more than ever before, the loving-kindness of my Heavenly
Father, the *goodness and severity of God.*

Yours, lovingly and gratefully,

HELENA.

"What a graceful little note, and on what a tiny sheet!" exclaimed
Margaret. "Who is this Helena? Any one I know?"

"You have never seen her, but she often visits me, and I love her
much. Her forte is in writing charming letters. I shall want you to
know her. But you want to write to Belle now, and I won't detain
you."

Margaret rushed off to her room, and rushed, as it were, a shov-
elful of hot coals at Belle, as reply to her letter. Then what receptacle
was worthy to hold this treasure? Her eye fell upon one object after
another, and rejected them, till it rested upon her Russian leather
mouchoir-case.

"The very thing!" she cried; pulled out the handkerchiefs, thrust
them, *en masse*, into a drawer, replaced them with the letter, and
then flew to hug and kiss Mabel, on whom she vented the feeling
she could not express.

. Ah, Margaret, you will have many, many such idols as you are
now making of Belle Heath! How many times they will fall off the
altar, and you will put them in their place again! What power they
will have to swell your heart with joy, to melt it into tears! And
yet—thank God that you have a heart! for even an aching one is
better than none at all.

"I want you to get dressed, now," said Mrs. Grey, "for I have
ordered the carriage, and am going to make some visits."

Margaret groaned. She did not believe in paying visits, except to very agreeable people, and was very apt to be silent and stupid in company, unless it was congenial. And this was not entirely her own fault. It belonged to her type of character as much as her gifts did.

She went off and dressed now, however, without a word of remonstrance, for she was in a happy mood; Belle's letter warming and brightening her.

As they drove from house to house, she chatted gayly with her aunt of a score of innocent, girlish things, and Mrs. Grey listened, and smiled, amused at her keen observation, her simplicity and naturalness. Her mother had so guarded her life that she was very ignorant of evil, and Mrs. Grey had kept up this care successfully.

"I know how I would arrange things if I had the management of them. I would go to see people I loved, ever so often, and have them come to see me. But I would have nothing to do with anybody else, in the way of visiting them. Why not? Why should those who do not love each other waste their time in meeting?"

"And what reason would you give those you neglected for your conduct?"

"Oh, I would speak the truth; I would just say, out and out, I don't love you, so I am not going to see you; you don't love me, and so you needn't come to see me."

"And how many friends should you have, at that rate?"

"Not so very many, but they would all be after my own heart."

"Well, now, let us see how your scheme will work. Here are two sisters; you love one, and can't bear the other. You make your frank statement to both, asking the one to come to see you, and the other to keep her distance; how much sympathy can exist between them after it? You probably will lose the friendship of both.

"Take another instance. You meet with a person with whom you fall in love, as you term it; she is more cautious than you, and hesitates to give her friendship until she knows you better. She asks questions about you of sister Number Two, who replies, 'All I know about her is, that she is very odd and very rude, and thinks herself capable of reconstructing society.' Now, the fact is simply this. We are all more or less dependent on each other. And therefore we must put up with some people who are not congenial to us, and they must put up with us."

"Yes, I see. Wouldn't it be nice to have an island which no disagreeable or stupid people would be allowed to visit! Everybody in it pleasant, and cultivated, and refined; like Belle, for instance."

"It might be nice, but not possible; and, if possible, not best. In the first place, there would be different opinions as to who would be eligible as inhabitants of your famous island. A. would object to B., and B. to C. Besides, life in this world is not to be just to our minds. We need the discipline of contact with uncongenial characters. But then, we are to stay in this world but a short time. By and by we shall go to a far more delightful and ideal spot than your island; an abode into which will be gathered the best, the wisest, the purest beings that ever adorned earth."

"Still, it seems hard to have to waste so much precious time in driving about from house to house. You have plenty of things to occupy every moment. You have your books to write, and a thousand other things to do; and as for me, with all the time I've lost, it seems almost wicked to be going to see people who care nothing for me, and for whom I don't care a fig."

"The time is not wasted, however. I seldom, if ever, make a morning visit without getting a new thought from somebody; and as for you, you must see something of the world, or be awkward and ill at ease all your life. But here we are at Mrs. Wallace's; she has some pretty little children; they may interest you."

Mrs. Wallace was a sweet-looking young woman, and was followed into the parlor by three girls, who soon gave evidence of being strong-minded females, though the eldest was not more than ten years old. They appropriated Margaret at once. One seized her muff and pelted the others with it. Another insisted on unbuttoning her gloves. A third wanted to know how much her hat cost. Now this may sound like exaggeration, but it is the literal truth. Their mother never seemed to realize that a forward, unabashed child is one of the most annoying and unnatural things in the world; she suffered these little girls, who were not bad children, to form these offensive habits, and victimized all her friends with them. When they had got all the entertainment out of Margaret she was able to render them, they thought she might be permitted to depart, and asked their mother, in audible whispers, how long "they" were going to stay. She whispered back, and Mrs. Grey, finding her too much occupied with them to attend further to her, rose to take leave.

"What dreadful children!" ejaculated Margaret, as they re-entered the carriage. "Aunty, you say you get some thought out of almost every visit you make; now what did you get out of this one?"

Mrs. Grey smiled.

"I know those children of old," she said, "and never had so comfortable a visit there before, as this time you were their prey. Well, my thought was this: How much depends on manners! These little girls are not bad children, and yet they are the terror of all their mother's friends. They ought to be kept in their nursery, and not be allowed to come into the parlor to torment visitors."

"Doesn't she know what annoyance they cause?"

"Perhaps she partially knows it, but fancies their great beauty will atone for that. We must not be hard upon her. The temptation to display those three beautiful faces is very great. We don't know what we should do under similar circumstances."

"Don't we?" cried Margaret. "I know what I should do. I should lock them all up in a box rather than let them behave as they do. Why, I would rather they were shy and awkward than bold and presuming as they are. I suppose people began by noticing them on account of their curling hair, and brown eyes, and bright speeches—for they are bright—and that spoiled them."

"Yes; and manners one can tolerate in a child of three, are intolerable in one of ten. However, these girls will outgrow these outside faults, I dare say, and grow up into agreeable and estimable women. Their mother has this one weak spot of wanting to display them;

but, in the main, she is wise and true, and will exert a good influence over them."

"Oh! but, aunty, you did not hear all that passed. They are not merely rude—they are conceited. One of them asked me if I ever saw such pretty hair as hers, and then had a dispute with another who declared hers was prettier!"

"Beauty is a snare, no doubt," said Mrs. Grey; "and I am afraid it is over-valued in that home. And now for the Grosgrains."

"Oh, those Grosgrains! *Must* I return their visit? We haven't a single idea in common. And they look down upon me so!"

"Yes, I can imagine that. But do not let it disturb you. They will not put on any airs in my presence, for I know, and they know that I know, whence they sprung. Their mother was brought up in a foundling hospital, and after she left it, learned a trade—that of tailoress. She was a hard-working, friendless girl, and had a certain kind of good looks as dowry. A young man took a fancy to, and married her. She kept at work at her trade, and made the first suit of clothes my Frank ever wore. They had no children for some years, so they laid up money, and began to live in more comfort than they ever had dreamed of doing. He had good business capacity, and she was ambitious. They kept rising in the world, and would have liked to have their early history fade out of people's memories. Then came these four girls, by whom they did the best they could. Women rise as men cannot do; they have quick, smart ways, and pick up a certain outside kind of good breeding, and the Grosgrains availed themselves of these advantages to the best of their ability. But the struggle to keep up on the one hand, and unaccustomed luxuries on the other, proved too much for Mrs. Grosgrain, and she sank under it. Now during her career as a woman of means, she had taken a young sister into her home, and educated her as far as money could educate, and it was natural enough for Mr. Grosgrain to marry her. She made as good a mother to the girls as she knew how to be, but in the best sense of the word never made ladies of them. As to Mr. Grosgrain, he had one talent: it was for making money, and money he made; but he had no culture, and no faculty for living in style; and the luxuries which were the delight of his wife and daughters, had no charm for him, especially as they were expensive. There was no end to the family squabbles on the subject of expenditures. He had five females to twit, and to snub, and to set him right—five females to spend his money and ruin him. He became a monomaniac, and worried himself to death on the ground of poverty. His departure was a relief to them all. They immediately went abroad and wandered all over Europe, during a long period. It makes one shudder to think of their being regarded there as representative Americans. Now I have not told you all this for the sake of talking, or to prejudice you against them. I only want you not to allow them to put you in a false position by looking down upon you. Observe a proper self-respect when in their company. You are far less a *parvenu*[1] than they."

"But, aunty, how did they get in with you?"

"Why, the first Mrs. Grosgrain, mother of the girls, used to come to me as tailoress, by the day, and would bring her sister to sew with her. Then when they became rich they fancied that that put us on a level. The present Mrs. Grosgrain has been instructed and snubbed by turns, until she has acquired a good use of language; and when they set up their carriage, and came and called on me, I thought it would be a silly pride in me not to return the visit. And I have a benevolent interest in them, for one thing. And then if it is any satisfaction to them to boast that they are, oh! *so* intimate with me, why not let them have it? It does not hurt me. If I should altogether turn a cold shoulder to them, they would think I despised them for their low origin. Now I despise nobody for accidents of birth over which they have had no control; neither do I bow down to royalty itself, unless it is as pure and high-toned as it is noble."

On arriving at Mrs. Grosgrain's ostentatious residence, they were informed that the ladies were all engaged. This was so far true, that they were engaged in peeping over the banisters to see who

1 Parvenu—an upstart; a man newly risen into notice.

their visitors were, in dressing-gowns and curl-papers.

"Now, girls, it is too bad," said Mrs. Grosgrain, as the cards were handed her. "Here we have lost a visit from Mrs. Grey! We really ought to be dressed at this time of day. There's no knowing when she will call again. And it is such a distinction to have her carriage at our door! I do hope the Van Tropes saw it."

"I can't bear her books," said Miss Grosgrain.

"Nor I," said Miss Mary.

"But it's the fashion to read 'em," said Mrs. Grosgrain, "and to like 'em, too. And when I think your marmer used to be a tailoress, and your parper—"

"Now do hush!" cried Miss Grosgrain, putting her hand over the maternal mouth. "Why need you be forever alluding to such things? You never let us have the ghost of a chance to forget them."

"If you had gone through all I have, I guess you'd allude to it often enough. Your poor parper and marmer, they—"

"Do, for goodness' sake, stop calling him parper! It is *so* American! Going abroad hasn't done you a bit of good."

CHAPTER 10

Mabel's "baby" (she never called it dolly) was almost always nestling in her arms. It seemed to fill the maternal element of her character, and though she was a wee little mother, a veritable mother she was, and it was amusing to watch her quaint ways with it. The march of improvement had taken up dolls, as well as everything else. What marvels of art are their generation, nowadays! Compare them with the stiff wooden monsters of fifty years ago, with their back hair done up like that of aged matrons, surmounted with high yellow combs! What a stretch of imagination is required to fancy these angular ladies' *babies*.

But now an event befell that nearly broke her heart. Baby's sweet blue eyes suddenly disappeared, leaving two empty holes in her face. From that moment all illusion concerning her vanished. The eyes of real babies never dropped down inside of them. So she begged to have it put away where she could never again be horrified by the sight. Margaret could not understand this. But Mabel had always shrank from the sight of unpleasant objects, and her aversion to her baby in its mutilated state was almost morbid. Still she bemoaned her loss sorely, and when Mrs. Grey, fearing she would make herself ill with crying, left the book she was writing, and everything else, and went to the city to replace the departed, nothing would induce the child to accept the offering, though it was the facsimile of the poor blue-eyed Mary.

Margaret spent a large part of the next day in making paper dolls for Mabel. Her nature was opulent; as she loved the few she loved to infatuation, so her gifts were prodigal. Never had a child so suddenly acquired a large family; their name was legion. Still, they did not supersede her darling.

"I want a yeal live baby," she said, amid her tears.

"So do I," said Margaret, "but I don't cry for one. And there are no live babies for sale, so I can't buy one for myself, or for you." Mabel said no more. She had been taught to pray for what she wanted, so she now stopped crying, went behind the door, and said, softly:

"Christ, will you give me a yeal live baby, with yeal eyes that can't drop out?" and came back composed and full of faith.

The next morning brought a line from Cyril Heath, announcing that the storks had brought them a splendid pair of twins, one for him and one for Belle. Margaret immediately wrote the history of Mabel's sorrow and Mabel's faith, and asked Cyril to give *his* baby to Mabel, which drew from him the following letter:

My Darling Little Mabel:—

I am so sorry to hear that your baby has lost its eyes, so I am going to tell you something. Mamma has had a present of a "yeal live baby," and so have I, and I am going to give mine to you; that is, I shall let you call it yours, and let you love it with all your might and main. At the beginning of your prayer tonight, ask God to bless your baby, and He will. Mamma sends you twenty kisses on your dear little mouth, and says she loves you, oh, ever so much. What fun we shall all have when you come home! The babies are such funny little fellows, with dark, curly hair, and big blue eyes! Good-bye, my pet lamb!

Papa.

"Now I know where my baby's eyes have gone!" cried Mabel, clapping her hands. "Christ took them out to give to my yeal baby. And I am going yight home, I am."

"No, dearie, you must wait till your papa comes for you," said Mrs. Grey. "Only to think! Two babies! How rich your mamma is getting! It is beautiful to have twins. I think I must go and see them."

"What, with going to the city to buy dolls, and make visits, and go to all sorts of meetings, and being on forty-one committees, and now a pair of twins," said Margaret, laughing, "I don't see when your book is to be written. Is it always so? When *do* you write?"

"Yes, it's always so, barring the twins. My dear, industrious people contrive to do a great deal in fragments of time that others waste. Writing books is only an episode in my life, not my profession. Nothing gives way to it. However, I must own that everything is giving way before this piece of news. To think of my Belle having twins! If they look alike, what a pretty sight they'll be!"

Margaret had never seen Mrs. Grey so excited, and was much amused.

"This is the very first minute I have seen you sit still and do nothing, since I came here," she said. "Oh, and here is a letter from Laura, with one inside for you."

Mrs. Grey took her share of the letter, and began to read it aloud, but suddenly stopped. "I forgot, dear, that you have a letter too, and must be eager to read it."

"I can wait, please go on; it is very entertaining."

Mrs. Grey finished reading, and said, "What a child she is, to be sure! And what does she say to you?"

Margaret, who had been glancing over her letter smiled, and read as follows:

Dear old Mag:—

Why haven't you written to ask me why I didn't write? You know perfectly well that I am in love with you, and yet you express no surprise that I do not pour out my soul on paper. Well, you must know that as soon as I reached home, and had set the family pendulum swinging again, I trotted out and bought a ream of foolscap on which to write my book. Mamma always buys hers by the quire. Of course I intended to write to you before I began my stupendous undertaking. But when I just ran up to the nursery to see that all was right there, I found all wrong. Pug was lying in his nurse's arms as red as a lobster, and of course I knew he had scarlet fever, and that Trot would have it, and that they both would die. Also, of course, I let them die, and began my book. You know I haven't any heart, only a large hole where one may grow, in time. Well, the two creatures were the sickest creatures I ever knew to get well, but I consoled myself with the fact that I had their portraits anyhow. Harry and I got a trick of sitting up nights with these twain small people, and he says I worked like a tiger over them; but then, he exaggerates awfully. They were not at all tired of this world, and were determined to stay in it; so here I am tied hand and foot to my nursery; and as to my book, there is nothing to show for it but that ream of paper; and that does look like business. I forgot to say that I upset a tea-pot of tea on my hand the first thing I did when I saw Pug looking so dreadfully ill, and that this is the first time I have held a pen in it since I came home. Some other pleasant little items occurred; my cook had a felon,[1] and was nearly wild with the pain, and my laundress went and got married in a tangent. And now, Mag, I've one thing to add, and it is this: I would rather have forty wild Indians, a rattlesnake, and a hyena, enter my nursery than scarlet fever.

Still, I'm going to write that book! and am

Your devoted admirer,

ONEY.

"Strange that I had not noticed not hearing from the child,"

---

1 Felon—a whitlow; a painful swelling formed in the periosteum at the end of the finger.

said Mrs. Grey. "But there are so many of them all that they drive each other out of my poor, forgetful old head. It will be a wonder if Georgy and Trot pull safely through. And how poor Laura's hand must have pained her! I must write, immediately, and warn her of the dangers of convalescence in this dreadful disease."

"Do you think she is really going to write a book?"

"I do not doubt that she will begin half a dozen, but whether she will ever finish one is another question."

"What a droll subject she had!"

"Yes; but I am not sure that she or anybody else can manage it. One might get fun out of it, though."

They both began now to answer Laura's letter; Mrs. Grey giving any amount of counsel about the children; Margaret, throwing care to the winds, and entering, with zest, into the pleasure, so new to her, of having friends to whom to write.

And not many days later, Mr. Heath came for Mabel. He was as impatient as a child to have her see the new babies, whom he considered marvelous beings, and of whom he was very proud. As to the child, she was eager to enter into possession of her share of the spoils, and Margaret felt a spasm of pain shoot through her heart when, with smiling faces, they took leave. She had loved Mabel so! Was she to be parted with in this way all her life, she asked herself, always giving amply and receiving sparingly? But one must not reason thus about little children. They know little about time and space; they have not learned to sentimentalize; they live in the present moment. Many a mother has experienced a pang akin to Margaret's, when returning from a journey, longing to fold her dear ones to her heart, the prosaic cry salutes her, "What have you brought me, mamma?" as if in bringing herself she had not done all a loving child ought to ask.

Mrs. Grey and Margaret now returned to their interrupted work, and the wintry days flew rapidly by. The weather continued mild until late in February, when the first snow of the season fell. But previously to this an event occurred which put a new aspect on life to Margaret. They had been to the city: Mrs, Grey to make visits to friends in hospitals there; Margaret to take her painting lesson, and on reaching the station found the carriage awaiting them, and the horses in a restive mood, which was provoking the temper of the old coachman not a little.

"What is the matter, Samp?" asked Mrs. Grey.

"Ain't used enough," returned Samp. "Needs to be took down."

"Any danger of their running away with us?"

"Never knowed 'em to run away."

"Nor I, either," said Mrs. Grey, "and yet I've a good mind to walk. What do you say, Margaret?"

"I say that it's too far for you to walk. Belle charged me to not let you overdo."

"Very well. But it's not too far for you to walk. I have a queer presentiment that something is going to happen. Suppose I drive, and you come home at your leisure?"

"No!" said Margaret decidedly; "if anything is going to happen, it must be to me, not you. But nothing is, except lunch." So saying, she sprang into the carriage, and Samp drove off.

· "I never saw you nervous, aunty, till now."

"And I am not nervous now on my own account."

Margaret understood, and was silent. After a few moments, however, she said:

"We fly over the ground like lightning. Can it be that Samp has lost control of the horses? Oh, aunty! there he goes! He's off the box! They're running away with us! We must jump out!"

"We must *not* jump out," said Mrs. Grey, in a tone that made Margaret pause. "It would be death to us both."

"What shall we do, then?"

"We must trust ourselves to Him who, if He can hold the winds in His fist, can certainly control these animals. And if He does not think it best to do that—if they rush on and plunge down the river-bank—why, it would be an easier death than martyrdom."

She was as quiet as if seated on her sofa at home.

Margaret grew quiet too. They clasped each other's hands and waited.

The horses flew on; they were nearing the river; now for it! They are over!

Neither knew anything more till they awoke as from a sleep, and found themselves at home; Mrs. Grey lying on her bed; Margaret being borne to her room on a door that hasty hands had torn from its hinges. The house was full, but by degrees faithful Mary cleared it of all but those whose presence was needed; and the physicians proceeded to examine the patients. Mrs. Grey's injury was on the head, but not serious. Margaret had a fractured ankle, and many bruises. Each forgot herself, and thought only of the other; but it was ten days before they met. Margaret was shocked when Mrs. Grey, with a face all colors, from the bruises on her head, was supported into her room, and made light of her own severer injury. It was comfort to see each other even in this unsatisfactory way, but Mrs. Grey had time to recover entirely before Margaret could leave her bed. And for a long time she was in too much pain to think or to feel much on any subject. But at last she said, abruptly:

"Aunty, did you expect to be killed that day?"

"Yes."

"And you were as calm as you are now."

"Yes, dear—why not?"

"And were you ever afraid to die?"

"Yes, very much afraid."

"And how did you get over it?"

"By realizing that Christ is conqueror over Death, whom He will, sometime, make His messenger to show me the way home."

"It was an awful moment when we plunged down the bank! I almost think I never really prayed in my life before! I don't know exactly what I believe about the world of the lost, but I heard a man say once that there will be no little children there—only grown-up sinners. And I don't want to spend my eternity with sinners. It makes me shudder to think of it. I want to spend it with those who were pure and good in this world, and have grown into greater purity in heaven."

"Margaret, my child," said Mrs. Grey, leaning tenderly over her, "do you call this the aspiration of an unrenewed heart?"

"No, aunty; I have been wanting to tell you that in that awful plunge down the bank, there came to me, as by a lightning's flash, *assurance of faith.* You know how I have distrusted and quarrelled with myself, and refused to believe myself a Christian, because light had come to me so gradually, that I did not know when it began to dawn. I might have gone on so for years but for the revelation of that moment."

"I have never doubted that your feet were on the Rock, my child; but, oh! how I have prayed that they might stand steadier there! You have made me very happy."

"It has almost killed me to say all this, aunty. And I don't want to say another word, or have you ask me any questions. Only I want to thank you for not plaguing me with exhortations. It wouldn't have done me any good. And I think a great deal more of how people act than of how they talk. One's words can cheat; one's life can't. I watched mother like a lynx, to find flaws in her religion, and sometimes thought I found them. Then I watched you in the same way; and, oh! what sermons you have both preached to me, when you were, very likely, reproaching yourselves for not doing more for me!"

By this time Margaret's face, long paled through sleepless nights and distressing days, had become crimson. To give even this beloved "mother-friend" a glimpse into her soul, cost her all the strength of her strong will. But what a new love had now sprung up between them!

CHAPTER 11

As soon as Mrs. Grey recovered her health and strength, she took up her abode in Margaret's sickroom, her mother's former "hospital," and devised endless ways of relieving the tedium of her long confinement. Margaret spent her days on one of the little white beds, and her nights on the other; the change was easily effected by members of the household, and was very refreshing. Mrs. Grey read to her, told her stories, played games with her, brought her fresh flowers and fruit every day, and was as companionable as a girl. Yet it cost her brave heart something thus to live over again Maud's illness, without alluding to it; only a mother who has ministered to a dying child can know at what a price. Once, when Margaret was suffering unusual pain, she broke down, and cried heartily; but for herself she shed no tears.

"My precious child," she said, "how you need your own dear mother now!"

"I wouldn't have her see me suffer so for the world!" cried Margaret. "As long as I live, whatever happens to hurt or distress me, I shall have one comfort—my darling mother never had to see this!"

Mrs. Grey made no reply to this exclamation, but took care to put it into every letter she wrote her children, till they had all received this hint how she wished them to feel after she had gone.

Meanwhile, letters and luxuries flowed in from them all. Belle wrote
about the children, especially Mabel and the twins; Laura kept up
her usual artillery of fun; even "the boys," Frank, and Rafe, and
Fred, wrote, when they found what a delight it was to Margaret.
Under ordinary circumstances, "the girls" would have relieved their
mother from the care they all regretted so much; but Belle was tied
hand and foot by her babies, and so was Laura, who had become
duly impressed with the danger still lurking about her nursery; the
daughter who came between these two (Grace) had her husband's
mother with her, of whom people said, "She means no harm, but
she is peculiar." She was so very peculiar, that it took all Grace's faith
and patience to endure her semiannual visits, which she looked forward to as she would to a fit of sickness. Old Mrs. Harrison would
never have got over it if Grace had deserted her for any reason whatever; yet if any one had accused her of being exacting, she would
have been surprised and felt insulted.

One morning, when Margaret was beginning to suffer less, she
said, earnestly:

"Now, aunty, I think I have taken as much of your time, to say
the least of it, as the case required, and I want you to go on with
your book. What a trial this long interruption must have been!"

"It has not been a trial, dear. You will understand why, one of
these days. I used to chafe and fret when interrupted in favorite
pursuits, but I have learned that my time all belongs to God, and
just leave it in His hands. It is very sweet to use it for Him when He
has anything for me to do, and pleasant to use it for myself when He
hasn't. There's no knowing what I have learned through these weeks
that I needed to learn, in order to have my book what He chooses
it shall be. Perhaps your fractured ankle has a mission to some soul,
which it will accomplish through my pen; who knows?"

"I think I shall write a book myself," said Margaret, demurely.

Mrs. Grey smiled interrogatively.

"It would be such fun years hence to read it over. Yes, I certainly
will write it. Come, aunty, you bring your pen and paper and set the

inkstand between us, and we'll both write. I am going to write down the nice things that have happened to me; the letters and presents I have had, and my journeys, and excursions, and all that. And I shall illustrate it with pen-and-ink sketches. It will be a bigger book than you ever wrote, if I live much longer, and you all go on being so good to me."

"I don't believe you can use ink; however, we'll see. That's a good idea of yours. I wish I had begun such a book at your age. It would be most entertaining reading at my time of life. Oh, what a volume of undeserved mercies."

"Well, I have a nice blank-book on hand which you shall have."

She went and hunted it up, collected her materials, and they both became absorbed in their work, until a little musical laugh from Margaret broke in upon the stillness.

"What is it?" asked Mrs. Grey. Margaret handed her the book by way of reply. She had written its title on the first page:

"My Book of Remembrance,"

and had drawn a picture of herself as a miniature angel flying down from heaven into a bright, artistic room.

"I remember my father's painting in which I was represented as thus entering the world, and how it was one of the last things mother consented to part with. She finally let it go to our landlord for rent. He refused to take it for a long time, declaring that he must have the money; when he concluded to consent to do so, mother called his attention to its title, 'The Advent of my First-Born,' and explained that it was my father's poetical way of stating a prosaic fact.

"'La!' quoth he, 'you don't say that's a angel, do yer? I always thought it was a *lightning bug!*'"

Mrs. Grey laughed. It rested and refreshed her to see Margaret's brightness beginning to return. But their books were not destined to grow that day, for Mrs. Cameron and Agnes came and staid an hour and a half, and then Mrs. Huestis drove them away, and Mrs. Cram stepped in for a minute and staid forty-five, and so it went on till dusk. Mrs. Cameron always had some important secret to divulge, and must see Mrs. Grey alone; Mrs. Huestis always wanted advice; Mrs. Cram invariably was in trouble and wanted sympathy; and as to them all they were not in the least to blame for taking so much of her time, for they all knew that *her* time was not her own. She had, long ago, consecrated it to Christ, and He used, but never abused it. Agnes Cameron amused Margaret, while her mother was in the library below, with scraps of domestic scenes, wherein she hit off, in a good-natured way, some of their household "ways," as she called them. One of her little brothers had a "way" of doing mischief, and his last performance was pouring a can of kerosene oil on the parlor carpet.

"Mamma spanked him for it," continued Agnes, "and he said, 'the whipping hurt, but I 'joyed pouring out the oil!'"

"What a little scamp!" said Margaret. "Your mother couldn't have whipped him very hard."

"Oh, yes, she did; she used her slipper. But he 'joys his mischief too much to care what she does to him. He put the kitten into a pot of hot soup; he drank a lot of sugar of lead; he pushed tacks up his nose, and into his ears; he scratched the piano all over with scissors; he threw papa's razor out of the window; he has poured ink all over himself twice; he climbed out of the window and hung there by his hands till mamma fainted away; and yesterday, when he wanted something she refused him, he climbed up on to the table, and walked across it, and helped himself."

"And what was done to him?"

"Oh, nothing. We all laughed, that was all."

"He would drive me crazy in a week," said Margaret, scandalized.

"No, he wouldn't. He is such a good-natured little fellow you couldn't help loving him."

Margaret would not dispute the point, but she thought it all the more a fraud upon the child to spoil him, when he was created with agreeable qualities.

"I would not laugh at his mischief if I were you," she said, at last. "He'll get to think it is nice and smart to cut up capers."

"Oh, he'll outgrow his ways."

Margaret had her doubts, but had too little experience with children to venture to offer any further advice. After what seemed an endless period of time, Mrs. Cameron and Agnes departed, and the short wintry day came to an end.

Margaret's book of remembrance grew in spite of interruptions, for all sorts of kind deeds and loving deeds kept rushing in, and sometimes after writing for a time, she would lie back on her pillow in silent ecstasy, that she, a little while ago, only an "incumbrance," was now literally surrounded with mercies. If every young person would keep such a record, there would be more smiling and more gratitude in this frowning, grumbling world.

And now she was to take the air, and glide over the smooth, white snow that fell just in time to cover all the inequalities of the roads. Samp had not been much hurt when he fell from the box, and new horses had been bought in place of the pair that had to be killed after the accident.

Mrs. Grey went with her, and both sat thoughtfully side by side, and quite silent, for they had each lived through a world since their last drive.

But on their return, Mrs. Grey said, "I have had a curious request made me during your imprisonment, and want to consult you about it."

"You are always having curious requests. How people do act."

"It is not their fault. I belong to 'people.' Well, here is a letter from a woman I don't remember ever seeing, though she says she once spent a summer in a boarding-house with me and mine. She wants me to come and examine her home-life, which she pronounces a failure, and tell her what is amiss. But read the letter before you give an opinion."

DEAR MRS. GREY:—

Some years ago I spent a summer at Newport in the "House on

the Cliffs;" among others, you were there, with your children. I was only a young girl at that time, but I was struck with the difference between your family and those of others; I did not understand then, nor do I know now, wherein this difference lay. But I am the mother of six children, the eldest a boy of fourteen, the youngest a baby. In deep humility, in bitter disappointment, my husband and myself have come to this conclusion: our boys and girls are exceptionally troublesome, or we are very bad managers. Our home-life is beset with disorder and discomfort, which is becoming intolerable. Well, can you, and will you, undertake the task of spending a day or two, more or less, as you think best, in our family? See for yourself where the fault lies, and act the part of a friend to us in the greatest emergency of our lives? It is asking a very self-denying act on your part; we realize that, but virtue has its own reward. Whatever strictures you may find occasion to make, will be thankfully received. We are unknown to you, but you are well known to us, and we put our cause into your hands.

Truly yours,
Lucy A. Thayer.

Please address Mrs. Neilson Thayer,
Box 298, New York.

"It's a nice letter," Margaret reluctantly owned; "but you mustn't go."

"Why not?"

"There are five hundred and forty reasons why."

"Tell me one."

"Why should you, who can speak to thousands through your books, be pinned down to one disorderly family?"

"Oh, that's no argument at all. If I were sitting on a pedestal, and had to climb down in order to help my brother, my sister, it might be a different thing. But I am not. My advantage over these younger people is, that I have longer experience of life than they have, and that's all."

Margaret smiled.

"I believe if the whole world knelt at your feet you wouldn't know it," she said.

"I don't think I should, for I *wouldn't* know it. And, Margaret, I think I shall go and have a long talk with these people; to do it, I may have to stay with them one night, as I suppose Mr. Thayer will only be accessible in the evening."

"Well, it's just like you to do such things."

"*That's* not the way to put it. It's just like God to make His children serve one another."

"Do go right away, then, and have it over with. You have spoiled me so, that I hate to have you out of my sight. However, I've plenty to do while you are gone."

"Oh, I should not leave you if you had not. Let me see, I must write to this Mrs. Thayer, to say that I am coming. Today is Friday— too late in the week; I'll go on Monday."

CHAPTER 12

The task that lay before Mrs. Grey was an uncongenial one, but she entered upon it cheerfully and hopefully; nobody who knew her, would need to be told that she went prayerfully, also. She found, as she expected, intelligent, educated persons in Mr. and Mrs. Thayer, and as he had retired from business, he had plenty of leisure to consult with her.

"Things have always gone wrong with us," he said, as soon as the ice was broken. "But we have at last reached a point when everything must be placed on a new basis. I have tried my best with the children; have talked to them by the hour together; have chastised them and indulged them by turns, but all in vain. And now," he added, his voice trembling, "I have just caught my eldest boy, Bob, in an act of theft."

"To a large amount?"

"Large for a boy of his age. And what makes it hard is, that I have been lavish with him in every way. I did not suppose he had a wish ungratified."

"*Ah!*" said Mrs. Grey, in a tone that declared she was beginning to see daylight.

"Bob is a good-hearted boy," said Mrs. Thayer, "but his character leans to shiftlessness. We have tried to tone him up, but if a child is born without a backbone, what can one do?"

"May I ask in what way you have tried to tone him up?"

"Certainly," replied Mr. Thayer, in a tone of surprise. "We have talked to him year in and year out."

"Does he like that?"

"No. He yawns in my face."

"Now, you want my honest opinion?"

"We do, most emphatically."

"Then, allow me to say that long talks to children seldom, if ever, do any good. A single, loving, wise word dropped just at the right moment, will do infinitely more. But something lies back even of this. It is parental character. Now I don't want to know from which of you two your boy gets his bias; perhaps it is from neither. But he is one of the sort who never should have a promise made him, and then left unfulfilled. He needs to see, every day, prompt, decisive action; what he sees will tell more than what he hears. And, I say it in all kindness, no human being who has his every wish gratified is in a process of toning up. Such luxury tends to enervate, not to strengthen."

"I meant it for the best," said Mr. Thayer, with a sigh. "I hoped to win the lad's heart by kindness. But I see how it has all ended in failure. Perhaps," he added, after a pause, "you ought to know the whole story. I am careless about money matters; don't like trouble, and have never kept any account with Bob. He got into the way of boasting to other boys how much he had at his disposal; how much more than any of them, and they dared him to prove that this was the case. In a great hurry one day I threw some loose bills into a drawer, forgot them, and perhaps never should have thought of them again, but a good friend of mine came and told me that Bob was exhibiting a larger sum at school than he thought it likely I had given him; and then the whole thing came out."

"What did you do?"

"I talked to him, and then thrashed him."

"Are you sure it is a good thing to thrash a boy of that age?"

"Why, could I do less?"

"Of course I cannot legislate in this matter; but you may depend there is a parental screw loose somewhere when a lad of fourteen has to be thrashed. Are you sure that you have kept him out of temptation by constant employment, for instance?"

"I never thought of that. Bob's a lazy fellow; he hates work, though he's fond enough of play, to be sure."

"It is a vital point to keep children busy," said Mrs. Grey. "Taste for this and that employment can be cultivated. Are you sure he would not like to learn drawing? Or the use of tools? Or music?"

"He has no natural taste for either."

"Then how does he spend his time out of school?"

"I don't know, exactly; I suppose he lounges about the streets more or less."

"What sort of boys are his intimate friends?"

"I don't know that either, exactly."

"I know," said Mrs. Thayer, "what boys visit him, but I do not know of what sort they are. He always sees them in his own room."

Mr. Thayer was here called out, and Mrs. Thayer turned eagerly to her guest.

"You see what my boy's father is," she said, "a kinder, a better man does not exist; but he never has known how to manage Bob, and most of the care of him has rested on me. And one parent is not enough for children. Still, I did the best I could, and Bob was obedient at any rate—for that I require of my children; but he slipped out of my fingers in this wise. I was just going out to pay some visits, when a boy came to invite him to dine with him. It was on a Friday, when there are no lessons, so I gave my consent, only directing him to put on a clean shirt, adding, remembering his indolence, 'You can go on no other terms. Go directly and dress, or you will get to romping about and forget it.' He promised, and I went out, returning in time to see him just ready to start in his soiled and crumpled shirt. I said to him, 'I'm sorry for you, Bob, but you know on what terms you were to go.' He began to cry, and the face of the other boy lengthened. My husband never had interfered before, nor has he ever since; but he interfered so decidedly then, and was joined so vehemently by one of his brothers who happened to be present, that it was next to impossible to hold out against them. Bob went off in triumph, and my authority was for ever ended. He has been growing worse ever since. His father meant no harm; but he did not foresee, as I did, what would be the consequences of this one mistake. Now, have you anything to suggest? Is our boy on the absolute road to ruin?"

"Before I reply, please answer one question. How much hold have you on his affections?"

"Very little. And since we have told him we could not love a boy guilty of his crime, he has grown surly."

"Is it true that you do not love him?"

"Of course not."

"Why then tell him so?"

"We are trying, in every way, to make him abhor the sin?"

"Poor boy! poor father! poor mother! What a series of mistakes!" thought Mrs. Grey. "Where *shall* I begin?" And then remembered she had begun in her closet.

"I know," she then said, "that some children are born with such amiable instincts, that they give little trouble to their parents and teachers, and become, therefore, their pride and glory. But this is the exception, not the rule. The *general* rule is that the more character a child possesses, the more he will be faulty. My impression is, that most parental difficulties result from misconception on two radical points. The first is a putting off of God's regenerating work to a period in their children's lives when they can intelligently help Him do it. The second is faith in self. Now I will not say that I know it to be the case that some souls are regenerated before they enter this world; I only suggest the thought for your reflection; but that the mass of mankind enter it unregenerate, is the belief of all who accept the Bible as Divine truth. This being the case, every parent who undertakes to mould and fashion his child into a model of morality and virtue with his own hands, makes a radical mistake.

Divine must precede parental work. Until a soul has been regenerated, labor spent on it is external, and cannot reach the roots of being."

Mr. and Mrs. Thayer listened with some incredulity, yet with the respect due to superior years.

At last Mr. Thayer said, "I must own that this theory is new to me, and that I am not prepared to accept, as I am unwilling to reject it. I have always believed that a soul must *will* to be born again, and that a child must reach an intelligent age before it would reach such a point."

"Do you believe that those who die in infancy are lost, because they never exercised faith in God, or willed to be His?"

"No, indeed."

"Well, how are they saved?"

"By special grace."

"And not through the exercise of faith on their part?"

"Certainly not."

"This concession, then, does away with the notion that faith is a redeeming virtue—a meritorious act. Consequently, a child can be regenerated before birth, at birth, or at an indefinitely early age after birth; the sooner the better. Instead of spending ten or twelve years in forming unholy habits, which it will require as many more to outgrow, it may begin from its earliest consciousness to form holy ones."

"Holy is a very holy word," said Mr. Thayer. "One hardly associates it with a laughing child."

"It is undoubtedly a very holy word, when applied to a veteran saint; but there has been a Holy Child on earth, the child Jesus; and in virtue of that fact, all our sons and daughters may, at any early age, become partakers of this grace."

Mr. and Mrs. Thayer were ominously silent. Mrs. Grey, therefore, proceeded: "Holiness in a young child is in its germ. It may mean little more than a genuine tendency to what is right. There will be faults, and foibles, and mistakes, perhaps falls; why not? Is it to be nearer perfection than its parents? They have faults and foibles, and make fearful mistakes; many of them have seasons of terrible backsliding, and falls that wring the hearts of all Christendom, if they have stood high enough to be seen by it."

"I have prayed for the conversion of our children," said Mrs. Thayer, "but expected it to come at some future time, when I wanted it to be a marked, unmistakable experience."

"Why not, just as rationally, put off their beginning to love you till they could give a good reason for it, and do it in a very decided way? It seems to me the most natural thing in the world for the children of Christian parents to begin to love Christ as soon as they hear who and what He is. Their love may be poor and meagre, and lack intelligence; but if it is genuine, it will wax stronger and stronger. If it does not exist at all, you can only work on them through the sentiment of fear; whereas love is the master-passion of the human soul."

"Oh," cried Mr. Thayer, holding up his right hand, "God is my witness, that I would give this hand to see my children converted unto Him! I never realized till now, what deep-seated yearnings I had for them. But I supposed they must go through some process first; distress of mind, repentance, faith."

"Faith they will have; faith that will put yours to the blush, if they are trained aright, with prayer. They may pass through painful processes later on in life, but not necessarily."

"But does not the Bible put repentance first?"

"It does, when addressing adults. I find no evidence that it thus addresses a child of two years. I believe that if Christ were now on earth, and should go into your nursery in order to save the two little boys there, He would not say a word about repentance; He would do something to make them love Him. Oh, how often I have rejoiced that the first parental words that fell on my ear were tender, affectionate ones about Him; that the law preached to me was, 'Do this because it will please Him! Don't do that because it will grieve Him.'"

"I am impressed by what you say," Mr. Thayer remarked, look-ing at his watch, "and could listen all night. But we have kept you up till eleven o'clock in our selfish interests."

"I have kept myself up in the Master's interests," she said, fervently.

As the family gathered together at breakfast the next morning, she took special pains to shake hands with Bob, and give him a smile. He was surprised and pleased, for he had vaguely connected this visitor with his own misdeed.

"They haven't told her, after all," he thought, and a faint spark of gratitude arose in his heart. "And she ain't one of the long-faced kind, either," he said to himself, as he glanced at her cheerful face.

There was a good deal of bustle after breakfast about getting the children off to school. One fretted about her luncheon; another at being directed to wear overshoes because he had a cold.

"Mamma," said the eldest daughter, "I'm going to have some girls to lunch next Saturday. And I don't want any of *you* in the room, either."

At this exhibition Mrs. Thayer blushed. She found it not so pleasant to have the children betray themselves to Mrs. Grey pres-ent, who was quite another person to Mrs. Grey absent.

Two or three little altercations arose, meantime, between the children.

"I don't see why you should have lunch all to yourself," said Julia, a girl of ten.

"Well, it's enough that I see it," retorted Esther.

"Mamma won't let you, I know; will you, mamma?"

"I've got to have an excuse for tardiness," said Esther, turning to her mother.

"Another excuse? I've a good mind not to give you any. Now, I can't have this. It is the third time this week."

And so on, and so on.

When they were fairly off, Mrs. Thayer burst into tears of min-gled shame and pain.

"You see how it is," she said. "Esther regards us as natural ene-mies, whom she cannot allow to share her interests. And her love of dress tries me, too. And there is Julia following in her steps. If it were not for the younger children I should have no comfort. It is strange that they should degenerate so; in their nursery I saw very little of the unlovely traits they are developing now."

"Well, now, Mrs. Grey, have you any counsel to give us?" asked Mr. Thayer. "We are ready to bear reproof and to amend our ways if you can suggest a change."

Mrs. Grey replied, very earnestly, "It is not so much outward change that you two need, as a new deep-seated principle within. I think you have dealt with your children too much on the outside. The first thing to *require* is obedience. The first thing for them to *acquire* is tenderness of conscience. All the lectures, and all the chastisements in the world will come to naught if this is lacking. A moment's reflection will show you that a time will come when parental law must cease, and that they must then become a law unto themselves. The best lock and key, the best bar and bolt, is conscience. Now we will allow that you have partially erred in this regard; what is the remedy for that and every other error? I maintain that the only remedy is prayer. The Divine hand can overrule your mistakes; no other can."

Mr. and Mrs. Thayer maintained an embarrassed silence.

At last Mrs. Thayer said: "Perhaps you have laid the axe to the root of all our difficulties. I do not think we have realized our human insufficiency till quite lately."

"Thank God, that you realize it now. The next step to such real-ization, is a laying hold of His strength. I have been watching Bob; he does not look like a vicious boy; if you manage wisely, he may never repeat the offence that has caused you such pain."

"And what would you counsel in regard to him?"

"I do not know. I have never had to deal with such a case. If he were my boy I should just go to God with my ignorance, and expect to gain wisdom how to act. But let me say, just here, that my experience with boys and girls forbids free use of money. As soon as they reach a proper age, they should have, if possible, an allowance, and be obliged to keep account of every penny of it. I should say in relation to Bob, that he should be indulged very sparingly, and obliged to restore to a mill all he has taken, even if it takes years to do it. This long discipline will do him good. 'The way of transgressors is hard;'[1] let him learn that so effectually that he can never forget it. One thing more. You have told him that you do not love him; go on in that path, and you will lose your boy. You must not only love him, you must let him know that you do by constant acts of kindness. God makes a distinction between the sinner and his sin; He loves the one and hates the other; we must do the same."

The unhappy parents began to feel their burden lightened.

"Then, you think there is hope for our poor boy?" they asked.

"I *know* there is just as long as you enclose him in your prayers. He will be as safe as an insect in a piece of amber."

"But the insect is dead."

"Yes, but how much better hath God made a human soul that cannot die?"

"I have not breathed so freely for a month," said Mrs. Thayer. "Will you give us some hints now about Esther? You see what she is, superficially; but she has good qualities, and far more character than Bob."

"How happens it that she wants to exclude you all from her pleasures?"

"I don't know; but she does, and so mortifies and grieves me."

"Have you always taken care to show sympathy with her in her pursuits, her friends, and the like?"

"Perhaps not all I might."

"I fancy this interest is all that is wanting. You might try and see. By the bye, have you any absorbing pursuit or friendship yourself?"

"Yes, I have many."

"Perhaps, then, you have unconsciously weaned the child from

1 Proverbs 13:15.

you by only half listening to what she has had to say about hers."

"Did you observe that she informed me that she was going to have friends to lunch, instead of asking permission?"

"Certainly."

"And what should you do in such a case? Reason with her?"

"No; I should simply provide no entertainment. As things stand, however, giving her warning to that effect."

"You have no idea how angry she will be."

Mrs. Grey was silent.

"And then how she'll tease!"

"The sooner she learns the uselessness of teasing the better."

Mrs. Thayer twisted her pocket-handkerchief around her fingers uneasily. At last she said:

"I can't tell you how I dread entering on this contest."

"There need be no contest. It takes two for that, and I don't propose a fight."

"What am I to do, then?"

"Do nothing while the tempest lasts. After it is over, speak to her kindly, but firmly; and state it as a simple fact that a new leaf is to be turned over in the family life."

"It won't do any good. Esther has such a will. I shall only provoke her!"

"You can't provoke her if you speak gently and lovingly."

"But I can't do that. When she has one of her tantrums I lose my temper."

"Then before you speak to her, speak to God. He will sweeten and humble you if you will let Him do it."

CHAPTER 13

rs. Grey's carriage," announced a servant.

"Oh, must you go so soon?" cried Mr. Thayer. "I am sure my wife needs more counsel."

"Let me countermand the carriage. Do stay one night more. You may save our children by doing it," urged Mrs. Thayer.

"I must send a telegram home if I stay."

"Certainly," said Mr. Thayer. "I will take it myself."

"Dear Mrs. Grey," said Mrs. Thayer, "I am so thankful to see you alone. You have opened a new world to me in regard to prayer. Beyond praying for my children night and morning, I have never consulted the Lord about them. I have always acted on the impulse of the moment."

"We come to grief, sooner or later, if we do that."

"But I am naturally impulsive, and look before I leap. I *cannot* always stop to think where I shall alight."

"If your watch is in good order, do you have to do more than wind it up every night to insure its keeping good time? Now if your soul is in a normal condition through the skill and goodness of God, and you do your part towards keeping it so by prayer, be as impulsive as you like. You'll keep good time."

"There is another trouble I have with Esther. She is too fond of dress."

"Most girls are. Their mothers teach them this by talking as if it were a matter of great moment, and by giving them articles of dress as holiday and birthday gifts, thus implying that this is the greatest favor they can do them."

"I have done this, but thoughtlessly. It never occurred to me that I was educating my girls into this folly."

She spoke in a weary voice, and at length added: "I am all out of patience with myself. I don't see but that I lie at the bottom of most of my children's faults."

"Fenelon tells us to be patient with ourselves, and he is right," Mrs. Grey said, gently, and looking with sympathy at the poor mother's flushed cheeks.

"And now about Julia," cried Mrs. Thayer. "She is naturally a nice child; but she is copying all Esther's ways. And before I forget it, I want to consult you about an incident that occurred just before you came. Julia is very energetic, and one day, when I was out, undertook to put my bureau in order. When I came in and found my room in an uproar—the bed, the floors, the sofa covered with heterogeneous masses of clothing—I was extremely displeased, and seized the child by the arm and marched her angrily out of the room. Whereupon she dropped a courtesy and said, 'Thank you, ma'am. You must have had a nice prayer-meeting!' I afterwards found that she had been preparing a pleasant surprise for me by putting my drawers in order. Ought I to say anything to her about it?"

"Yes, you ought to ask her pardon."

"Ask her pardon! Ask a child's pardon!"

"Why not? She has her individual rights as you have yours."

"But to degrade myself to a child of ten years!"

"To ennoble yourself in her eyes. The degradation was in losing your temper."

"Well—well—*well!* This home has got to be pulled all to pieces and built up again, if we are to follow your suggestions."

"Pull away," said Mrs. Grey, smiling; "the sooner the better.

And now won't you let me see the little nursery people?"

Mrs. Thayer's face cleared as she led the way to baby and his brother, both large for their age.

"What splendid boys!" exclaimed Mrs. Grey.

"Are they not? And the others were just as fine, apparently."

Mrs. Grey took the baby from his nurse's arms and kissed it.

"I should think this room would be a city of refuge, with these innocent creatures in it," she said.

"Yes; doesn't it *rest* one to see little children before they are spoiled?"

"You speak as if spoiling was inseparable from development; as if life were intended to be all retrograde."

"Oh, I thought I should find you ladies here," said Mr. Thayer, entering the room. "Suppose we adjourn to the library."

"Let me take Mrs. Grey to my room first, to see the children's portraits."

Mr. Thayer assented, and they all proceeded thither.

Bob, Esther, and Julia had been grouped together and beautifully painted by an artistic hand.

• "I never saw a finer face than Bob's," said Mrs. Grey, "nor sweeter ones than those of the girls; it is hard indeed to think such children can turn out ill."

"Yes," said Mrs. Thayer, "I little thought when these portraits were painted, how Bob was going to break my heart, and Esther refuse to obey."

"Mrs. Grey," asked Mr. Thayer, abruptly, "do you think that children properly trained, invariably turn out well?"

"There are exceptions to all rules. Some children seem to enter the world with such low tendencies that no amount of wise training avails to uplift them. But no case is hopeless that can be carried to God."

"I want to ask one question more. Do you find us, as parents, exceptionally full of mistakes, and our children exceptionally bad?"

"I believe all parents make mistakes. They find out, sooner or later, that they cannot, of themselves, train their children right, and so cease making the experiment, and seek Divine guidance at every step. I see no evidence that yours entered this world materially more depraved than others. But whatever the case may be, you have no reason for discouragement, if you can once make up your minds to distrust yourselves and leave all to Him who giveth to all men liberally and upbraideth not."[1]

Thus with line upon line and precept upon precept, Mrs. Grey tried to show to her eager listeners, that the first step towards reforming their children was a thorough reform in their own lives. She then took leave and gladly returned to her own peaceful home, where so many of her own rules had long been put in practice. Margaret was awaiting her in brilliant spirits, and everything settled down into the old routine; the one busy with scores of interests beyond her own; the other living in an imitation of her as yet remote, but yet original and unique.

Meanwhile Mr. and Mrs. Thayer found that it was no easy matter to change habits formed through fourteen years, and still went on making mistakes. Yet a radical change was taking place in their souls, which the children soon began to feel and to comment on.

In the first place, Mr. Thayer began to speak to Bob with a kindly yearning in his voice that startled and puzzled the boy. It was plain that his resentment was over, and that he was feeling pity instead of anger. What could it mean? Bob was full of curiosity and anxiety. Did this tenderness portend some coming penalty of the law—perhaps? Was he to be sent to a Reform school, or to jail, or what? His mother changed too. Julia, between whom and himself a certain kind of intimacy existed, took him aside one day, and said:

"Does mamma look sick to you?"

"She looks as if she cried a great deal."

"But does she look as if she was going to die?"

"To die!" he repeated.

"Yes, to die," said Julia.

1 See James 1:5.

What heart lay developed under the lad's vest died within him. This, then, was the penalty that lay before him; his crime was to kill his mother!

"Who says she's going to die?" he asked, roughly.

"No one says so, but I know she is. Read *that.*"

Bob took the little note the child handed him, and read it in silence:

MY DEARLY LOVED JULIA:—

Not very long ago your energetic little hands undertook to arrange my bureau drawers for me. Coming in suddenly I misunderstood the disorder of my room, and drove you from it angrily. It was wrong; I am sorry for it; I have asked God to forgive me, and now I ask you to forgive your poor, faulty

MOTHER.

"I'll bet she *is* going to die," said Bob. "Never knew her to do anything like that before. I've been an awfully horrid fellow. I wish I hadn't."

"I've been horrid, too," said Julia. "And *I* wish I hadn't." ·

"You've been splendid compared with me," said Bob. ·

"Let's go and tell Esther," suggested Julia.

"What for? She won't care."

"You seem to think she's a heathen Chinee," said Julia.

"So she is, sometimes. But not always."

Esther was accordingly taken into confidence, and expressed a wish to box their ears for a pair of ninnies, until she read the note, which struck terror to her heart.

"I don't feel at all nice," she said. "Though I'm not as bad as many girls. I know Mrs. Mather pays Melville five dollars a month if she isn't saucy to her. And Jane Waite tells fibs. And Jemima Watson threw her mother's watch on the floor and stamped on it."

"What for?"

"Because she couldn't get an example right. Julia, I wish you hadn't shown me that note. It was real mean in you. You knew it would stick in my throat."

Meanwhile Mrs. Thayer was looking forward with anxiety to the day of Esther's proposed lunch party, and the storm that was to follow the announcement that she should not sanction it. Great, therefore, was her surprise when Esther came, voluntarily, to say, in a nonchalant way, put on to hide some real feeling, that she had changed her mind, and did not intend to invite the girls.

"I am very glad to hear it," was the reply, "for I did not intend to provide lunch save for the family, as usual, and you would have had to recall your invitations. Henceforth, when you wish for an indulgence of this sort, come and ask my consent."

The quiet dignity and firmness with which this was said, impressed Esther with such a sense of amazement that she was in no state to wage war.

The family leaf was thus turned over without signs of affray; yet, He who seeth in secret witnessed many a struggle with self and pride, and evil habits on the part of the parents. It is not so easy to own that one's whole theory of domestic life has been wrong; not a trifle to drop all querulous tones, sharp reprimands, and hasty penalties. Again and again they were tempted to try new theories; to imitate this and that successful experimenter; to go on searching books and other human counsel. But every such attempt ended in a failure, and at last they went together hand in hand, confided all their interests to God, and resolved henceforth to consult Him and Him alone in every emergency. And now they found rest of the sweetest kind, and a new influence was shed abroad in the house. It is simply impossible to live this life of trust without influencing children powerfully. The young Thayers were too young to be utterly spoiled, and gradually the new principles that controlled the parents began to act upon them. Rome was not built in a day, neither is a human character suddenly so formed. It took time and patience to undo the work so ill-done; but the Holy Spirit so often wooed was lovingly won. He came and brooded, like a peaceful dove, over the disordered household. There is not a more upright man in Wall Street than Robert Thayer. His character was ripened by the discipline of labor through which he had to pass while earning the means to restore the sum feloniously appropriated, and that one act of dishonesty was his last. For parental prayer stood between him and temptation; and through Heaven-taught wisdom his conscience is as tender as a little child. Esther is living a peaceful life of faith in a nursery of her own, and Julia's energies are legitimately spent in true Christian work. As to the three younger children, they never gave their parents, with all their natural depravity combined, an hour's heart-ache; they were not models and not prigs, but just happy, bright, lovable fellows who had heard very little about law, and a great deal about the Gospel; who knew how to fish, and gun, and garden, and play, and frolic, and also knew how to pray when the right time came. More might be said, with truth, but it never answers to paint too close to nature.

Those who do not understand the life of faith, fancy it to be all mysticism and effeminacy. But while it is mystical to the mere looker-on, to its possessor it is almost homely in its practical details; touching every point of life from worship to service, from service to worship, claiming the whole being for Christ, and spending and being spent for those whom He came to redeem.

CHAPTER 14

Margaret wrote to Belle and to Laura about the new light and life that had come to her, though it cost her a great effort to do it. In reply, she received four or five pages from each; Belle wrote in great delight and earnestness, saying, she had never doubted for a moment that she was as safely in the ark as herself.

"Isn't it strange, darling," she went on, "that you did not see what I saw so plainly, that your love to me was really love to Christ? There is nothing in me to call forth such passionate devotion, and I knew it, all along; and how I have prayed that you might have the bliss of knowing that your Beloved was yours, and you His."

"'Bliss!'" re-echoed Margaret, "bliss is no word. It's *heaven!*"

Laura wrote one of her lively, domestic letters, full of "Pug" and "Trot;" and Margaret, while enjoying it, wished she could, for once, get a glimpse into her soul. She was just returning the letter to its envelope, a little chilled, when she perceived a scrap upon the floor that had fallen from it. In contained these words:

"And thou maun speak o' me to thy God.
And I will speak o' thee."[1]

---

1 *Thou Hast Sworn by Thy God* by Allan Cunningham.

"Ah, *she's* all right!" was Margaret's joyful thought. "I begin to think she's as good as Belle, only different."

A few days later, as she sat at her easel, she suddenly felt herself seized from behind, and squeezed by somebody's arms.

"Take care, or you'll get covered with paint," she said, as soon as she could speak, and in a moment more, saw Laura's bright face, and Pug and Trot in the rear.

"Where's mamma, you naughty child, you, and what do I care for paint?"

"Aunty has gone to the city to see a lady, or on the whole, two ladies, in some hospital."

"I'll warrant it. Well, the doctor said the children must have change of air, and so I've brought them home. Pug, put your arms round aunty Mag, and squeeze her till she can't breathe; and Trot, do you do the same!"

Margaret held out her arms, and the children sprang in.

"How good it is to feel your little arms," she said. "I've just been hungry to see you. And I'm ever so glad to see you, too, Oney."

"Of course you are. Where's that good, old soul, Mary? Oh, here she comes! Well, Mary, how are you? We've come to make you lots of trouble. Haven't the children grown?"

"Why, yes, Miss, only Miss Laura is small for her age."

"So are you, Molly," cried Laura, laughing.

Mary laughed, too, and tried, furtively, to slip a bit of cake into the children's hands.

"Ah, at your old tricks, I see. Very well, if you undertake to make them ill you'll have to nurse them, that's all, for I am worn out."

"You do look completely used up," said Margaret, beginning to scrape her palette.

"What are you doing, child?"

"Why, you don't suppose I am going to paint when my pets are here?"

"Nonsense! Their nurse is here. Now, I tell you, once for all, you shall go on exactly as if we were miles away. You say you are going to give each a picture at Christmas; and how are you going to do it if you let everybody hinder you?"

"I don't call Pug and Trot, 'everybody;' I can't do any more work today, anyhow."

"Well, you can tomorrow, for I am going to the Astor Library."

"To the Astor Library? What for?"

"I have a sudden thirst for information before I begin my book."

"Your book for mothers? Oh, Laura, the idea of going to the Astor Library about that!"

"Oh, that scheme fell through."

"What a pity! It was such an original one."

"So is sin. But one has to get rid of it."

"Did you write nothing at all?"

"I wrote a little bit. I'll show it to you when my trunk comes. I thought it was a capital idea, and was going to make mamma write a preface for it. How is she, anyhow?"

"Very well, if one may judge by her actions."

"I suppose that means being at everybody's beck and call."

"Yes; first, she had me to nurse, and then she went on a pilgrimage to a family of strangers."

"People she knew nothing about?"

"She knew they were in great trouble, and judged, by the letter they sent her, that they were respectable, more or less educated people."

"Here comes the dear old thing, skipping like a young roe!" cried Laura, who had been to the window half a dozen times. "Now Pug and Trot—goodness! what *have* they been about while we were talking?"

Sure enough, what had they been about. Each, armed with a brush, had been daubing away at Margaret's canvas—their hands, faces, and dresses all colors.

"Oh, Margaret! they've ruined your picture!" cried Laura, in dismay.

"Oh, Laura! they've ruined their dresses!" cried Margaret; at the same time her enthusiasm about the children cooled down not a little. Here was a week's work destroyed.

Meantime, Mrs. Grey entered on this scene of dismay, and she and Laura were too glad to see each other to pay much heed to the children. Margaret rushed off after a bottle of turpentine, and old Mary, and Laura's nurse; and between them all, and a bowl of soap-suds, decency was restored, and the little ones made presentable, though not fragrant. The unexpected scrubbing, and a faint sense that they had been in mischief, gave them a somewhat awe-stricken look, which gave way, when grandma kissed them, to relieved smiles.

"It's all my fault," said Laura. "I ought to have warned you that these creatures are always up to something. How much harm have they done to the picture?"

"Oh, never mind the picture," said Margaret, who was herself minding it a good deal, but was trying to wrench her heart back to the little culprits.

"I am delighted to have you come home, Laura," said her mother. "You look worn out."

"I dare say. But it's only want of sleep. I shall be all right in a few days. Pug and Trot are two little plagues, but somehow I didn't want them to die. Did I, poppets?" she said, pulling the children to her knee.

"Here's your trunk," said Margaret; and Laura flew off to pay the expressman, and to unpack it.

"You poor child," said Mrs. Grey to Margaret, as soon as Laura had gone, "your picture is ruined! And I must say you have borne it beautifully."

"It may have looked beautiful on the outside," replied Margaret, "but it wasn't at all so inside. I could have slapped the children, I was so provoked."

"Jean Paul says, that an angel, incapable of feeling anger, may well envy one who can feel, yet control it."

"I would run the risk of being an angel if I could," said Margaret.

Laura now returned with her arms full. "This shawl, mamma,

I knit for you; also this afghan, which is to keep your dear old feet warm. And, Margaret, this Madonna is for you, chicken!"

"For me!" cried Margaret, flushing with delight. "Oh, it is worth a thousand of the daub the children spoiled. How came you to get it for me?"

"I couldn't help it. I can't love people and never give them anything. Dear me, what fun it would be to go through the streets and chuck something into everybody's hand!"

While this was going on, Pug, who had escaped from the nursery, was busy fumbling in his mother's pockets, and soon possessed himself of her purse, the contents of which, with a magnificent air, he went and poured into Margaret's lap. On perceiving this, Laura, with a peal of laughter, caught up the child and kissed him.

"Oh, Laura, how can you encourage Harry's mischief?" cried Mrs. Grey.

"He means no harm," said Laura. "He is a chip of the old block. He does nothing on the sly, but it is his instinct to give. This isn't the first time he has picked my pocket, is it, Pug, you young scamp? Oh, you needn't undertake to give it back," she ran on, as Margaret offered her the money. "I always regard it as providential when Pug robs me and never touches the trash he has given away."

Margaret looked embarrassed. Mrs. Grey shook her head.

"You needn't shake your head, mamma," said Laura. "You let me do this very thing when I was a child, and it did me good. You think my ways with the children all harum-scarum, but they are not. They are founded on philosophical principles. If there is anything I hate it's prig fathers, prig mothers, and prig children."

"I suppose there is no medium," said Mrs. Grey.

"There's no nice one," said Laura. "Well, now, about my book. It fell through—or, rather, it died of scarlet-fever."

"You promised to let me see what you had written," said Margaret.

"I'll read it to you and mamma. You could make nothing out of my scrawls. My idea, if you remember, was to write a receipt-book for young mothers, and you thought it a capital idea, mamma. But such things are easier said than done. I meant to classify everything under different heads, like a medical-book; and then when a mother wanted to know how to act, in an emergency, she could look at the index and find directions instanter. Now listen:

"'ILL MANNERS

"'*Diagnosis*. Patient objects to saying please, and forgets to say thank you; slams doors; slides down the banisters; interrupts conversation, etc., etc.

"'*Remedy. Rx*. Of maternal politeness, 1 lb.

"'Of parental ditto, ¾ lb.

"'Of firmness, ½ lb.

"'Of line upon line, 8 oz.

"'Mix intimately, and form into thirty pills, which are to be given according to symptoms.'"

"What a girl you are!" said Mrs. Grey, laughing.

"Who, do you suppose, would buy such a book?"

"I would, for one, if I were not already running over with wisdom. Shall I read any more?"

"Yes, go on."

"'SELFISHNESS

"'*Diagnosis*. An acute disease, that, if neglected, will become chronic and incurable; patient begins to show disinclination to wait upon papa and mamma; wants the best seat by the fire; steers for the biggest apple.

"'*Rx*. Of parental benevolence, 1 lb.

"'Of essence of Bible, 1 gall.

"'Bottle, but do not cork, that the delightful aroma of this liquid may fill the house.'

"There! I shall not read any more of this nonsense. I have a scheme for another book, which I am quite eager to begin immediately."

"I shall put my veto on all brain-work," said Mrs. Grey, "until I see you looking like yourself. The best thing you can do now is to lie down and take a nap till dinner-time. I believe I shall have to do the same, for I am very tired."

"Why *will* you go about waiting on other people, and wearing yourself out, mamma?"

"Dear Laura, long before you reach my age you will understand. You will see that 'this world's a room of sickness,' and must have its nurses as well as its doctors, and I can truly say,

"'I have often blessed my sorrows,
That bring others' griefs so near.'"[1]

"You are the nicest old thing in the world," cried Laura, with a tremendous hug, and several admiring pats on her mother's back. "I mean to have ten children exactly like you. But I am not going to bed in the day-time; you may depend on that. There, lie down on the sofa and let me cover you with the afghan."

Laura looked so refreshed the next day that her mother could not find it in her heart to make an invalid of her, or forbid her visit to the Astor Library. Armed with pencil and paper, therefore, she set gaily forth, and was soon seated at a table with eight or ten volumes before her, out of which she got some amusement, but nothing serviceable. She went back to her mother rather crestfallen.

"I could have saved you all this trouble," said Mrs. Grey, "if you had told me what you wanted;" and going to the nearest bookcase she took down several books which exactly met Laura's wishes. The result will be seen by and by. Margaret, meanwhile, had begun a new picture in place of the one defaced by the children, and as the three sat together reading, painting, chatting, they formed a trio almost any one would have enjoyed watching. Laura feeling the

1 *True Honors* by Adelaide A. Procter.

relief of her children's convalescence, was particularly happy.

"How nice it is to be at home," she cried. "I shouldn't mind living a hundred years if I could always have things just as they are now."

"Nor I," said Margaret.

"Nor I," said Mrs. Grey, smiling; "but things won't go on a hundred years just so, nor should we live a hundred years if they did. It is better to leave our destiny in wiser hands than our own."

And then a pleasant silence settled down upon the group, each busy in her own way, and each, in her own way, very happy.

CHAPTER 15

The next morning Mrs. Grey settled herself comfortably near the fire, to enjoy one of the luxuries in which she indulged herself—the daily paper. She liked to know what was going on in the world. But as her eye ran leisurely from column to column, it was suddenly arrested, and she seemed turned into stone.

"Oh, mamma darling, what is it?" cried Laura, running to her side, and seizing her hands. "Why, you are as cold as ice!"

Mrs. Grey tried to speak, but could not; she pointed to a paragraph, however, and Laura read:

"It gives us great pain to announce that the President of the —— Bank is under arrest on a very grave charge. His books have been seized, and are to be thoroughly examined. We make this statement reluctantly, trusting that Mr. Grey will come triumphantly forth from this ordeal."

"What horrid, shameful stuff and nonsense!" cried Laura, indignantly. "Oh, mamma, you look ten years older than you did."

"I have lived a hundred," faltered Mrs. Grey.

"Why, mamma! you don't mean that you believe any of these lies?" demanded Laura, amazed.

"Oh, I don't know what I believe. I am stunned."

"Frank Grey accused of crime? Frank Grey under arrest? I don't believe a word about it!" cried Laura. "He is utterly incapable of anything wrong!"

"Don't say that, my child. We are all capable of *every* thing wrong if left to ourselves. Try to think for me. I am so bewildered. Oh, I have been too proud of that boy. And I have been too cold and unsympathizing towards distracted parents. I needed this blow. When does the next train leave?"

"At 10:40. Yes, of course you must go," said Laura, overawed by her mother's anguish. "And Mary must go too, you are in no state to travel alone."

Mrs. Grey made no remonstrance; for the first time in her life, she became passive in the hands of others, and let them act for her.

"Mamma, you weren't like this when darling Maud died," said Laura.

"When darling Maud died," repeated Mrs. Grey, dreamily. Then after silent reflection she said, "Maud died; yes, but Maud was not accused of crime. To lay away a lovely child in the grave is nothing—nothing, by the side of this horror."

"Such a man as Frank can live down disgrace," said Laura.

"Disgrace!" repeated Mrs. Grey, "what care I for disgrace? It is sin against God that makes me shudder; the bare suspicion that my boy has wounded my Master." And now, as if the mention of that sacred name was a gigantic power, her passing weakness disappeared, and the prompt, resolute, strong woman stood equipped for her journey.

And on the way to her son, her prayers rushed like the engine that bore her to his presence, straight to their end, and she began to reproach herself for her want of faith.

"Am I to fancy that my children can break through the hedge my prayers have built about them?" she asked herself. "Suppose Frank has been sorely tempted, am I to forget that he belongs to a covenant-keeping God?"

Day and night they flew on; at one station they were joined by Cyril Heath.

"Belle thought I should intercept you," he said, cheerily. "I hope this miserable business is not weighing upon you, *mother,*" tenderly using this word for the first time.

"The shock has been terrible," she replied; "I never could have believed I so little knew what trouble meant."

"You do not mean to say that you have the slightest suspicion that these rumors have any foundation in truth? I have none, nor has Belle."

"I am afraid my faith in human nature is not as strong as it was twenty years ago. But I ought to have faith in God as a Hearer of prayer, and thought I had."

"You have the strongest faith of any one I know, except my dear Belle," he said decidedly. "This shock has staggered you, but you will get over it. Ah, here we are! And whose bright face is that in the crowd—if it isn't Frank's? Hurrah!"

In a moment Frank bounded into the train, his face aglow with health and happiness.

"I knew you would come," he said, "and I made a nice calculation as to when. But I did not expect you, Cyril. How are you, old fellow? Come, here's the carriage, and Lily in it, waiting for you."

"What a ridiculous old goose I am," said Mrs. Grey to herself. "The idea of distrusting a man with such a face."

On reaching home Frank could hardly do enough for the travelers, to show his appreciation of their sympathy.

"The charge came upon me like a thunder-clap," he said, "and at first I was inclined to treat it as a joke. It is the work of a clerk, whom I had discharged for dishonesty, and who thirsted for revenge. He was under suspicion for a long time before I could convict him of theft, and then he begged so hard for mercy, and expressed so much penitence, that I forgave him. I had no right to employ him, however, for the money under my control was mine in trust for others, and not to be risked. The injury he has done me is a temporary one; that done to himself is irreparable."

"Has he a family?"

"Yes, a poor old mother and three sisters dependent upon him."

"We must do something for them, poor things."

"Yes, of course. They are in great distress. As to myself, the main question after all is, have I a clear conscience; I am sure, mother, you never doubted that, who trained it with such care?"

"I distrust everything but God," she replied, "and even my faith in Him wavered when I read that terrible paragraph. All my prayers for you, all my instructions and labors, seemed for the time thrown away."

"That is like your mother's usual self-distrust," said Cyril Heath, "not want of faith in you, Frank."

"Thank you for that suggestion," said Mrs. Grey. "Well, we must send dispatches to Laura, and Margaret, and Belle, at once. You ought to have seen Laura's righteous indignation! It isn't a bad thing for people to find out how they love each other, through some emergency like this. How do you suppose a mother feels when she hears that her firstborn son is under arrest? Were you really suspected to that degree?"

"Yes; and I am at large now only on bail."

"And how soon do you expect to clear yourself?"

"I don't know; there may be complications I do not foresee. But I shall come out all right in the end."

"Do you stand, with your friends, as you did before these charges?"

"With most of them I do. There were any number of them ready to go bail for me to any amount. Outsiders may look at the matter differently. I have taken a very decided religious stand here, and that has prejudiced some men against me, who are very glad to make a handle of this thing to injure the cause of Christ. I am inclined to think that, sooner or later, every one of His faithful disciples will have to suffer something, not only for, but *with* Him; if we do aggressive work for Him, we must expect aggression in return."

"I am glad you have learned that."

"Well—yes, but I have been swallowing a bitter pill. If I was ever proud of anything, it was of being the very soul of honor. If I could commit the most tempting sin on earth, unknown to all humanity, unknown even to God, I wouldn't commit it."

"My dear boy, I believe you. But it won't do to be proud even of sinlessness. Our only true attitude before God is one of absolute, constant self-distrust. I have known of men standing on as apparently secure ground as yours, and fancying they could never be moved, fall at last."

"Into ruin?"

"No; a redeemed soul can only fall partially. In the midst of his deepest degradation, he can look on Christ, and say to the Tempter, 'Rejoice not over me, mine enemy; when I fall I shall arise again.'"[1]

The affair proved more annoying than Frank Grey had believed it could be. There are any number of people who respect a man while he is up, who will kick him when he is down. Every detail of his life was paraded out for public inspection; all that was most sacred to him was fingered by soiled hands. But for his mother's presence, and faith and prayers, he would have been overwhelmed, for his wife was unto him in this sea of trouble, just what she would have been if he were struggling in mid-ocean, a drag, a dead weight.

But it does not hurt a true soul to be tested, even by fire. It comes out stronger, surer, safer, better fitted than ever for the true purposes of life.

After a long, hard struggle, Frank Grey came forth from the conflict with as clear a record in his hand, and as pure a light in his eye, as was ever known to mortal man. But there was no unseemly triumph, or blowing of trumpets on his part, or his mother's. Both felt that they had been humbled under the hand of God, and walked softly before Him. And in this mood she wrote an eloquent letter to Mr. and Mrs. Thayer, owning that the sharp experience of the past weeks had quickened her sympathy with them in their parental cares and trials, and assuring them that they might rely upon her friendly services, should they again be needed.

1 See Micah 7:8.

She was now at leisure to cast a scrutinizing, but kindly eye at the little world she had so suddenly entered, and saw much that needed correction. Some of the children were like their mother, and she got along with them comfortably enough. But she had next to no control over the others, and had to coax, manage, and bribe them into the little proprieties a mother should require. The table was not neatly arranged; the children's clothes were untidy; dust lay everywhere. The most incomprehensible thing about it was, that Frank, who used to be fastidious about all such matters, did not seem to care how things went. The boys helped themselves to what they wanted; the girls had their wardrobes as nearly in common as their different ages permitted.

"Frankie, dear," his mother would drawl out, "aren't you afraid so much mince-pie will make you ill, as it did last week?" And "Frankie, dear, would you mind beating that drum out of doors; it makes my head ache to have it so near." Or,

"Frankie, dear, Cyril says those are his mittens; take them off, do, and let him have them; I can't bear to hear him cry so."

She had got a habit of whining and crooning over them, of which she was unconscious, in fact she was not conscious of any of her defects. Frank had always said his wife must be amiable, and in one sense Lily was so; but she had not strength of character enough to get angry on, and in her ill-ordered household she was beginning to grow, not morose, not crusty, but nervously peevish.

Mrs. Grey kept congratulating herself that she had come to see all these evils, and then kept asking herself what she was going to do about it.

She concluded, at last, to begin on a very small matter.

"Lily, dear, do not let my being here confine you to me. You must be wanting to use this delightful weather for your spring shopping."

"There isn't any hurry about that."

"You know hot weather may be upon us any day. I have written to Laura to do Margaret's shopping for her at once."

"I don't think it will be hot. I hate to have to see to dress-making."

"I'm afraid Frank keeps you low in funds."

"He gives me all I want."

"Wouldn't it be well, then, to dress the children a little better?"

"I thought you believed in dressing them simply."

"I do. But they need not be shabby, dear."

"It is a great deal of trouble to keep them looking nice. Frank and Cyril get holes in their knees the first thing I know; and the girls tear and stain their dresses so that I can't keep them looking decent."

"Well, I shouldn't mind doing the spring shopping for you," said Mrs. Grey, briskly. She hated shopping, cordially; but these ragged children must be taken in hand by somebody.

"Shouldn't you mind it, really?" asked Lily, brightening a little. "It tires me to go out, I go so seldom. And I wish you would take the children in hand, as well as their wardrobes. I can't do anything with them."

"Nor can I do much in the little time I am here. But if you will try not to be hurt, I will make a suggestion to you. These turbulent boys are too much for you, and are wearing your nerves all out. They would be better off away from home, provided you could find just the right place for them. And, if you and Frank think best, I will take Gabrielle home with me, and see what I can make of her."

"Would you, really? What a relief it would be! She and Annabelle torment me and each other. Frank does not see enough of the children to know how they behave. He makes them obey him, and on Sundays does the best he can for them; but somehow our home isn't peaceful and pleasant, though I have such a good disposition, and am never angry with the children."

"Frank is not confined to his business all day; could he not contrive to look after the children more?"

"I don't know. He is on ever so many committees, and is superintendent of the Sunday-school, and our minister wants him here and there and everywhere. He is so energetic and bright, and people think so much of him, that he has no time. Then the letters he has to write! But if the children do anything *very* bad, he lets everything go till he has seen to them."

"Frank would not have married this poor, languid, inefficient woman if I had had the faith I ought," thought Mrs. Grey. "But she is not accountable for gifts never afforded her, dear child."

That evening Lily went early to bed with an attack of neuralgia brought on by one of her fruitless attempts to subdue Frank. Mrs. Grey seized the opportunity to talk with the boy's father on the subject of sending him from home.

To her surprise, he at once yielded to her suggestions.

"You understand human nature well enough," he said, "to know that while I may allow that my wife has disappointed me in some things, I can't stand it to hear a word said against her, even by you. I love her; and though I wish she had more energy of character, and kept my house and my children in better order, I would not change her for any other woman I know."

"I should hope not!" was the reply. "And I think if the three elder children were off her hands she would have better health, and look after the house more."

"I shouldn't like to send Gabrielle to a boarding-school," he said.

"Nor would I have you do it. I propose to take her home with me."

Grateful tears filled Frank's eyes as this unexpected offer fell upon his ear.

"Oh, mother!" he cried, "if you knew how many times I have wished this could be! If our eldest girl could be trained by you, this home of ours would, by and by, be transformed."

"I cannot work miracles," she replied, "but I am more than willing to try to benefit Gabrielle. Now about the boys; have they any vices?"

"No, indeed. They are just two great hearty, healthy, noisy fellows, not at all obstinate when I take them in hand, but too much for their delicate little mother."

"Are they truthful?"

"Yes. Never knew either of them to tell a falsehood."

"Then I think I can kill two birds with one stone. Belle and Cyril have a hard time with his insufficient salary, and I think they might be induced to take charge of your boys. Cyril needs more books, and Belle needs a good seamstress; you can afford to pay a fair price for advantages money alone could not purchase. I don't think they would, on a mere pecuniary consideration, burden themselves with new cares. But they do not live for what they can get, but for what they can do."

"You have made me almost a boy again," he replied; "you have lifted my greatest cares off my shoulders."

"Well, do write to Cyril tonight, and I will write to Belle; then, if they agree to the plan, the boys can start with me, and be left at Lancaster."

Frank wrote his letter, and Mrs. Grey wrote hers; this was Belle's reply:

Dearest Mamma:—

When your letter first reached us, I thought the project almost insane, and so did Cyril. But we prayed over it, and altered our minds. I would not take any other boys in the world; but dear Frank always was my favorite brother, and if I can help him in this emergency I will. Poor little Lily never was made to cope with such embodiments of health and mischief as Frank and Cil; but I am now in excellent health, and will do my best for them. How little I foresaw that my daily prayers for these children were going to bring them under our roof! Pray for me, darling mamma, that I may win their confidence and love, and be as true to them as to my own precious ones. As to Cyril, you know his doctrine—that it is the mother who should rule the house, and beyond setting them a perfectly beautiful example and frolicking with them, he will do nothing for them. Give a great deal of love to Frank and Lily. Of course you will stop, on your way home, to see our babies. I think we are just about as happy in each other, our children, our work, everything, as we can be. If you don't believe it, come and see!

Your loving, devoted

BELLE.

Lily's neuralgia confined her to her room six weeks, during which time she suffered so much that Mrs. Grey had to attend to everything; and she took the opportunity to reconstruct the household. Perfect order and cleanliness reigned supreme; inefficient servants were replaced by reliable ones; the children were made neat and tidy, and Frank took his meals from a bountiful, well-ordered table, with great satisfaction.

All this took more time, thought, patience, and energy than any man can imagine. It is part of woman's lot to do a large amount of unappreciated work. And the sick-room claimed attention, too. Lily had no relatives living to come to care for her when ill, and it was a great relief to be nursed by experienced hands. Mrs. Grey and Mary took the whole charge of her; bore with her faint-heartedess and childishness, prepared her food, kept her in fresh and dainty white dressing-gowns and caps, and at last pulled her through. They were veterans in sick-rooms, and had long worked manfully together.

CHAPTER 16

The three children were highly excited at the idea of leaving home, and, on the whole, delighted. The preparations for their departure were soon completed, and on a pleasant spring morning the party set off. Lily could hardly conceal her relief as she took leave of them; she was not fond of children, though, of course, she loved her own, more or less; and these vivacious young creatures wearied her beyond everything. She hated care and trouble and exertion, if, indeed, she had life enough to hate anything; and when Frank declined to take leave of them on the train because he knew he should disgrace himself by crying, and did cry, like a big school-boy, as he saw them drive off, she gave him up as a problem too hard for her comprehension.

The village in which Cyril Heath was settled was a manufacturing one, and full of activity. His house was a large, old-fashioned, ugly structure; but he and Belle together had made it home-like and pretty within doors, and as no part of it was kept in state and shut up, it smiled a welcome to every guest. Belle was awaiting her mother with a baby on each arm, and a face all smiles and delight. She let the three children loose into the garden immediately, where they were soon joined by Mr. Heath, who chased them up and down the walks with all the joyousness of a boy.

"It's splendid here," said Frank, Jr. "I never mean to live in a city again."

"Nor I," said Cil.

"Is it as pretty as this at grandma's?" asked Gabrielle.

"It's a thousand times prettier," replied Mr. Heath. "Have you never been there in the summer?"

"No; only at Christmas, and at Aunty Maud's funeral."

"Oh! then you have a great pleasure before you. Have you all had gardens?"

"No, no, indeed!"

"You boys must have some at once."

"To dig in ourselves? How jolly!"

"Would you like to see my workshop?" asked their uncle.

Wouldn't they, though? *Any*thing to work off their steam! Taking twenty steps when one only was needed, they scampered at his heels, and arrived, breathless, at a small room in which was a carpenter's bench in perfect order, a turning-lathe, and other objects, as new to the boys as Paradise was to Adam.

"Now, I sha'n't want you fellows meddling with my tools," said Mr. Heath, as the children began to finger and play with whatever they could lay hands on. "Useful things are not meant for toys. I shall have another bench made adapted to your height, and whenever you give your aunty special pleasure, shall give you a tool, till you acquire all you need."

"Papa hasn't any workshop," said Frank.

"But he's got a bank," said Cil. "Have you a bank, uncle?"

Mr. Heath replied that he had not that article, which greatly relieved the two.

While this was going on, Mrs. Grey was admiring the babies, lovely little creatures as need be, and rejoicing over Mabel.

"You will have a hard time with the boys, I am afraid," she said. "Poor Lily was no more fit to grapple with them than if they were giants."

"I suppose it will be hard, at first. But I already love them with a new kind of love—the love of possession. To all intents and purposes, they are mine now. How nice it was that Laura was at Greylock when you left! You wouldn't have liked to leave Margaret alone so many weeks. To be sure, she could have come here."

"Not very well, because of her lessons."

"True; I had forgotten that. Now come upstairs, please, and look at the boys' room."

"Why, you *witch!*" cried Mrs. Grey, "when did you do all this?"

For the room was not only neat and fresh and home-like; it was adorned with illuminations, pretty engravings, and other agreeable objects which had cost, not much in money, but a great deal in time.

"If I am a witch I learned it of you, mamma," said Belle. "Besides, Cyril helped me. He made the bedsteads, and the washstands, and the brackets, and picture frames. And the illuminations I made years ago. Don't you remember the mania I had for that sort of thing at one time?"

"I had forgotten it. How nice these upholstered boxes are."

"Yes, Cyril made those, too; and I had chintz left from a piece you gave me ever so long ago. Come, now, and see my room. It has been altered since you were here."

"What a pleasant room! How has it been altered?"

"Cyril took away the partition between it and the next one, and put up this linen-closet. See, isn't it nice. He did it all with his own hands, and then I painted it."

"Not since the twins came?"

"No, indeed. It was more than a year ago."

"Are these illuminations, also, things of the past, too?"

"Why, yes, mamma. Don't you remember trying to impress those truths on us children, and having these very illuminations hung at the foot of our beds, so that we could see them the first thing in the morning?"

"Yes, I do, now you speak of it."

"How many, many times I have read them!"

" 'WRONG LIVING LEADS TO WRONG THINKING.'

" 'WRONG THINKING LEADS TO WRONG LIVING!' "

"Yes; one whose life is practically wrong will soon form a theory to adjust to it. And one who starts with a false theory will, inevitably, end with evil acts."

"Soon after we came here, Cyril preached two sermons, taking those illuminations for his texts. There were several persons in the congregation who thought it was no matter what they believed, provided they were sincere. And there were others who took the ground that they were just as well off out of the church as in it, and so gradually slipped back into the world they had promised to forsake. But these are only specimens of the errors he has had to contend with—growing out of wrong thinking on the one hand, wrong living on the other. Still, we have some of the very salt of the earth here."

During all this time Mabel had followed them about, keeping close to her mother's side, the perfect image of undemonstrative devotion.

"It is you and Maud over again," said Belle, responding to Mrs. Grey's intelligent glance. "Mabel and I are just in love with each other. The other children will be home soon. Just look into their bureau-drawers. Now I have trained them as nearly alike as I could, and see the difference. Everything in Amy's possession is in apple-pie order; and unless I see to it every day, Alice keeps hers topsy-turvy."

"Never mind. Habit is second nature. Ah, here they come!"

Two smiling little girls came, somewhat shyly, forward; but grandmamma soon made them at ease with her.

"Have you seen the babies?" was one of the first questions.

"Yes, indeed. But they are asleep now."

"Which do you think the prettiest, mamma's baby or Mabel's?" was the next.

"Dear me! I didn't see any difference. They looked exactly alike to me."

"How funny!"

"Run down into the garden, now, my darlings, and find your cousins."

The little ones darted away like gold-fish, and in a few minutes had renewed their acquaintance with each other.

"Don't you think it would be a good plan, mamma," asked Belle, "to let the boys run wild for a week before sending them to school? They are racing in the garden like young colts. Dear me! What is that?"

'*That*' was the sound of four noisy feet rushing up the stairs, with such a racket as had never been heard in that house. Both babies woke up in a twinkling, and began to cry.

"Now I shall make short work with that sort of thing," said Belle, as soon as she had quieted them. "The boys may make as much noise out of doors as they choose; but such rushing, and tearing, and stamping will never do within."

"Of course not. It does not add to their happiness or comfort to be boisterous like that, one iota; and it destroys the peace of the whole household."

Here came an Indian war-whoop, and bang, bang, bang downstairs, with a door slammed tremendously as a *finale*.

"Well, I don't wonder Lily's nerves gave out," said Belle, "if that's the way she lets the boys tear up and down. Why, our boys never went on like that."

"No; I would not allow it. If boys are to become gentlemen, they must begin in the nursery. I have been astonished at the uproar most of them are allowed to make. One of the first things to teach Frank and Cil, is, that they are to form the habit of regarding the comfort of the household."

"I must go down, now, and see about tea," said Belle. "Poor Frank, how he will miss his boys!"

Shortly after the tea-bell rang, and the three young Greys, their hair flying, their hands soiled, their feet covered with mud, rushed in, hungry and eager.

"I want to sit next to grandma," said Gabrielle.

"No, I am going to sit next her," said Frank.

"Neither of you will sit next me with such hands and faces," said Mrs. Grey. "I thought I convinced you of that before you left home."

The children looked a little crestfallen, and beat a hasty retreat to their rooms, where they made themselves presentable as fast as they could.

After tea they were going to rush out again, but Belle detained them.

"I want to tell you something funny before you go out," she said. "Some years ago—ten, perhaps—I went to visit an institution for the deaf and dumb, and enjoyed everything I saw. But when school was dismissed, and the boys came running downstairs, I did not know but I should become deaf myself, they made such a noise. I did not know, before, that one set of fellows made more noise than others; but it seems they do, because they have no idea of sound. Now, you two young men are not deaf, and if you choose to listen to yourselves, you will hear what needless racket you make."

The boys looked in her smiling, kindly, but determined face, and saw they had no help for it but to give in.

"Alice said she knew we woke the babies this afternoon," said Frank, "but Cil had got my hat, and run after it, and I tumbled up to take it away; I'm real sorry I woke the babies."

"Oh, *that's* not the point. If there wasn't a baby within a mile, I should not approve of your tearing and shrieking like Indians. You may have just as much fun and frolic as you like; the more the better; but I mean to make two little gentlemen of you at the same time. There! be off with you all into the garden, and have as good a time as you can."

This was one of thousands of lessons that Belle had to teach day after day, week after week. She made her little sermons as short as she possibly could, and as quaint; and the mixture of earnestness, and banter, and fun, with which she assailed their bad habits, told upon the lads.

But there was work to do below this surface-work. She had to teach them the life of faith in Christ, a kind of teaching so eminently the province of woman, and to this end had to efface some impressions that had been falsely made in their nursery days. Long before they comprehended her teachings, her courage and patience were put to their full test. But she was a woman mighty in prayer, and day and night the name of every child in the house was mentioned singly to God.

Thus wisely and kindly Providence provided a remedy for Frank Grey's mistaken choice in his wife; thus He will rectify all such errors of judgment for those who put their trust in Him.

CHAPTER 17

Mrs. Grey knew perfectly well, that the task of training Gabrielle would be a most self-denying one. Those who never felt the sweet pain of putting self down in order to help a human soul to rise, have only touched life on the surface; have never been down into its depths; *she had.* So it was cheerily she entered upon this new labor of love, throwing her heart into it without a thought as to how her own interests were to be affected by this invasion of her home.

Gabrielle was fourteen years old, and as her mother had never done much thinking for her, had acquired a habit of thinking for herself. During the first few weeks of her stay at Greylock, her grandmother let her drift pretty much as she pleased, studying her, meanwhile, and seeking wisdom from above. The child fancied this state of things was going to last, and was well content. As the spring opened early, and was a very warm one, she adopted a hammock that swung on the piazza as her pet luxury, and there she lay during a large part of the day, reading novels. In the pang of parting with her, Frank thoughtlessly gave her more money than any child should be entrusted with, and she, consequently, laid in a stock of unwholesome dainties, which she fed upon while reading. Very soon this effeminate life began to tell. She woke with a headache, was peevish and irritable about nothings, and at times had a "dumb devil," when it was next to impossible to get a word out of her. It was evidently time to take her in hand, which Mrs. Grey did, on this wise.

"My child," she said, kindly, "have I done anything unkind to you since you came here?"

"I don't know's you have."

"Well, you speak to me as if I had. So I think you can't be well. How much exercise did you take yesterday?"

"Not any; I was tired."

"And how much the day before?"

"Not any; I wanted to read."

"But you know I wish you to walk every day."

Gabrielle was silent, and looked sullen.

"There is another thing; I saw a piece of candy on the piano just after you left; was it yours?"

"I suppose so."

"Have you been in the habit of buying candy at your pleasure?"

"I have a right to spend the money papa gives me."

"Yes; but while you are under my charge, it must be spent according to my judgment, not yours. Now I am not trying to plague you; I am trying to find out why you are irritable about everything; and if you have eaten much candy, that, with want of exercise, may be the trouble."

Gabrielle looked down morosely, and made no answer.

"Won't you tell me all about it, dear?"

No answer, only portentous frowns.

"Very well; I see you are not in the mood to listen to me. I will pray that you may be more docile another time. And, mark this: I forbid you eating any more candy without leave."

With a toss of the head that said: "We shall see!" Gabrielle retreated to the hammock. Mrs. Grey, greatly pained, looked after her till she was out of sight, when Laura, who had been concealed by a curtain, came forward.

"It isn't right for you to be treated in this way, at your age, mamma," she said. "If Frank and Lily spoil their children, they ought to reap the fruits, not you. I have been meaning to tell you that old Mary says Gabrielle is nibbling at sweet things all day long, and continually coaxing the cook for more. No wonder she is cross."

Mrs. Grey said nothing; at least nothing heard by human ears; but presently rose and went to Gabrielle's room, and examined her bureau-drawers, which she found in confusion, and whence she abstracted a quantity of pernicious articles. Later in the day Gabrielle detected the fact, and came to her defiantly with—

"I am going to write to papa to let me go home."

"Very well, my dear."

The child, expecting a conflict such as she had often had with her mother, was startled by this cool rejoinder, and at last began to cry.

"I am very sorry for you," said Mrs. Grey.

"No you ain't sorry either. And my head aches awfully, and I feel sick. I wish I was at home."

For answer, Mrs. Grey took her by the hand, led her up to her room, applied remedies with tenderness, and sympathy, and skill, and at last helped her to undress and go to bed. She slept better than she had done for weeks; had some beef-tea for her breakfast, and the devil of indigestion was exorcised, for the time.

Laura was going home now; she and the children were now quite well, and Harry could stand his loneliness no longer.

"Mag and I had delightful times together while you were gone," she said, as she took leave, "and if she gets out of the tangle of all those lessons, I shall want her to make me a good long visit. You will have your hands so full with Gabrielle that you won't miss her. Mamma—"

"Well, dear."

"I wish I hadn't been such a bad child."

"You weren't bad. You had fits of ill-humor that I did not understand, and therefore mismanaged; I know now that indigestion often lies at the bottom of what looks like moral delinquency in children.

Keep them well, and they'll keep themselves good-humored."

"Oh, I'm careful enough about Pug and Trot, as need be!"

"It's enough to make them ill to call them by such hideous names."

"Well, what could I do? Could I call my husband 'the old Harry' to distinguish him from the young Harry?"

"There, go, you incorrigible child!" cried Mrs. Grey, kissing her good-bye. Laura drove off, laughing, and the children laughed in concert, they knew not why.

Gabrielle was in a much more docile humor now, and Mrs. Grey explained to her the laws of health that made the open air, and exercise, and plain food essential to every one, but especially so to growing children.

"I do not intend to treat you in an arbitrary way," she said, "because I happen to have it in my power to do so. What I do will be for your good, not to gratify my self-will. I took away the dainties from your room because, in your condition, they were poison for you; when you are quite well you shall have some of them, from time to time, as a part of your dinner; never between meals."

Not more than a month passed, when Gabrielle had another sick headache. It soon became apparent that she had gone back to her old trick of eating, at all hours, on the sly. When she recovered, Mrs. Grey said to her:

"When your father was a boy, there was not a key turned in the house to hinder his helping himself to forbidden sweets. I could trust to his honor. Now, am I to consider you so far his inferior that I must furnish myself with bolts and bars?"

"Mamma did not lock up things, either. It wouldn't have done any good if she had. And we ate whatever we pleased."

"And were continually having ill turns. Now, my child, you are old enough to act like a reasonable being, and you must see that you bring on these sick headaches by your want of self-control. I want you to do me one favor, of your own accord give up tea and coffee."

"Oh, I can't!"

"With God's help you can."

"No, I can't. He won't help me about anything. Old Mary says she should think He would hate me, I plague you so much."

"Oh, I don't think old Mary said that!"

"Well, maybe she didn't. She said something like it."

"My poor child, He hates nobody on earth. And now, if in spite of all your fractious, disobedient ways, I, only a human being at best, love you, how do you think *He* feels?"

"I think He can't bear me. And I don't believe you love me, either. But papa did, and I mean to ask him to let me come home."

"So you have said a dozen times. If you think you had better go, and that you will be happier there, and more likely to outgrow your faults, I shall not prevent you."

"You won't ever let me have my own way, and mamma did."

"And were you becoming a model eldest daughter to her?"

"Nobody *could* be a model in the house with Rosabelle. On the whole, I'd rather stay here than go home. Rosabelle is just *horrid!*"

"I can't talk to you any more now. I must pray more and say less."

"I want to go to Ellinor Lathrop's party."

"I have told you, once for all, that you cannot go."

"Then I think you're real mean."

"Gabrielle!"

The girl was startled by the righteous indignation, mingled with dignity, with which she was addressed. Accustomed for fourteen years to look down upon her mother, she fancied she could browbeat her grandmother also.

"You may go to your room now," said Mrs. Grey. "And let me tell you that if you wean my heart from me, you will lose one of the best friends you ever had."

For once Gabrielle found she had gone too far. There is a limit no child should be allowed to pass, and she found herself confronted by it now. She flew to her room, and began letter after letter to her father, pouring out her grievances into an ear that had always listened to her with sympathy. But what would be the use of complaining to him about his mother, whom he loved and revered? Suddenly she bethought herself of Margaret; wouldn't she take her part, perhaps? There was another rush here and there, and at last she found Margaret in her own room studying.

"Grandma won't let me go to Ellinor Lathrop's party," was her abrupt beginning.

"Why, I know that. You and she discussed it at breakfast."

"Yes, but I have teased her since then, over and over again, to let me go, and she won't."

"Of course not when she had once refused."

"Mamma would let me go."

"Aunty is your mamma now. And I can't imagine what makes you such a naughty girl when she is so kind and good to you."

"Do you call it kind and good to thwart me about everything?"

"Gabrielle, I want to tell you something. You've got a guilty conscience. That's what ails you. You are all the time doing something wrong when you know better, and that keeps you unhappy."

"I am not unhappy."

"Yes, you are; and you grow more and more so every day."

"Grandma is awfully mad with me."

"Now I know that isn't true. And you ought not to talk so. The idea of saying aunty is 'mad!'"

"Gabrielle, why are you here?" asked Mrs. Grey, in a tone of surprise. "Did I not send you to your room?"

Gabrielle made no answer, but moved sullenly away.

"Oh, aunty," said Margaret, "it doesn't seem right for you to be fretted in this way!"

"I am not fretted, dear. I foresaw all these troubles before I came home. The child is trying a series of experiments with me, to see if she can't tame me down. When she once finds that the attempt is useless, we shall get on better."

"Aunty—"

"I know what you wanted to say. You wonder I do not go to the root of the matter, and try to lead her to Christ. I am praying that she may be drawn to Him, but until she learns to submit to me, it is useless to expect her to submit to Him. Her father thinks the same; and I have his full sympathy in every effort I make to do her good."

It must not be supposed that Gabrielle was always unruly and always in disgrace, and that she had no pleasant traits of character. Almost everybody has agreeable little ways that cannot be transferred to a book; and this girl, at times so rude and self-willed, had her gentle, even winning moods, and won love and good-fellowship. Nor was it strange that at an age when young people are apt to be unlovely if they have not been handled aright, she resented the sudden bit and curb of her new surroundings, and fancied herself ill-used. Mrs. Grey did not, in the least, lose heart. She knew she was not working in her own strength, and knew, by long experience, that though for a time the Lord answers never a word, He invariably does answer in His own time, and that that is always the best time. About a number of Gabrielle's faults she said nothing to her; too much fault-finding is almost worse than none; but she deplored them before God, and then tried to meet them with contrary example.

There was no good school in the neighborhood, and as soon as under her care and rule the child's health warranted it, she had a daily governess come from the city to give her lessons; and finding she was fond of music, Maud's long-silent piano was opened, and the air was filled, now by the accomplished hand of the master, now by the unmelodious bang of the pupil. Things went better now; Gabrielle had no time for idling; every hour brought its own occupation, and regular exercise, wholesome diet, and agreeable occupation broke up the habit of picking and pecking at dainties, which had been so pernicious.

She caught, too, some of Margaret's tastes, and instead of thinking about dress as a matter of great import, would content herself to put on a woodland rig, quaint, yet not ugly, and go off with her in quest of the gems Nature is always flinging lavishly about. They came home from their expeditions with baskets running over with ferns, mosses, lichens, grasses, and nobody knows what not, till their rooms looked verdant with beauty. Margaret got up a mossy bank with red berries nestling in it here and there; Gabrielle must have one, like yet not like it, for no two hands work on one and the same line; and Margaret had a rustic basket hanging from every possible point, and Gabrielle hasted to do the same. Mrs. Grey looked on with delight at all this. No utterly spoiled character riots in such simple pursuits, and she who begins to love Nature, begins to grow cold to all that is artificial. While in that house personal neatness was made a law, dress was never talked about as much more than a necessary evil to be attended to twice a year, and then forgotten. And now that she had taken to ornamenting her room, Gabrielle found she must keep it in order, and learned, too, that she had not a little executive power in the matter of arrangement of furniture and clothing. She began to observe, too, that though grandmamma would not scold, she could and did punish, and that invariably, when infringement of a rule required it. Later on she perceived a regular system of rewards going silently on. After a week of exceptional docility, an invisible good fairy would leave tokens of her presence in her room; now it was a vase for flowers; now a little photograph; now a paper-weight; it was not always possible to tell who this good fairy was; but whoever it was, knew just what she wanted.

So the summer bloomed and budded and bore fruit, and faded into autumn, and autumn froze into winter. There was rarely a conflict now; Gabrielle was too busy to find time for them, and too fond of the deeds of the good fairy to run the risk of one when she could help it. Mrs. Grey was not in the least surprised when, one day, the girl came shyly behind her, put her arms around her neck, and whispered, "Grandmamma, I wish I was a Christian!"

"So do I, my dear child," was the reply. "And why not become one, this minute?"

"I don't know; I've tried ever so many times."

"Tried how?"

"To be good."

"Is it said anywhere in the Bible that being 'good' and being a Christian are synonymous terms?"

"I thought it was."

"We have our Lord's own declaration that there is only one good Being in the universe, 'that is God.' Salvation is not offered to good people, but to bad ones."

"Well—I am *so* bad that I don't believe it is meant for me."

"The Bible says, *'there is no difference.'* Everybody has got to come to Christ on one level."

"Some are worse than others."

"True; but when it comes to our relation to Christ, we all stand shoulder to shoulder. I have spent a large part of my life in believing on and working for Him, but that does not entitle me to one atom of His favor. I must go to Him, every day, just as you must go now, denouncing, renouncing myself, and receive Him, by faith, as my only ground of hope."

Gabrielle looked puzzled, and was about to raise another objection, but they were interrupted, and the conversation was not renewed till the next day.

CHAPTER 18

Gabrielle knelt that night at her bedside, with a latent, but strong, desire to walk, not by faith, but by sight. She wanted to hear an audible voice from heaven to assure her that she might feel sure of salvation. Mrs. Grey had had large experience in dealing with souls, and soon detected and brought this to light when they next met in her dressing-room.

"I wish there was something I could *do* to make God love me," the child began.

"My dear, there is something."

"What is it?" was the eager demand.

"Believe on His Son, Jesus Christ."

Gabrielle's countenance fell.

"I can't believe, I don't know how!" she said.

"My child, if I should tell you that I was going to take you to drive this afternoon, you would believe me, should you not?"

"Yes, indeed."

"That would be having faith in me."

"Yes; but it wouldn't be loving you, and God says we must love Him. Even if I can believe in Him, I can't make myself love Him. I am sure I would if I could."

"If it is true that you cannot love Him, then He will not condemn you at the last day."

"It's all perfectly *horrid!*" cried Gabrielle, bewildered and excited.

"Don't say so, my poor child!" said Mrs. Grey, drawing the girl to her and kissing her burning cheeks. "Christ is altogether lovely, and all His paths are peace. He puts no difficulties in your way; you make them yourself. Now let me ask you one question. Have you not asked our Lord to save your soul?"

"Yes; hundreds of times."

"And has He refused hundreds of times?"

"He must have, for I am not saved."

"Will you prove to me that you are not?"

"Why, if I was saved I should be full of joy; and instead of that I am full of misery."

"Well, now, here are two poor men, brothers, and they are homeless, and friendless, and weary, and heavy-laden; but a rich man dies and leaves them each a fortune. One of them learns this to be the case, and is relieved of care and want; the other has not heard of his good luck, and therefore is, to all intents and purposes, as poor as ever."

"You mean that I may have faith and not know it, and so my faith is of no use to me?"

"It brings you no present peace. Of course it would save you in the end; but meanwhile you would lead a dark, joyless life."

"Sometimes I feel as if I had been changed a little," said Gabrielle, thoughtfully. "But my feelings are not alike two hours going."

"Of course not. A thousand things vary our emotions. The Bible says nothing about feeling this way or feeling that, in order to be saved. It says *'believe.'*"

"I think, though, that it would be easier to believe if I felt more. I keep hoping that sometime I shall feel so much that God will pity and forgive me."

"In other words, you keep hoping to make yourself agreeable to Him by a great display of emotion. Do not be hurt at my saying this. Human nature is supremely self-righteous, and is not willing to take salvation as a free gift. I beg you to decide for Christ now, with your *will;* having once done that, your heart will follow fast enough."

"But suppose I begin and don't hold out?"

"Begin thus. Say to God: 'Let me not wander from Thy commandments;' and He will reply: 'I will put my fear in your heart that you shall not depart from me.'"

"Then there are so many things to give up if I become a Christian," said Gabrielle, evasively.

"There are no good things to give up, and there are thousands to gain. I cannot preach to you below the gospel-standard, which says that the friend of the world is the enemy of God."

"Well, He elects some people to save, and rejects others. How can I know that I do not come under the last head?"

"By electing Christ as yours, at this moment, when His Spirit is striving with you to that end. I can't tell you how it pains me to see you tampering with divine truth as if it were a straw. I believe this temporizing, argumentative temper comes from a league between Satan and your own evil heart. If you do not take care you will grieve away the Holy Ghost. For my part, I would rather offend than grieve a friend."

"Do you mean that the Holy Ghost is my *friend?*" Gabrielle asked, in great surprise.

"Certainly. Otherwise why should He hover around you as He is doing now, offering you the greatest prizes of life?"

"Why should He love me? Why should He offer me prizes? I have never so much as given Him a thought!"

"I do not know. I can only say: 'Even so, Father, for so it seemed good in Thy sight.'"[1]

"Then I won't hold out against Him another minute, if God will take me, just as I am, a dreadfully naughty girl! He may have me and welcome! Only I wish I hadn't done so many things I am ashamed of."

1　Matthew 11:26.

Some weeks later she came shyly again behind her grandmamma and whispered:

"May I join the church next Sunday?"

"'If thou believest with all thine heart thou mayest,'" was the fervent reply, and Gabrielle slipped timidly away.

Everybody knows that, as a general rule, young people cannot talk to their nearest friends about their souls when they will confide in strangers. It ought not to be so. A warm-hearted mother once said that she began to talk to her children about Christ when they were *three weeks old!* by which sweet little exaggeration she only meant that she gave her confidence, and won theirs, at the earliest conceivable age.

Mrs. Grey perfectly understood that, taking Gabrielle at a disadvantage, she could not expect her to sustain to herself the relation of a little child, and that she would be painfully shy should she try to penetrate her hidden life. Indeed there was little to penetrate. The child apprehended dimly the path on which she had entered. All she knew about herself was, that whereas her chief aim once was to have a nice time, and that in her own way, her earnest desire now was to be "good."

Mrs. Grey's life, far more than her instructions, had dropped, as a seed, into soil prepared for it by the hand of Him who hears and answers prayer. Nor did she at once emerge into a saint, with all the holy aspirations and activities of mature life. She was a child still, and needed pruning, grafting, and weeding. But the root of the matter was in her. That tiny spark of grace that sometimes seemed to her and to her friends to have died out, was there; it flickered, and was often invisible to mortal eyes; *but it was there*, and had her soul been at any moment required of her, that grace, small though it was, would have been her humble passport into the company of the redeemed.

Mrs. Grey's pastor at this time was quite an inexperienced man, and he would not venture to admit any young people to his church till he had seen their parents or guardians. He came now to see her with reference to Gabrielle.

"I think the root of the matter is in the child," she said, "and that she may safely unite with the church. But, if you will allow me to say it, these immature young Christians need a great deal of looking-after. Taking them into the church is like taking plants into shelter. But shelter is not enough. *All* the conditions of growth should be observed, or instead of blossoms and fruit, we shall have stunted or effeminate growth, or what is worse, no growth at all."

"One object I had in calling today," he returned, "was to ask you if it would be possible to gather our young people about you once a week for Christian counsel?"

Mrs. Grey cast her eye over her already overcrowded life, and shook her head.

"I think I am playing the school-ma'am quite as much as is good for me," she said, with a smile. "Sometimes I am almost frightened at the multiplicity of things I am undertaking to do. However, the work you propose looks very attractive; I might spare one evening in the week."

"They are almost all confined to their studies in the evening. Perhaps we should have to steal a piece of Sunday."

"Oh, I don't see where."

"Nor I; unless I succeed in carrying out a plan I have in my mind. My theory is that there is too much preaching, and too little doing, of the word. Men of business, for instance, have next to no time for Christian work, and their piety falls to sleep in consequence. If the church would organize some plan for setting everybody at work on Sunday afternoons, pastors and all, I think we might soon begin to expect the coming of our Lord. By the bye, you love to deal with difficult cases; I wish you would take occasion to talk to Mr. Morrison. You have had great experience, and I have had next to none."

"It takes more than experience to reach a polished moralist," she replied. "It needs the Holy Spirit. I doubt if there is anything we can do but pray for him. He is so intrenched in his own virtues that he is farther out of reach than most hardened sinners."

"I know it; but there are his poor wife and those six boys to be thought of."

"You have been among us so little time that you are, perhaps, not aware that he is my brother."

"Indeed, I was not aware of it."

"He is my half-brother; we had different mothers. At the time of his birth, and for many years following, our father was not a Christian; his training was different from mine. Our mothers were as unlike as possible, and I can't begin to tell you how it pains me to look at his perfectly useless—because Christless—life. I think he will be saved at last; too much prayer has been offered for him to permit his being lost; but oh, how much he has thrown away!"

"He is an interesting man; he would be very useful in the church; I wish I could see him identified with it."

"I will make one more attempt to move him. My heart yearns over those dear boys."

A few evenings later saw her closeted with Mr. Morrison, a fine-looking man, with complexion almost as pure as a baby's, clear blue eyes, and a noble head, crowned with waving white hair. They talked a while about his boys, and his plans for their future; then she spoke, naturally, for her heart was full of it, of the special religious work then going on in the church.

"It is mere excitement," he said; "it will not last."

"Time alone can prove that. In my own case the excitement has lasted fifty years, and I see no signs of its passing off. Robert, you can't think how it distresses me to see you coming to church, Sunday after Sunday, with a regularity that might put many a professor to the blush, yet never advancing beyond that point."

"I should like to ask you one question, Emily. Haven't I heard you say you were almost certain of my salvation?"

"Yes, I have said it. But salvation is not the sole end of man; his first end is to glorify God."

"Well, don't I glorify Him? Point out any word or deed of mine that is sinful, if you can. Am I not fair and square in all my dealings?

Do not I give, liberally, to the poor? Am I bad-tempered? Am I a backbiter?"

"We have gone all over this ground scores of times," she replied. "If mere morality glorifies God, then I must allow that you are living up to all His claims. But the Bible is our standard, and we learn there that Christ rejected a man who had kept the law from his youth up."

"I never could see the reason for that. I have always aimed to lead a blameless life, and think I have."

"To be saved by a blameless life one must never have transgressed in a single point. Now you do not pretend that you never once transgressed?"

"I know it would be a lie to stand up in a prayer-meeting, and say I was the chief of sinners, as so many do."

"Did St. Paul lie when he called himself the chief of sinners?"

"I suppose he knew what he was saying. I do not pretend to be St. Paul, or saint anybody; but to pretend I am a great sinner, when I know I am not, would be mere nonsense."

"That is as far as I ever get with you. You say you believe the Bible; let us see what that says."

"Oh, I know what it says; that every man is, by nature, a great sinner; granted, but all are not equally depraved, and it has always been my nature to be upright, faithful, and true. What would you have more?"

"A great deal more. Morality is not Christianity."

"You think I am not a Christian because I never joined the church. But I consider myself a better man than half your professors. If I ever do set up to be a Christian, I mean to put most of you to the blush. The way old Mr. Whitcomb gets up and whines over his 'coldness' makes me smile."

"I don't like whines any better than you do. But I want to call your attention to a fact you overlook. Allowing that your life is blameless, let me judge you by that life. Its whole history is *forgetfulness of God*, and that issues in final condemnation, however faultless your record in regard to man. You are not honest and upright and amiable to please God, therefore He scarcely looks at this exterior, fair as it is in your eyes."

"Prove that I forget God, if you please. Is it forgetting Him to go to church twice every Sunday? I do not make the pretension that some men do, but I defy them to find me wanting in any virtue."

"Let us define the word 'forget' before we go any farther. It implies heedlessness, does it not?"

"I suppose so."

"Then one who forgets God is heedless towards Him. You go to church every Sunday; outwardly this looks well. But the Divine eye penetrates to the heart. Does He find a true worshiper there?"

"You cannot prove that He does not."

"I cannot *prove* it, it is true, but I must judge of the state of your heart on Sundays, by what I see of your life on weekdays. Now, I see no Christ there."

"I believe the Father judges me more leniently than you do. He finds no fault with my worship."

"Does He not? Read what is said in prophecy and afterwards repeated by Christ, of those who worship God with the lips while the heart is far from Him."[1]

"While my outward life is spotless I am not afraid of my heart's not keeping step with it. Besides, there is nothing malicious, or unkind, or severe in my heart, that God should look upon with displeasure. It is not mere sentiment He wants. He wants a good, honest, manly life, and that He gets from me."

"If He gets from you all He wants, why does He declare you must be born again?"

"I know most men need regeneration, but I feel no need of any such change, and never did."

"My dear brother," said Mrs. Grey, with difficulty suppressing her tears, "I see that further argument is useless. You are living for yourself and not for Christ, though He has died for you. You are

1 See Isaiah 29:13; Matthew 15:8–9.

training your sons to outward morality like your own. But all your souls are in jeopardy. There are those who have gone far beyond you; they have prophesied in Christ's name; cast out devils in His name; done many wonderful works in His name; and He has said, 'I never knew you; depart from me, ye that work iniquity.'"[1]

"At any rate," he returned, "you are religious enough to satisfy the most exacting Being possible. If I fail to enter heaven through my good works, I can plead yours."

"Mine!" she cried. "There isn't one on record!"

"Oh, if it pleases you to take that view of your life, well and good! It seems to be a part of your creed to believe yourself a sinner."

"It is, indeed, my creed," she replied, "and I find that creed in the Word of God. One ray from it darting through your soul would reveal to you depths of evil of which you are now unconscious."

"'Where ignorance is bliss, 'tis folly to be wise,'" he said, smilingly, and rose to go.

Defeated and grieved, Mrs. Grey went to the Refuge of her soul, to plead once more on behalf of this deluded man. But for a time "He answered her never a word."

---

1 Matthew 7:23.

CHAPTER 19

Christmas came upon Greylock before they were quite ready for it; it seemed to come earlier every year. Margaret had worked very hard to get a picture done for each of the grown folks, and though she had undoubted genius, and wrote poetry with her artistic brush, of course her work was more or less crude.

Once more the house flung open its doors, and the scattered family came trooping in. They were a clannish set, wonderfully fond of each other, and willing to take any amount of trouble in order to accomplish this yearly meeting. Everybody found Frank's three elder children marvelously improved in health and behavior, and he and Lily could hardly believe that these three well-bred, gentle, and obedient young creatures were those who went forth from them like so many unruly colts. Belle's twins were now ten months old—a lovely age—and she was positive they could say "papa," a point on which the rest of the family were doubtful. Mabel was as devoted a lover as ever; there was no room for her in her mother's lap nowadays, but she still stood always close at her side, except when Margaret beguiled her away.

"How long did it take you to paint all these pictures, Margaret?" Laura one day asked.

"A long, long time, small as they are," she replied. "I can tell you, painting means *work.* "

"It is a great comfort to us common mortals to see genius plodding along the highway like the rest of us," said Laura. "By the bye, that reminds me that my book, such as it is, is done, and I am going to read it aloud for your delectation the first stormy day."

"Whose? Mine?" asked Margaret.

"Not yours in particular; all you girls in general."

"And leave us boys out?" cried Frank.

"You boys won't be left out with my consent," said Harry. "*I* think it's a capital story."

"Of course *you'd* think it capital if it was 'Mother Goose,'" said Laura. "Don't any of you believe a word he says. It isn't half so good as it ought to be."

The stormy day was close at hand, and the whole family met in the library, amused at the idea of "Oney's" writing a book, and secretly afraid they might have to quiz it. The ladies had their work, and were, therefore, out of mischief during the reading. But the gentlemen kept Mrs. Grey in a constant state of scandal the whole time. One unscrewed her inkstand and looked in; another took up and laid down her paper-weights, and always in the wrong place; another upset a bottle of mucilage, hoped she didn't know it, and furtively wiped it up with his handkerchief; another bent a leaf-cutter Margaret had painted for her, and every moment she expected to see it snap in two. Now and then, to Laura's vexation, they whispered to each other, and now and then a mamma was called out, and the reading had to be suspended. But she kept at it manfully, and by degrees, as the "boys" became interested, they let the library-table and its contents alone.

And this is Laura's story:

Eric

"It is of no use, I cannot stand; you see the ankle is fractured."

"But the Signor will perish if he lies here on the ice."

"Is there, then, no hope that one of the other sledges will come to our rescue?"

"None whatever. We are quite off the usual route; nightfall is approaching, and there is but one way of escape from death—if the Signor will permit me to take him on my shoulders."

"Impossible! You could not bear such a burden a single rod."

"The Signor does not know the young men of Dalerna."

"Nay, I will not suffer you to make the trial. Go, my good Olaf, and leave me to my fate. It is not needful that both of us should perish. Take my watch to my wife, and with it, present her with my parting salutations. My purse I give to you; by its means you can marry some blue-eyed maiden, and tell her Fortune had a smile for her when it played such a freak on me."

The young man colored with indignation.

"You do not know our muscles, stranger; neither do you comprehend our scorn for money won by cowardice," he said coldly.

And, without another word, he proceeded to burden himself with the disabled traveler, who, after making a feeble resistance, yielded himself to his fate.

This scene occurred on the frozen surface of the Gulf of Bothnia. A party of Italians, weary of their own luxurious clime, had come to these northern regions in hope of stirring their blood by adventures and perils. Several ladies of the party remained at Upsala in tolerable comfort, while their husbands and brothers, expecting to find the gulf a smooth and glassy expanse, hastened to cross it in sledges in pursuit of a new sensation. With great difficulty they procured sledges and horses with their drivers, from the country about Grisselhamn, a little town whence they proposed to set out on the expedition. It was also necessary to provide themselves with huge coats of bearskin, before encountering the cutting blasts to which these foreigners were unaccustomed.

Thus equipped, the party set forth in high spirits. Instead, however, of smooth surface over which they had expected to glide as on the wings of the wind, they soon found, to their dismay, that they were toiling over a rough and dangerous series of masses of ice, by means of which they were jolted and bruised to the last degree of endurance. Again and again they were thrown from the sledges, whence they went rolling in all directions. To add to their dismay, the horses, fancying these strange objects on the ice to be veritable bears, became every moment more and more unmanageable, and one of them, wild with terror, at length took flight. Several of the occupants of the sledge drawn by this horse were scattered along the way, and were gradually rescued by their fellow-travelers. He who remained at the mercy of the terrified horse, kept his seat with the utmost difficulty, and watched, with anxiety, every motion of his sturdy young driver, Olaf Stein, whose strength seemed to be giving way. Mile after mile they flew over the jagged ice-field in awful silence; awaiting at last in breathless suspense the fate that seemed inevitable. When both were thrown violently from the sledge they lay insensible on the ice, while the horse, now left to himself, rushed onward and was heard of no more.

Olaf was the first to recover, and by his aid, his companion was also so far restored as to attempt to rise to his feet. But what was his distress to find that one of his ankles was fractured, and that he must sink back again to the hard and icy bed on which he had already lain until almost benumbed.

It was at this point that he was generous enough to concern himself for the safety of his guide, while hopeless of his own; and that Olaf, with equal generosity, resolved to rescue him or perish in the attempt.

The task he had assumed was severe. They were quite off the usual track; night was approaching, and the cold becoming intense. He toiled on in a sturdy kind of patience, almost instinctively taking the right direction, until at length he had the joy of finding himself on the track whence the terror-stricken horse had diverged. Very shortly, the other sledges came in sight, and the party made the best of its way back to Grisselhamn. The injured traveler was made as comfortable as was possible under the circumstances, and Olaf was sent to Upsala to bring thence his wife, with her maid. The poor fellow had himself sustained a severe injury when thrown from the sledge, and was also exhausted by his toilsome homeward route. But he set forth at once on the journey to Upsala without a word, and under his escort, those he sought returned with him to Grisselhamn. Fortunately, he was not as entirely ignorant of the Italian language as were his new charge of the Dalecarnian speech. He had wandered repeatedly so far as the northern part of Italy in order to dispose of various little articles of his own handiwork, as well as those of his neighbors. His share of the profits of these adventures had enabled him to purchase the horse he had just lost, and by whose means he supported himself. This, therefore, seemed an inauspicious moment for falling in love, and of proposing to himself to take a wife. But love being a sentiment not particularly subject to order and rule, poor Olaf had to yield to his fate. This fate was black-eyed, and brown, and its name was Viola, and she who possessed these attractions was the little maid whose duty it now was to take charge of her master, with such aid as Olaf could render. Nursing was new business to the hardy young peasant, but he was glad of occupation, and thankful for a task that kept him near Viola. She, on her part, felt supreme contempt for black eyes, from the moment she met the first kind glance from Olaf's blue ones; if he proved an awkward nurse, why, there was all the more for her to teach him. Besides, it was not long before she discovered the severe contusion he had received in his fall, and felt it absolutely necessary to take his aching shoulder under her charge, and to treat it with a vast deal of needed and a vast deal of needless compassion and care. Though his nature was honest as the day, Olaf for once was willing to make the very most of his bruises, since Viola was thus led to pour out upon him such floods of pity as would soon lead to love. When, therefore, the fractured ankle was healed, and the Italian party ready to return home, and Olaf was pressed to ask what favor he would wish in return for his services, it is not so strange, considering what human nature is, that all he asked was permission to make a Swede of the little brown maiden who, in his eyes, was the only maiden on earth.

Her mistress, a spoiled child of fortune, received this proposal with indignation; said she could not live without Viola, who knew all her ways, and for whom she had done so much, and that, at least, she could not spare her until their return to Italy. When her husband overruled all these objections by reminding her that he owed his life to Olaf, she ceased open argument and resorted to secret strategy.

"How do you expect to live in this villainous climate, you silly child?" cried she, when Viola, with downcast eyes, owned her wish to do so. "You will absolutely perish with the cold. Then think what food you will have to eat! Instead of grapes, and melons, and figs, you will have that abominable bread made of bran mixed with bark and resin! I tasted a bit of it one day, and the very thought of it sickens me. You think Olaf will provide you with flour? Nonsense! And then to sit and spin, spin and knit, knit from morning till night! Why, even the very children in their cradles are taught to work, and I have seen them, myself, knitting all the way to school. What do you say? That you are never so happy as when at work? And that work for one you love will be sweet! You cannot really pretend that you love that great clumsy fellow with his round face like the full moon, and his breeches and knee-buckles, and odd little caps. Now, Viola, that is actually too absurd! Think, now, there was young Oglio, who had such a passion for you; think of the cruelty of forsaking him for this stranger."

"I cannot forsake that bad man, for I always hated him, and never would listen to him," cried Viola. "And if the Signora thinks I am only fit to marry such a little, idle, impertinent coxcomb, then the Signora thinks very ill of me."

"But then the conscience of the thing, Viola! To renounce your religion just to gratify a mere freak of fancy which you will outgrow in less than a month! Really, when I think of it, I feel that I ought to use the authority given me by your poor mother on her death-bed, and absolutely refuse my consent to this crime."

"Renounce my religion! Our holy mother forbid!" cried Viola.

"Olaf will surely embrace it so soon as he comes under my influence. He already says I can wind him round my finger."

"It is very silly in you to repeat such nonsense. Ah! if you but knew men as I do. The winding is all on the other side, I assure you."

"It *was* silly," replied Viola; "I hope the Signora will pardon me. But it is so long since any one was so good as to love me! It is so lonely, so sad to be an orphan in this great world, so full of fathers and mothers."

"None can be so sad or so lonely as they who peril their souls as you are about to risk yours," returned her mistress, severely.

Viola became very pale, but was silent, and at that time no further conversation took place. At her next interview with Olaf she related to him all that had passed, and begged to know if in marrying him she should be forced to renounce the religion in which she had been brought up.

"Nay," said Olaf, smiling, "I do not intend to be so hard a master, little one."

Viola was satisfied. "I shall soon convert him," she said to herself.

"I will not frighten her," was Olaf's secret thought. "The little thing loves me dearly; I shall soon hear no more of her beads and mummeries. We shall go to church every Sunday; by and by we shall have children; they shall have dark eyes and dark hair, and be Lutherans, every one of them."

So in spite of obstacles, true love ran smoothly with the twain into wedded life.

Olaf was put into a position to earn his bread and that of his wife, and after taking leave of their friends, he bore his little treasure to his home, where his aged father and mother yet lived. Viola's life had been hitherto spent in a sunny land, which had for her little real sunshine. Her parents died when she was quite a child, and the mistress into whose hands she then passed was too self-absorbed to ask the question whether this human being had emotions and passions like her own. Now she went from seeming luxury to the real luxury of being beloved. Olaf's father and mother opened their hearts and took her in without delay; they liked her quaint, lively ways, and her foreign habits were a pleasant marvel, breaking in on the monotony of their hard lives. She, for her part, was young and flexible, and adapted herself readily to her new duties.

So their domestic life moved on harmoniously in the main, and Olaf took great delight in teaching his wife to speak the language of his own people, and in hearing her pretty, foreign accent which gave a charm to everything she said. She learned with marvelous rapidity, and the long winter evenings, full as they were of necessary work, gave leisure for reading, also. There was only one point on which the two differed seriously, and this was a vital one, their religion. At first Viola began with great zeal to use various arguments with Olaf to convince him how much she was in the right and how far he was wrong, but he would not argue; he only laughed at her, called her his little one, told her what beautiful hair she had, and the like. Then Viola would turn pale and look displeased, but soon would whisper to herself, "But he loves me!" and in that sweet conviction recover her good-humor. Meanwhile she watched his honest, Christian life with increasing respect. She could not help seeing that in his measure, religion reigned over every detail of his existence, nor fail to contrast it with that of her mistress, who, while faithful to fast and feast, and scrupulous as to prayers and masses, did not hesitate to indulge herself in falsehood and passion.

It seemed strange to her that she had been able to respect the religion of one whose violence through many years of her servitude had left visible marks on her flesh; then reproaching herself for such thoughts she did penance in secret, and redoubled her zeal on behalf of her husband.

With early May came spring, with buds and blossoms, and Viola welcomed the home of her adoption in its new dress. She surprised her husband by appearing one Sunday morning in the national costume worn by the Dalecarnians on all holidays. For the first time he asked her to go with him to church, and for the first time she was in the mood to gratify him. Hitherto, she had resolved, come what might, never to set foot within that dangerous spot, but on this, of all days, should she and Olaf worship apart? Had she not a sweet secret to whisper in his ear that would make him love her better than ever, and would it be so very great a sin just for that once to kneel with him? So with her heart throbbing beneath her new costume, the prettiest little peasant of the whole picturesque scene, she entered the church with mingled curiosity and fear. Watching Olaf, to do as he did, she stood, with folded hands, to utter, silently, a few words of prayer, then seating herself, she cast timid glances about her. The aspect of the congregation was earnest and reverent. So many rosy, blonde children she never had seen, and coming back from higher thoughts to everyday matters, especially to the subject that at this time lay near her heart, she hoped her little daughter—for surely it was to be a little daughter— might be just like a fair, sweet child who sat opposite, with large blue eyes like Olaf's, and hair almost silvery in its soft beauty. And then she smiled to herself to think how quaint and charming her child should look in a little costume of its own, embroidered with her own hands; but after all, would it not be best to have a boy? would not Olaf like a boy? Of course he would! Then it should be a boy tall and strong and ruddy; not the slender, dark-eyed little fellow she had pictured to herself in years gone by, when dreaming of a home and children, but a real Swedish yeoman, with buckles on his shoes and a picturesque holiday suit like his father's. She laughed as this image presented itself to her imagination: a little low laugh, but Olaf heard it, and turned quickly and looked in her face. Tears of vexation filled her eyes. "Oh, Olaf," she whispered to herself, "you would forgive me if you knew why I laughed, I am sure you would!" Olaf's countenance was serious, but he looked down kindly on his little wife, who sat abashed beneath his glance, recalling her wandering thoughts.

"Here I have been trying so long to convert him," she said to herself, "and after all he is far better than I am. Nothing could make *him* laugh in church!" Thus humbled, Viola entered into the service with all her heart, and listened to the sermon with eager attention, striving to catch its meaning, though only able to do so in a dim and misty way, so new was the language. There were many old people in the congregation, some of whom slept through the whole service, while others coughed; there was also no small variety of babies, who cried whenever they saw fit, and were pacified with onions by their mothers.

"I never will bring my baby to church," thought Viola, "and on no account will I feed it with onions! But here I am again, as wicked as ever, and not listening to the sermon at all. Ah, I will pinch myself black-and-blue till I learn to fix my thoughts better! Oh, Jesus—the Jesus Olaf loves—come and help me to be good!"

This prayer went forth from the very depths of her heart, and an answer came at once. It seemed as if scales fell from her eyes at that moment, and she felt her soul united to Olaf's and those of the true souls about her; felt the points of union and forgot the points of difference, and with all the warmth of her nature, gave herself to Christ. Ever after, this beautiful Sunday lived in her mind and in that of Olaf's as the bright spot in their lives, for thenceforth there was no discussion, no 'my religion,' and 'thy religion' but a gradual, quiet union of belief and practice.

"There's the lunch-bell!" said Mrs. Grey, as Laura finished the last sentence. "We'll hear the rest after we have sustained ourselves with oysters and other creature comforts. Gabrielle, my dear, please don't drag on your father so; you may love him to your heart's content, but you needn't eat him up."

Gabrielle would once have fired up at even as good-humored banter as this, and Frank was astonished to see her loosen the hold she had on his arm, and let him follow his mother's significant glance, and offer it to his wife.

After lunch there was an hour with the little ones, and any

amount of fun and frolic, headed by the Rev. Cyril, whose specialty it was to be a bear, and go round, on all-fours, after a shrieking, laughing, scampering crowd.

At length, order was restored, the family group reassembled, and Laura continued her story.

CHAPTER 20

Some months later, as Olaf held in his big arms his first-born son, Viola shyly whispered:

"It was to have been a girl, but for your sake I decided it should be a boy. Thinking of it on that blessed Sunday, I laughed, wicked little creature that I was. He is not like you, neither is he like me; indeed he is very ugly; but who cares? We shall love him just the same!"

"Nay, I will not have him called 'ugly,'" said his father, "for he has your hair, Viola, and my eyes, and haven't you told me a thousand times you fell in love with me on account of my blue eyes?"

"In love!" cried Viola; "now, Olaf, you are too absurd. As if anybody *could* be in love with such a big, burly, giant-like fellow! Why, how should I, half a mile below you, see up so high as to know the color of your eyes, unless indeed I climbed a ladder on purpose?"

So saying, Viola pulled the giant down to his knees by her bedside, laid his great head on her breast, and patted and caressed it, while railing at him and his eyes and his baby to her heart's content. Olaf received these mingled attentions with purrs of satisfaction, and went on his way with the calm conviction that however his wife and child might look to other people, there was no doubt they were both as near perfection as need be.

In spite of her happiness and of Olaf's cares, however, Viola did not recover from her illness very rapidly. She missed now many comforts to which she had been accustomed; some dainty to tempt her appetite, or the luscious fruits of her own land. Her brave, true heart, and Olaf's affection sustained her amid these new demands on her fortitude; when strength failed her she made up for it by patience and energy, and though she accomplished it painfully, she did accomplish as much as other vigorous women of her class. Olaf worked diligently to procure for Viola such alleviations as he could think of; but always accustomed to a life of the utmost simplicity, many of her real wants, had they been expressed, would have seemed to him most puerile.

The child received the name of Eric; Viola thus honored and gratified Olaf's father; but she promised herself that her second child should bear the name of her own mother.

Little Eric, at six months old, had reversed the apparent gifts of his birthright. His dark hair fell off, and was replaced by a crown of luxurious golden curls; his blue eyes became steel-colored, then a soft brown, like his mother's; he was a marvel of the beauty of two races. And as his character developed he proved the truth of the saying, that mingled races produce the finest strain of nature.

In his very babyhood the neighbors said he was no common child, and, of course, Olaf and Viola thought so too, though they both said, as they thought they ought to say, that he was like all the other babies in the world. Viola, indeed, knew little about children. She had neither brother or sister, and the mistress with whom she had spent most of her life could not bear the sound of a child's voice. Eric was, therefore, an object of great curiosity to his young mother; a little mystery whom she was never tired of studying. She and Olaf had some pleasant strife together as to the first language the child should speak; naturally enough, he chose that which he heard most frequently, and spoke his first lisping words in her musical tongue. His grandmother thought that for a Swedish boy to speak Italian was nothing less than a miracle, and prophesied that such a child would die before its time. There was her old neighbor,

Stenbock; her son died of knowing too much, and of having his hair left to grow till it hung down all over his shoulders like a yellow veil; she hoped Viola would not let Eric's hair grow in that fashion, though, to be sure, its having once been dark might make all the difference in the world.

But when Eric soon proved that he could talk Swedish almost as well as herself, the good grandmother shook her head, and hoped, with secret misgivings to the contrary, that this was not some wicked spirit come in human shape to ruin them all. Viola concerned herself very little with such fancies. Everything the child said or did amused her, but she had too little experience to know how individual this little creature was; how imitative and yet how original. As soon as he could speak plainly, Eric began to go singing about the house, as his mother did. He caught both words and air without effort, and when he sang, seemed as unconscious as a bird on the wing. Then one day, as Viola sat at work, using her needle with great rapidity, she was suddenly aroused from her absorption in it by Eric's long silence; unusual quietness in an active child usually means mischief brewing, as every mother knows. Looking up, she saw Eric seated gravely opposite her, with a bit of cloth fastened to his knee, and imitating her every motion with precision. He had fastened his thread to a pin, and was making this pin move in concert with her needle, only, of course, his movements were only a pretence, while hers were real. She threw herself back in her chair to laugh at her ease at this comic scene; whereupon Eric, with no little humor twinkling in his eye, threw himself back likewise, and laughed in unison with her.

"You little monkey, how dare you!" she cried, half vexed and half amused; but Eric looked at her with such an open, innocent face, that she saw he meant no harm, and if a monkey, was a harmless one after all.

But now the whole household was kept busy and merry with the incessant activity of this quaint child. Nothing escaped his observation. He coughed like his grandfather; he made believe knit, and took snuff like his grandmother.

When Viola shook her head at him, he would instantly turn upon her that open, honest face, free from guile and malice, and obey forthwith. No one who caught that glance could help forgiving the unconscious child and taking him into his confidence.

Viola, meanwhile, attained the desire of her heart—a little Swedish maiden with rosy cheeks and fair hair, the very funniest miniature of Olaf. Eric, of course, cried when the baby cried, or at least lifted up his voice in perfect imitation, and crept when the baby crept, as if going on all-fours was man's normal mode of loco-motion. At the same time he constituted himself her guardian and protector. All the songs he had picked up he sang to her as she lay in her cradle, and as she grew older he repeated to her, with mar-velous accuracy, all the tales he had heard in his short life. Then the tenderness Olaf poured out on Viola, Eric lavished on his little sister; words sacred to husbands and wives who love each other, and which they never mean to let fall on profane ears, will sometimes escape; such words and tones the boy treasured in his memory per-haps many long months, and then showered them on Carina with all manner of courtesies and gallantries. She received them without much response, but with sweet content, for her instincts told her that when Eric said he loved her and could not imagine how he ever got along without her, he was not just "making believe."

There was no school in the neighborhood, and Viola was too ignorant of the language to teach Eric to read. His grandmother, therefore, undertook this task, which proved to be only a pleasure, he learned with so much ease, and was so joyous and cheerful over his books.

His fine ear enabled him to catch her tones, so that when he first began to read aloud to his father the effect was almost ludicrous; by degrees, however, as his mind developed, he read with great spirit, like, yet unlike, all he had ever heard. By degrees the peculiarities and talents of this strange boy began to be much spoken of; strang-ers who passed that way made the excuse of needing refreshment, in the hope of seeing for themselves some of his performances. Viola received them with true Swedish hospitality, as her husband wished her to do, but she never could succeed in making Eric understand what was desired of him. His unconsciousness saved him from vanity; what he said and sang, and what he did, were all as natural and simple as childhood could make them.

There had been one great inconvenience in his imitative propensities; since his early babyhood they had not dared to take him to church. They knew that the whole congregation would be excited to merriment should he have the opportunity to watch the grotesque gestures of the pastor in the pulpit. Eric had already caught them, to a certain extent, when the minister made his visits at the house; but bad must not be suffered to become worse. When he was four years old, however, Olaf resolved that his boy should be cured of a habit which would make him disagreeable, now that he was ceasing to be a child. He, therefore, set himself seriously to work.

"Eric, do you know what sort of an animal a monkey is?" he demanded.

Eric began eagerly to tell all he knew, which was not a little.

"Well, and should you like to have everybody say you were a monkey?"

"I don't know," replied Eric, reflectively. "It wouldn't turn me into a monkey to have folks say I was a monkey. And if I really was one, why, then I should have a great long tail, and I could hang to the branches of trees, this way; look, father, I'll show you how!"

"Has the boy really no sense of shame?" cried Olaf, angrily.

"Leave him to me, I will manage him," said his grandmother.

"Do you know, Eric, how nice and pleasant it is to go to church? There are all the good people together praising God. They sing like the angels, so that one actually sheds tears when one hears them. Now, would not you love to go and shed tears at church, listening to such beautiful music?"

"I shouldn't want to go there to cry," returned Eric. "I should like to go and sing like an angel, though."

"But if we let you go you will not be contented with singing.

You will be getting up on the seat, making your arms go like our dear pastor's."

"Should I?" said Eric. "But, dear grandmother, couldn't you tie my arms with a string?"

"Fie! now you are talking nonsense. And great boys four years old should not talk nonsense."

"Yesterday, when I asked for another piece of oaten cake, you said I ate too much for such a little boy," said Eric, thoughtfully. "But it is a long while since yesterday; perhaps I *am* a great boy now."

"Well, well, child; but now suppose we take you to church with us tomorrow, will you behave yourself like a little man, and not fall into any of your tricks?"

"I don't know," said Eric, mournfully. "Maybe I should. I never do any tricks on purpose. They come and make me."

"Who come and make you?"

"The Trolls, and all of them."

"Now who has been teaching the child such wicked nonsense?" cried Olaf, starting to his feet. "Oh, mother, I would not have believed this of you!"

"Don't be angry with mother, Olaf dear," said Viola, gently. "She can't help believing things she has been taught all her life."

Olaf was silent. He felt angry with his mother, and wanted to reproach her. But that must not be in the presence of that keen-eyed child, who would remember every look and tone.

"Eric," he said at last, "you will go to church with us tomorrow, for our pastor will have it so. But there are no Trolls in God's house, therefore if you are not a good boy I shall know whose fault it is."

"You will be a good boy, Eric, won't you now?" said his mother, coaxingly.

"Yes, dear mother, I will," replied Eric, in tones so perfectly like her own, that, as usual, they all burst out laughing.

With such management the only wonder is the poor child was not ruined at once. But He who commits little children to the hands of inexperienced and ignorant parents—and are there any earthly hands that are not such?—He overrules the mistakes and corrects the errors. Eric had been used all his life to be coaxed, threatened, laughed at, praised, and argued with, in multitudes of cases where a single word of parental authority was all that was needed.

The next day was a bright, cheerful Sunday, and the whole family set off for church in good spirits. Eric was full of curiosity to know what going to church could really mean. He helped pack the basket of dinner, and made himself useful in many ways a less-observing child would not have thought of. On entering the church he watched carefully to see what his father and mother did, and perceiving that they stood for a moment with folded hands, engaged in silent prayer, he, too, closed his eyes and moved his lips, with an aspect of great devotion. When they were all seated, his eager gaze at the unwonted scene around him repaid his mother for bringing him with her. She enjoyed his surprise and pleasure, and showed her sympathy with him by pressing the little hand she held in her own. Nothing was lost upon him, and he responded at the close of every prayer, like a veteran, until that preceding the sermon; for a moment his attention wandered, and he sat lost in thought, till suddenly arousing himself, he uttered a vigorous "Amen" that was heard all over the church, and which broke in upon the text which the pastor was repeating in solemn accents. Viola laughed; Olaf pretended not to have heard, but changed color in spite of himself; the grandmother shook her finger at him, and Eric, amid these contending influences, felt half pleased and half frightened. He now, however, was attracted by the sermon, and the manner of its delivery; he sat erect, silent, almost breathless, a picture of awe and of ecstasy. Gradually, seeing him so absorbed, Olaf and Viola began to feel easy about him; Olaf gave himself up to enjoyment of the sermon; Viola attended to Carina, who continually asked if service were most done, and whom she invariably answered; the old grandmother fell asleep, and the grandfather began to take snuff. Eric unconsciously rose to his feet, climbed up to the seat, stretched forth now this arm, now that, clasped his hands, looked heavenward, and, in short, copied every motion of the pastor with unerring accuracy. The pastor, instead of serious faces, saw endless smiles; he was first surprised, then displeased; his gestures became animated with these emotions, and Eric faithfully repeated them, till, by degrees, nearly the whole congregation was in an uproar. The poor little fellow was ignominiously pulled down from his throne, and borne out of church by his exasperated father, who could hardly wait till he got him to a safe distance, before he gave him a most severe thrashing. He was interrupted in this labor by a hand laid, with force, upon his arm, and turning resentfully to the intruder, was ashamed to find himself confronted by the pastor's wife.

He pulled off his cap, and saluted her, and Eric, in the midst of his pain, did the same.

The Fru Prostinna looked kindly down upon the little boy, and instantly reassured, a frank smile lighted up his ingenuous face.

"You were severe with the poor child," said the Fru Prostinna.

"It was because I forgot to have my hands tied!" cried Eric eagerly. "I brought the string, but when I got inside the church and saw so many people, all dressed in holiday clothes so gay, and the Prost with his black gown and big ruff, and heard the singing and praying; oh, I forgot my string! But here it is," he continued, drawing it from his pocket, "and next time father will tie my hands."

The Fru Prostinna smiled.

"Well, my little fellow," said she, "I think it would be better to tie your hands than to break your bones, and you may thank me for hurrying after you out of church, to see that you were not killed outright. Play about now, while your father and I have a little talk together."

As soon as Eric was out of hearing, Olaf began to apologize for his severity to the child.

"It is the first time I ever laid my hand on him," he said, "and it shall be the last."

"Do not say that, Olaf. Correction is as necessary in our days as it was when Solomon forbid the sparing of the rod. Rather resolve never to strike him again in anger."

"Why, I could not strike him at all, if I were not angry," said Olaf. "For though he is wild in his way of mocking everything he sees and hears, he is a good boy in other things; a merry, pleasant boy as need be."

"Yes, I know. I have heard all about that. And if I were you, instead of reproving or laughing at this habit, I would turn it to good account. His active nature craves employment; now the next time you manufacture any of those pretty baskets you used to make, lay materials and tools within his reach, and see if instead of imitating, in a superficial way, all your motions, he does not really produce a facsimile of your work."

This was a new idea to Olaf, and it gave him pleasure. "Ah, if Eric had the Fru Prostinna for his mother, she would train him so wisely and discreetly; whereas, Viola is never the same person one day that she is the next. She lets the children do so many things I was not allowed to do at their age. And the Fru Prostinna would have made a man of Eric. Not a hard-working peasant, a great rough fellow like myself, but, who knows? a clergyman perhaps, with his parish and his schools, and his farms and his houses!"

And Olaf began to feel aggrieved, and as if Viola, in being of his own rank in life, and uninstructed and capricious, had done him a wrong and deprived him of the chance of giving a refined and educated mother to his children.

But when she came, at the close of service, to meet him, dressed in her becoming holiday costume, her red bodice and white cap, her face looked, as it always did, home-like and very dear. He laughed at himself for the foolish thoughts that a momentary ambition had awakened, and as they sat on the grass, eating their dinner together, told her what the pastor's good wife had said to him.

"But you only make baskets and things of that sort in the winter evenings," said Viola. "And such work as you are doing now, he cannot possibly do. But my work he can learn, and that he shall do forthwith."

So the next day, when she swept her house she put a little broom into Eric's hands, saying, "Sweep now, as I do. Don't just move your brush in the air; do just as I do, and make the floor clean for mother."

Eric obeyed, and when he saw that his little brush helped to beautify the floor, he used it with delight, singing joyfully to himself the while, and doing his work with his mother's exactitude. So it was in almost all the details of the day; and when, in the afternoon, she sat in her well-ordered room, in her clean, fresh dress, and began to sew, she gave Eric, not a bit of waste cloth, but part of a little garment, saying:

"See, now, dear Eric, when I sew I join these pieces together, and make your little sleeve. But when you sew you make nothing. You only move your arms as I move mine."

Then Eric watched her more closely, and saw that she pulled her needle through her work, now in, now out; imitated her with joy, and really made the little sleeve. Viola showed it to his father in the evening, and they all thought it a wonderful affair, as it indeed was, for the stitches were not the unwilling, irregular workmanship of compulsion, but the result of a taste that must indulge itself in aiming at perfection. Eric, himself, was not satisfied with his sleeve because it was not so nicely done as his mother's, but she laughed at the idea of his expecting at his first attempt to equal her needlework, of which she was very proud.

A few weeks later, two little arms came to fill the little sleeves; the baby-boy to whom they belonged, was beautiful from his birth; even Viola was satisfied with him, though she would not own it. Eric did not cry in imitation of his brother, as he had done with his sister; he knew better, now; besides, he was too busy to waste his time in watching him, except when bidden to do so. His father had been occupied at intervals during several weeks in manufacturing articles which Viola needed about the house: a table, two chairs, and a little bedstead for Carina, who must give up her place by her mother's side to the baby. Eric could hardly contain himself till he had made miniature furniture of the same pattern. To be sure, he pounded his fingers and cut them, and met with all sorts of difficulties, but that made no difference; chairs and table and bedstead he was resolved to make, and make them he did; and then his mother made a little doll of the right size for the furniture, and the whole establishment was given to Carina. His father was astonished at this performance, which he could appreciate better than he could the needlework. He began to find great pleasure in taking Eric with him to his work, and in answering his endless questions, which were daily becoming more and intelligent. He was obliged to work very hard, now that there were so many little children, for though the grandfather owned the house in which they lived, this was all they possessed, except the small bit of land which had been bought at the time of his marriage, when Olaf hoped to add to it; but that he had never been able to do. Shortly after the birth of the third baby, the grandfather began to suffer seriously from rheumatism, particularly in his hands, so that by degrees he became quite unable to do work of any sort. Olaf must do double duty; but it was some relief to see Eric growing every day stronger and more useful, and to look forward to the time as not far distant, when he would materially help in the support of the family.

To be sure, the neighbors all said among themselves, that Eric would be Jack of all trades, and master of none; such prodigies, they were sure, never turned out in the end to be anything wonderful; and after all, he wasn't so much of a marvel as he might be.

Olaf, however, determined to have Eric's education hurried forward as speedily as possible. But how was this to be done? Viola knew how to keep her house, to bear children, and to be a good, loving mother to them; but beyond these duties she could not go. Her education was far inferior to that of the peasantry about her; she could neither read nor write. The grandmother had taught Eric to do both, and had made him say the catechism every Sunday till he knew it past ever forgetting one of its ponderous words; but this did not satisfy Olaf; he was sure he ought to do more for this boy who had been endowed by nature with such varied powers.

CHAPTER 21

While the subject was under discussion, the Prost came driving over from the village, to make known that he had secured a teacher for the neighborhood, who would collect the children together for instruction, as ought to have been the case long before. The family rejoicings were great; but the question now arose, how was the boy to get to the school? A Dalecarnian mother would easily have led him thither, with her baby strapped upon her back; but Viola was not strong enough for such an undertaking. But as the grandfather's rheumatism had only disabled his hands, he volunteered as escort, and as the old man and the child went to and fro together, many were the godly instructions that fell into the receptive, youthful soul. Not to be entirely outdone by her husband, the grandmother every morning plucked a clover-leaf for the boy, to insure good luck. She was yet in the prime of life; tall and strong and ruddy; she could work on their bit of land like a ploughman, and understood all the petty economies peculiar to the hard lives of her country-women. Bark-bread, revolting to Viola, nourished her powerful frame, and the bracing air of her native valley gave color to her cheek. But for her, Viola could never have endured the hardships of her lot.

Olaf, meanwhile, had, during the winter evenings, manufactured a sufficient quantity of articles to justify another pedestrian trip to Italy, but when he spoke of it, Viola clung to him, with tears, entreating him not to go. But he yearned for change; the novelty of domestic life was over; the spirit that had brought Viola's master and his friends to the North, urged him to the South.

"Don't cry, little one," he said, "I sha'n't be gone long, and shall bring back what will make us comfortable for a long time. Pray for me, night and morning; take the communion faithfully; watch over the boy's soul in my place, and see that his grandmother reads the Bible to him every day."

Eric watched the parting between them with his usual keen observation. Why did the mother cry, and the father smile, he wondered; and why should his soul be watched over more than Carina's? And where was his soul, after all?

"Carina mia," he said solemnly, as he started for school next morning, "you should put your arms around my neck and weep when we part, like the dear mother. And I shall watch over your soul, as the father has watched mine."

"Was there ever such a boy?" cried Viola.

Eric gave her one of his guileless smiles, and said:

"No, never," exactly as if he were talking of some third party; and then, with the usual good-bye kiss, proceeded on his way.

Everybody they met on the way to and from school was hard at work, save very aged men and women, who, however, were not idle, but might often be seen seated amid groups of fishermen, or peasants at work in the fields, reading the Bible aloud. Eric marked, and inwardly digested, this, and though he had not yet learned to read well, could pretend to do so to perfection. In his father's absence his grandparents read a chapter to him every day; he would then take the book and, by a wonderful act of memory, with his eyes fixed upon the page, repeat word for word to the bewildered Carina.

As Olaf pursued his solitary way, his thoughts dwelt fondly on his little home, and proudly on his boy. But when he reflected that his education would, at best, be limited, and that he would grow up to a heritage of economy and care, he sighed, and wondered why nature made such mistakes—lavishing gifts upon the poor, to whom they were of no use, and often withholding them from the rich, to whom they would have been so welcome.

He made his way once more into Italy, and disposed of his wares quite readily—more so than ever before, because he now spoke Italian readily. His weary shoulders were gladly relieved of the heavy pack they had borne, and he now bethought himself that he might indulge Viola with some memento of her native land. But what should it be? It was an event in his life to make a present, and he felt almost ashamed of himself for being so sentimental. While he stood stupidly scratching his head, a merry, musical voice fell on his ear, that was so like Viola's that he started and turned, almost expecting to see her before him. It was a young girl, daughter of the man to whom he had sold his wares, and she was asking if he did not mean to carry home some gift to his wife, unconsciously hoping that he hadn't one.

Olaf felt that he could confide in one of Viola's country-women, and in a few words told her the dilemma he was in.

A quick flash of intelligence lighted the girl's face, and she began searching among the heterogeneous articles scattered about, and finally held up, in triumph, a small picture, in which Italy's beautiful blue was the color that chiefly caught the eye.

Olaf knew little about art, but had some general idea that even this small study was beyond his means. But the musical tongue ran merrily on; he should have it for her country-woman for a mere song, and it would warm her heart to see a bit of her own sky.

"Yours," she said, "is bleak and cold. I would not live there; it would kill my heart!"

At the same time she would have tried the experiment under the guidance of such a genial-looking man as Olaf, provided he had no wife.

"And now," she said, "something for the boy, with his blue eyes and rosy cheeks."

"Black eyes and olive cheeks, like thine!" cried Olaf.

The girl blushed and smiled.

"Would this please him, think you?"she asked, producing a miniature palette, on which were fastened cakes, in water colors—a cheap affair, such as, however, has gladdened many a child's heart.

"And, stay, here are brushes, likewise—a gift to the Swedish boy with my eyes and hair."

Olaf received the little gracefully-offered gift, and took leave, the young girl following his sturdy figure with her eyes as long as it was in sight.

"The saints grant that the father does not miss the picture, and beat me for as good as giving it away," she cried; "and if he does, Antonio shall paint him another. Ah, Antonio, if your eyes were but blue, and your cheeks ruddy! If you were tall, and straight, and strong, and not as black as a raven, and round-shouldered, and bow-legged! And still painted divinely!"

Olaf proceeded rapidly home, and greeted his wife in a way that procured for Carina, on the part of Eric, embraces, kisses, and asseverations not a few. But when the picture was produced, and Viola saw this bit of her native land, a strange complication of emotions she could not understand made her burst into tears. A sense of the beautiful had long lain dormant in her soul amid the stern scenes about her. Now came reminiscences of sunshine, birds and flowers, and delicious fruit; of works of art seen in the house of her master at Rome, and dimly appreciated.

"Thou wicked picture, to make the dear mother cry!" said Eric, rushing at it with a stick of wood. "I'll kill thee!"

But as his eye fell upon it, his hand dropped at his side, and a new soul illumined his face. They laughed at him, they shook him, they tried in every way to divert his rapt attention, but all in vain; he stood like a devotee before a shrine, and lost to all beside.

"Let him alone," said Olaf, at last. "He has gone clean daft over a picture no bigger than my hand!"

Indeed, he and Viola had enough to talk about, for they had had no correspondence during their absence, as Viola could not write.

"I have had a strange proposition made to me," said Olaf. "Before selling my wares, who should I stumble upon but your Signor and Signora. The Signor recognized me at once, and made friendly inquiries about you. The Signora was, at first, very haughty and distant; but after a while became more gracious, and spoke of you in a way that made me proud of you. She says she is out of health, and sad, and lonely; and that if we would all come to their villa, near Rome—you to be to her what you once were, and I his valet—they would make it a great object to us."

"And I suppose our children count for nothing," said Viola, indignantly.

"Yes; they seemed to think the children could stay with their grandparents. But isn't it a pity now that we could not go just for a time, and earn money to educate the boy?"

"Olaf, I am ashamed of you," said Viola. "Leave our children, and go and live in that idolatrous land!"

"But you hate so to spin."

"I adore spinning."

"And the bark-bread is so nauseous to you."

"It is delicious."

"And you have no grapes, no peaches, no melons."

"Grapes, and peaches, and melons! Ugh! Disgusting things!"

Olaf listened, bewildered, but convinced.

"I thought," he faltered, "that you had often said you used to revel in luxuries; but it seems I was mistaken."

"Indeed you were, you bad child. Talk not to me of Counts and villas. Did I not enter Paradise when I left them?"

"Then the picture does not please you? My mind misgave me when I bought it. But the maiden who selected it was like you, Carissima, and had me round her finger."

"The picture is bewitched; it has driven the boy mad. Eric, come to me!"

The boy woke from his dream of ecstasy and bounded towards her.

"See what the father has brought thee! Put in the thumb—so; no, no, the left thumb; hold the brush thus; ah, I have seen men paint in my country. Bring me a cup of water, and a bit of paper; there, my little man, now thou art an Italian, not a Swedish boy, and shalt paint Carina."

The boy looked at her, and then at the colors, delighted, confused, trembling, as she made some inartistic dabs upon the paper; then suddenly seized the materials and began to work himself, making a rude imitation of the picture that had so entranced him. Amid their homely, hard-working life, his parents ceased to heed him. He was out of mischief, and they had much to think of and much to do. Days, weeks passed, and Eric painted on; always at the one subject, never weary, never impatient, but discarding one copy, only to begin on another.

At last the Prost drove up in great state, and was in the midst of a solemn harangue, when his eye suddenly fell upon a row of pictures pinned to the wall.

"What is all this?" he cried, imperiously.

"The boy only does it in his play-hours," said Viola, apologetically.

"The boy!" repeated the Prost. "Unhappy mother!"

Viola trembled, and caught at the nearest chair.

"What is the matter?" she gasped.

"The boy is a genius!" he hissed in her ear.

"Is it my fault?" she asked, piteously. "Did I create him? And what *is* a genius? Is it anything to come between him and salvation?"

"Yes, woman, it is. Take these colors away from the child; give him no more play-hours, and set him at honest work. What has the son of a peasant to do with genius, I should like to know?"

"We will do all we can to cure him of it," said Olaf, in deep humility.

The Prost departed, leaving the frightened household fluttering behind him, like poultry besieged by a fox.

When Eric came home from school the terrific announcement was made to him that his beloved colors were his no longer; that the mother had thrown them into the fire, and the grandmother raked hot coals over them. The boy uttered not a word, and did not shed a tear. He was like one stunned. But there was something awful in his childish silence.

"Eric," said his mother, "we have not done this in anger. But the Prost willed it, and who dares resist the Prost?"

"Mother, what have I done to anger the Prost?"

"He says you are a genius."

"Is that something very bad?"

"Oh, yes! Very, very bad!"

"But you said the dear Lord would not let me be bad, if I prayed to Him. And I have prayed six times, and four times."

"Well, you must pray fifty times."

"Yes, I will."

He went and knelt down, and folded his hands, looking upward and said:

"Thou, dear Lord, I did not be a genius on purpose. It came its own self. Help me not to be one any more."

But his pale, sorrowful little face smote his mother to the heart. Her spirit rose in rebellion against the Prost. Why should he come with this terrible and mysterious accusation against her godly boy? She lay awake long that night, thinking what was to be done, and the next morning, as soon as Olaf had gone to his work, she said to the grandmother:

"If you will take care of the little ones for me, while I go to the village, I will spin for you as long as you require."

"And what errand have you at the village, child?"

"The Prostinna is always kind; she will make me understand what is evil in the boy; as for me, I see no evil in him, and my heart is breaking."

"Yes, go, thou good child. And the dear Lord go with thee!"

The Prostinna received Viola with great sympathy, when she learned that she had come in sorrow; but when she heard her artless tale, could with difficulty repress peals of laughter.

"You do not understand the Prost, my poor child," she said, as she could trust herself to speak. "The boy is a gifted boy; he will become a great man; there is nothing to be alarmed about."

"But the Prost called me an unhappy mother," objected Viola.

"Yes, for when your son has won a name and riches, and is abroad in the world, he will despise, nay, he will forget you; you will see him no more."

"It is not true!" cried Viola, proudly. "No, thank God, it is not thus my boy will demean himself. And how should having great gifts come between him and salvation? Are not all gifts from the Lord?"

"They are; and it is their abuse, only, that makes them perilous. Now let me advise you how to manage the boy. Give him the best education you can; keep him pure, and simple, and pious; and leave the rest to God. He can take care of his future, and, if you trust Him, He will."

Viola thanked the kind lady, and went home relieved, though after such a humiliation as that of the previous day, not proud.

"Eric, my boy," she said to him, "if you trust in God, and pray to Him every day, as long as you live, it will not be an evil thing to be a genius. The Pastorinna says that to be one means nothing evil, but only that you have wings hidden away in your shoulders that will grow and grow and grow till you are a man, and then they will unfold and be two great, white, strong pinions, that will carry you all over the world, if you like; and that sounds to me like being an archangel, such as we read about in the Bible."

The boy slipped his hand under his blouse, and felt his shoulder.

"I think I feel a very, very little wing growing," he said. "But I sha'n't want to fly all over the world; I shall fly up to heaven to see the dear Lord."

Viola's heart gave a great bound of pain.

"You would fly away from us who love you so?" she cried.

"Only to see the dear Lord," said Eric, solemnly.

Then an inward voice spake to Viola, and said:

"Better that than off into the wide, wicked world; better that than name and fame and riches, and a despised, forgotten mother! Even so, Father, if so it seem good in Thy sight."

Laura stopped reading, folded her manuscript, and looked shyly about her.

"Oh, Laura! you don't mean that you killed that beautiful boy?" cried Belle.

"How could I help it?" asked Laura, the tears running down her cheeks. "He *would* die! I tried all I could to have him live, and so did his father and mother, and all of them. But the wings grew and grew, and he mounted upward, and passed through the golden gate; but he left it ajar for Viola."

"Mamma, you'll have to look out," said Frank. "Laura is catching up with you rather too fast."

"I like to keep step with those I walk with," she replied, with a smile. "She may catch up, and welcome."

"I never did you any kind of justice, Laura," said Belle.

"That was not your fault. How *can* one do justice to a butterfly, as long as it's an ugly chrysalis?"

"But, Laura, how could you have the heart to take both Eric and Viola away from Olaf?" asked Margaret.

"Poor Olaf, indeed!" cried Laura, "just as if men never survived the loss of their wives. I have no doubt that by the time the first year was out he trotted down into Italy and married that pretty little Italian girl who reminded him so of Viola, and who took such a fancy to him."

"But she was a Romanist," objected Belle.

"So was Viola; yet he converted her. On the whole, I think I sacrificed her in a proselyting spirit."

"Well, what put Eric into your head?" asked Cyril Heath.

"What puts anything into anybody's head?" she responded, saucily. "And when I had got him on my hands, I didn't know what to do with him, and his death was a mercy."

"I am going to have this story published," said Harry. "I'm right proud of my wife."

"Suppose I put it into my book," said Mrs. Grey.

"Would you, mamma?" cried Laura, eagerly, "That would be splendid. How can you bring it in?"

"Very easily. It is not so far off my track that it will at all interfere with it."

"Well, Miss Oney," said Belle, "so you're an authoress at last. But I don't envy you. I would rather be the authoress of these babies, than of any book I know."

"So would I," cried Margaret.

"So would I, you dear old geese!" said Laura, laughing. "But I have to put up with what comes to me."

CHAPTER 22

I want a bit of talk with you, Frank," Mrs. Grey took an opportunity to whisper on the way to the dinner-table.

"All right," he replied. "Shall it be in the library, after the rest have gone to bed? Or right after dinner, in your dressing-room?"

"Right after dinner," she replied; and as soon as the meal was over, they disappeared.

"Now for my curtain-lecture," he said, as they seated themselves by the fire.

"I want to speak a word for your poor Lily," she said. "You began by loving her extravagantly, and educated her into expecting this sort of thing could last; now you are transferring your attentions to Gabrielle, in a way that must hurt your wife."

"Gabrielle has grown charming," he replied, "and it is delightful to have her again."

"That may be; but you may depend upon it, I understand my sex better than you do, and that no woman wants to see a girl put into the place once hers, even though the girl is her own child."

"Lily never complains of it."

"No; but she droops under it."

"I don't like the idea of her being jealous of Gabrielle."

"That's not the way to put it. It is not jealousy. You lavish on

Gabrielle, by the hour together, caresses you used to lavish on Lily, and she would have to be made of stone not to feel it. You must bear with me, my son, when I say that I don't like it. Whatever defects you may find in her, you cannot undo the past. You fell desperately in love with her, and married her; now you owe it to her to keep up that affection."

"Our affections are not under our control."

"True; but they are under God's control, and He can make all right between you twain."

"It never crossed my mind to ask Him to do that. But, mammy dear, who says I am alienated from Lily? Loving Gabrielle does not involve indifference to my wife."

"You ask who says it? *I* say it, and say it with pain. I did hope to see my sons loyal to the wives they themselves chose, however they might be disappointed in them. Lily has never wilfully annoyed you, and she gives you all the affection she is capable of giving, and wants yours in return."

Frank sat thoughtfully looking into the fire, and at the same time searching his own heart. At last he said:

"I thank my dear mother for her timely faithfulness. I see now that I must have wounded Lily in many ways. I shall ask her pardon, and start afresh. She little knows her indebtedness to you."

"What's going on here; secrets?" said Fred, who had knocked and been admitted.

"I have had my dressing, and now you may come and have yours," said Frank, rising.

"There's hardly a chance to get in a word edgewise, when Frank is at home," said Fred, taking possession of the seat he had vacated. "And I'm sure he doesn't love and admire you more than I do. I want to tell you, as I could not in a letter, what a happy family you have made of us. We took all your lessons to heart, and the improvement in Kitty is marvelous. She is a very interesting little creature, and a great amusement to us. Hatty keeps a journal, and records all her bright speeches."

"I am glad of that. You must let me see it. Every mother ought to keep one, if she can."

"Did you keep one about me?"

"No. You never said anything bright enough. It wasn't your forte to make smart speeches. Frank and Belle made enough to cover anything wanting in the rest of you. Tell me all about the baby now. Do you know Hatty has never written me once since it was born, and that all I know of it is that it is a boy?"

"Is that so? Why, I took it for granted Hatty had written. Well, he's a magnificent fellow, exactly like me."

"Shall I ever get the conceit out of you, you foolish boy?" she said, looking up at him with loving eyes.

"Yes, a magnificent fellow! Almost as big as Kitty, but not at all like her. He has a thick head of hair, dark eyes, and the prettiest little dumpling of a chin, with a dent in it. Kitty nearly eats him up. He's a good-natured chap, too, always laughing and crowing, and kicking up his heels. I tell you what, mother, it's great fun to have a dear little wife and two splendid children. Hatty says she means to have ten."

"I don't see but I shall have to add a large wing to this house if that is the case," she said, much amused and pleased.

"But they must all be getting together in the library, and we had better join them."

"Yes, I suppose so. What were you and Cyril talking about at dinner? I only caught a word or two."

"Oh, I was consulting him on a series of articles I was requested to write for a magazine."

"Didn't I hear something about editing one?"

"I dare say. That was one out of dozens of similar propositions."

"They keep you as busy as ever, it seems. And Laura is following in your footsteps. Wasn't it a little tall in her to read her own story, though?"

"No; there's nothing tall about her. She's just as fresh and unspoiled as a rose-bud."

"I'm glad you think so. I can't bear to think of either of the girls as being like the common feminine run."

They descended to the library, and found them all prepared to play some game of wits, with pencil and paper.

"Oh, here come mamma and Fred," said Belle, gaily, "and they are two of the brightest at this game. Where are the pencils? I have no pencil."

"I bought a box last Christmas," said Frank. "Surely they can't all be gone."

"Oh, I'll get them," said Margaret. "I remember putting them in one of the drawers in the library table. Yes, here they are. But they need sharpening."

Thereupon, out came half a dozen penknives, and the gentlemen prepared the pencils with great zeal. They were all, from Mrs. Grey down to Gabrielle, fond of these innocent little games, and some of the inspiration of the moment was so bright that Laura provided herself with a blank-book, and took copies of them, that years later were read, with great applause, at one of the Christmas gatherings.

"I want Belle to hold a Bible-reading some evening," said Cyril Heath.

"Oh, I couldn't," cried Belle, shrinking back.

"What's a Bible-reading?" asked Frank, interested at once.

"Belle has learned the English system, and holds two every week; one on Sunday afternoon for myself and the children and servants; one for a company of from twenty to thirty ladies; both in our own house; and they are delightful. I believe that if they were held all over the land, our country would be revolutionized. I never enjoyed the study of the Bible as I have since we began it in this way. The children enjoy it, too."

"Let us have one tomorrow evening, by all means," said Frank. "And that will be something you can join in, Lily," he said, turning kindly to his wife; "you who dislike games so."

Lily felt the unaccustomed tones, and gave a grateful look.

After they went to their room that night, Belle said to her husband:

"How could you propose my holding a Bible-reading with all those men?"

"Because I think you do it so nicely. Still, if you prefer it, I will conduct it as long as the boys are at home. After they go I hope you will take it."

The next evening they all gathered around the library-table, each with a Bible in hand. Old Mary came, with her spectacles, very curious to know what was to be done.

Mr. Heath chose the sixty-third Psalm, and called upon Frank, Jr., who sat next him, to read the first verse. But Frank had not found his place, and Gabrielle read for him.

"Now, in the ideal Bible-reading," said Mr. Heath, "the reader makes a remark, or asks a question."

"I should like to ask, then, why David and others put the word 'my' before the name of God, so often?"

"I think there are two reasons. In those days a large number of gods were worshipped, and it was natural enough for men to distinguish between them through the possessive case. Besides, the old saints all had assurance of faith. They not only loved God, but they knew they loved Him."

"The moment we put the possessive case before a thing, it assumes a new interest for us," said Belle. "In prayer we say 'my' and 'our,' and I don't know that it would not be more reverent if we did it in conversation. Some people have a flippant way, or what seems like it, of saying, 'I told the Lord thus and so, and He said so and so.' Wouldn't it sound less familiar if they put it 'my Lord'?"

"Perhaps so," said Mrs. Grey, "At any rate we must have assurance of faith, if we are to grow in grace."

"Why must we, grandmamma?" asked Gabrielle.

"Because, if we keep digging up our seeds to see if they've sprouted, or how many roots they have, we are in danger of destroying what vitality they have."

The children all looked at each other with conscious smiles.

"I lost all my beans that way," said Frank, Jr. "Shall I read the next verse, uncle?"

"Oh, no, we have only touched a corner of the first one yet."

As it turned out, this one verse served them for study an hour; an hour enjoyed by the children as well as the elder ones; and all who engaged in this exercise for the first time, were delighted with it. Mrs. Grey resolved to start a reading among her neighbors; Laura said she should do the same for hers; Margaret wondered if she could get courage to hold one with half a dozen young girls of her acquaintance, and found she could.

Meanwhile, Mrs. Grey received a note from Mrs. Grosgrain, imploring her to come to her as soon as possible next morning.

"How fortunate that I have kept up the acquaintance," she said, running over the note. "Now comes a chance to do them good."

"Grandmamma," said Gabrielle, "you are not going to see those kind of people, and leave us, when we are having such nice times together?"

"That kind of people, not those kind. And of course I am going, for they are in trouble."

"It's too bad. Everybody thinks you are made to look after them. And I was in hopes you would finish reading that German story to me."

"I suppose you don't include yourself among the 'everybody'?" said Frank, laughing.

"But, papa, we had just got to the most exciting part."

"I'll read the rest of it," said Margaret.

"You'll want to be painting."

"No; I don't paint in the holidays."

"Oh, no, you don't."

"I wonder if mamma ever thinks of herself one minute at a time," said Belle, as her mother retired to make preparations for the early expedition of the morrow. "It is a real sacrifice to her to lose a whole day of our visit; but she has trotted off to get ready, like a girl.

And she'll be thrown away on those Grosgrains."

"Yes, just thrown away," repeated Laura. "I wonder she doesn't see it."

"I dare say one of them has put her thumb out of joint," said Margaret, feeling like anything but an angel towards the Grosgrains. "To think of leaving all of you to go to see such people. However, I don't know that it's any stranger than the way she lets herself be interrupted when she is writing."

"Writing isn't her profession, you know," said Belle. "It never was. She used to write as long ago as when we were babies, and yet did not neglect us."

"I am doing the same," said Laura. "I mean to go on writing, but Pug and Trot won't suffer from it. Of course scribbling is a mere recreation. My profession is to be a good wife and mother, as I am sure mamma's was. As to you, Margaret, you are a genius, and must make up your mind never to marry."

"Thank you," said Margaret, dryly.

"Why, you don't mean to say that it isn't enough to be an artist!" cried Laura, a little dubious as to what the dry tone meant.

"If by being an artist I have got to kill off my heart, and live for fame, then an artist I won't be," returned Margaret. "I am in no hurry to be married; and if I decide to be an old maid, it won't be without children, I can tell you."

"And where do you expect to get them?"

"By begging, borrowing, buying, or stealing them," said Margaret, her good humor returning at the thought.

"What, and bring them here to live?" asked Gabrielle.

"No, indeed. I must earn a home of my own first."

"Papa says you will make a great name for yourself," pursued Gabrielle.

"What do I want of a great name?" cried Margaret. "It is the very last thing in the world a woman ought to seek."

"So I think," said Belle.

"But suppose she gets it without seeking?" asked Laura.

"Look here, Laura," said Margaret, springing up, "let me feel if you have a pair of wings sprouting. It is my private opinion that you have, and that it is you, not I, who is to be famous. And how stupid I was, the first time I saw you, to fancy you just—just—"

"A goosey-gander? Yes, I was perfectly delighted to see how you measured me after the first ridiculous talk we had together."

"I don't think it's nice to belie one's self as you do, Laura," said Belle. "Even your own mother never knew you till this story of yours opened her eyes."

Laura shrugged her shoulders.

"I shouldn't care to be so shallow that people could read me at a glance," she said.

"One is not necessarily shallow because transparent," said Belle.

"Margaret, how nearly done is mamma's book?" asked Laura.

"So nearly that I think I hear it ringing the doorbell now. I saw an expressman just drive up. Yes, here comes the parcel. Might we open it, think?"

Laura replied by cutting the cord and throwing it upon the floor, whence Belle picked it up and wound it around her fingers, and put it away in her mother's string-box.

"How beautifully it is got up," said Laura. "But why wasn't it out at Christmas?"

"Aunty thought it would be," said Margaret, "but there was unexpected delay. Oh, are you each going to read it to yourselves?" she added, in a disappointed tone, as she saw each take possession of a volume. "I thought we should read it aloud. Aunty, your books have come," she cried, as Mrs. Grey here entered the room.

"Indeed? Just in time for me to take one to Mrs. Grosgrain."

"Pooh! Always Grosgrain!" thought Margaret; but took one of the volumes and folded it carefully in a fresh sheet of paper, and placed it on the library-table, and the next morning reminded Mrs. Grey to take it with her.

CHAPTER 23

Mrs. Grey proceeded on her way, on a bitterly cold day, when so much ice had formed in the harbor that crossing the ferry occupied hours instead of minutes. Foreseeing that return before the morrow would be impossible, she sent a dispatch home to that effect, and at last, weary and benumbed, presented herself to the Grosgrains.

She found them too absorbed in tribulation to concern themselves about her condition, and all talked together with briny tears, telling an incoherent story, out of which she at last got at these facts:

A young man, to whom Miss Grosgrain had engaged herself on board the steamer that brought them from England, had so won their confidence that they were gradually led to put their entire business affairs into his hands. He conducted them, for a time, so well that they congratulated themselves that their fortune had ceased to be a care to them. Recently he had received letters from his mother summoning him to take possession of a large property, to which he had become heir through his father's death, and had urged to have the marriage celebrated at once, and that they should all accompany the happy pair to Europe, there to live in almost regal splendor. Charmed with the prospect, they sold their palatial residence, their horses, plate, furniture, and prepared for a grand flight. But when all was in trim, one little item disappeared—namely, the foreign lover—who forgot to refund the sums in his hands, the result of the sale, and had also contrived to possess himself of their whole fortune. Whither he had disappeared they failed to learn; and here they were, huddled together in a house no longer theirs, as miserable a group as one need to see.

Why had they sent for Mrs. Grey in particular? Well, with a vague hope that she would help them in some way; she had the reputation of being everybody's right hand. And she had come to help them, and listened with real sympathy to their story.

"Have you done everything that can be done to arrest the fugitive?" she asked.

"Yes; he has fled to some country where he will be safe, and live in luxury while we starve here."

"You have your jewels left; they will carry you along till you have time to bethink yourselves what to do next."

"Oh!" groaned Miss Grosgrain, "our jewels are gone too. Our seamstress, Jane, whom we trusted as we did each other, disappeared at the same time with—with that wretch, whose name I never will speak as long as I live—and took almost all our valuables with her. No doubt she was his accomplice, and has left the country with him."

"It will be necessary, then, to seek remunerative employment," Mrs. Grey said, as cheerfully as she could; "now let me see what gifts you have."

"Employment!" shrieked the girls. "What a disgrace!"

"Why call it disgrace, when thousands of women are engaged in it? Refined and well-educated women, too."

"So I tell the girls," said Mrs. Grosgrain. "If we set still and do nothing, we shall starve."

The quartette was too full of dismay to correct the maternal grammar, and listened in gloomy silence.

"We never had to work for our living," pursued Mrs. Grosgrain, "but the girls' marmer had to, and she was a master-hand at tailoring.

And they've all took after her. Mary can make as handsome a bonnet as any milliner, and so can Flora; and the others can cut and fit beautifully."

"But there was a deal of money spent on your education," said Mrs. Grey, turning to the young ladies; "could you not open a school?"

She knew they could not, but thought it best to make them face the situation for themselves.

"They never took to their books," said Mrs. Grosgrain. "And they never thought to come to this. But they're all handy, like their marmer."

"Then the hands must come to the rescue," said Mrs. Grey, looking brightly into the sad faces around her.

"What a disgrace!" cried Miss Grosgrain. "We who were born to so much better things!"

"I think we were all born to the lot in which we find ourselves," said Mrs. Grey, kindly. "Poverty is no disgrace, nor is work; I would rather see one of my daughters employed as a housemaid, than living a life of ease and luxury and pleasure. In the one case I should hope to see her forming a useful character; in the other I should expect to see her a mere cumberer of the ground. Now, you have asked me to advise you, and I will try to do it. Have you any friends who will aid you until you begin to support yourselves?"

They shook their heads mournfully. Their money had plenty of friends; personally, they had none.

"We have to leave this house in a week," said Mrs. Grosgrain. "The party that owns it is going to pull it all to pieces."

"I would as lief die, as to work for my living?" cried Miss Grosgrain.

"Providence has not given you the choice," said Mrs. Grey, gravely. "And all that looks so distressing now, may, through Him, become a benediction."

"I had a little money hid away," said Mrs. Grosgrain, brightening up. "I always mistrusted that our luck wouldn't always last, and now and then I hid gold pieces away. But my memory has failed of late years, and I don't remember exactly where I put it. 'Twa'n't all in one place, and when we sold out I forgot all about it. If we could stay in the house long enough, I guess I could find some of it."

"To whom did you sell out?"

"To James J. Sheldon."

"Ah! He is a friend of mine. I can easily persuade him to allow you to stay. He could do nothing to the house in this cold weather."

"Still, it isn't likely if we find the money that it will amount to anything; and, for my part, I wish I was dead."

Hereupon ensued fresh bursts of tears all around.

"My dear," asked Mrs. Grey, seriously, "where should you be if you were dead?"

"I could not be worse off than I am now," was the sullen answer.

"You must excuse the way she talks," said Mrs. Grosgrain. "She never had no trouble before, and it sets her ag'inst everything. I'm older, and don't feel so bad. If it wasn't for seeing the girls so full of trouble, I should say I hadn't felt so comfortable these twenty year."

Poor Mrs. Grosgrain, do you know the reason? You have been snubbed more than "twenty year" by these four young women, and now they let you alone, and you are jogging on in such English as you please; and what a relief it is! Take an old hat, and the more you brush it, the worse it looks. No amount of labor could make a real lady out of one whose instincts were not refined. It was not going to be the hardship to her to descend to what she sprang from, as to these girls who had never been there with her. To make a long story short, however, Mrs. Grey never rested till she had found employment for them all. At first their pride fell flat, and they struggled against their fate in a way that put all her energy to the test; but contact with her strong and steadfast nature at last told upon them all. In the strictest sense of the word, she rescued them from the ruin to which prosperity was leading them; or, rather, she fell in with the Providential plan for their rescue, and helped carry it out.

Now, why all this self-sacrifice and labor for five ill-bred, ill-tempered women, with whom she had not five thoughts in common?

Well, she saw in them now what she always had seen—human beings to be saved or to be lost; she had kept up an acquaintance with them for years, on the mere chance of sometime finding an entrance to their souls; and she found it "after many days."

Even most of her children did not understand this; they loved and respected her too much to call her Quixotic, yet fancied such people as the Grosgrains unworthy so much long patience, such journeys to and fro, such letters, such lines upon line. But they could have found ample explanation for all she did in the twenty-fifth chapter of Matthew. The fact is, the Grosgrains err in their way; but we err in ours when we draw our sanctified garments about us and pass by on the other side. An eagle may have a more ruinous fall than a butterfly, because he flies higher.

Meanwhile, there fell a shadow upon Greylock, and every-body in it. Belle's devoted little lover, Margaret's little pearl, fell sick. Only the mother observed the change in her at first, it was so nearly imperceptible; but as time passed, all had to own that there was a mysterious change, with no marked symptom of disease, except increasing silence and lassitude. Everybody's virtue came to the front now. They told her stories, they sang to her, her father and uncles walked the floor with her by the hour together when a strange restlessness was soothed by it. The elder children moved about the house on tiptoe; the younger ones, not quite up to the situation, but impressed by it, whispered to each other that they would play the "softest plays" they knew. The physician, early called in, was puzzled and helpless. Yet all were full of hope save Mrs. Grey and Belle. They did not tell each other what they feared, yet each saw it in each other's eyes. As the little creature became increasingly nervous and sensitive to noise, it was obvious that the household must be reduced in numbers, and, very reluctantly, most of them departed for their own homes.

Margaret's inexperience with children kept her long free from grave anxiety. There were days when Mabel would brighten and become as animated as ever; a new toy would give her pleasure, and she would take it to bed with her. Such days encouraged her inordinately.

"How strange it is that the doctor does not give her a tonic, when he sees how weak she is!" she kept saying. "Nothing ails her but want of strength."

She and Belle divided the nursing between them, and the one was as tender and devoted as the other, with this difference: Margaret was full of hope, and Belle full of misgivings.

"*Where* are you sick, my darling?" she asked, again and again, and the plaintive, weary little voice invariably answered: "Nowhere; only *so* tired, *so* tired."

"Cyril, I can't bear this suspense any longer," Belle said, at last. "As soon as I know what God wants of me, He shall have it, if it breaks my heart. You must make the doctor tell what he thinks."

"He seems completely puzzled," was the reply. "But I will ask him; and if it would be any relief to you, request a consultation."

"It would be a great relief. Cyril, Mabel is *very* ill."

"My dear, you exaggerate the matter. I have seen any number of sicker children, and known them to get well. I don't see, as Margaret says, why no tonic is given her."

"You will find out, if the doctor is frank with you. If my fears are well founded I know the reason."

"I did not know you had any definite fear."

"I have; and so has mamma, though she has not said so. We think there is some insidious disease on the brain."

"The brain!" he repeated. "Oh, Belle, what would you do without your devoted little worshipper?"

"What every one does who believes in Christ," said Belle, bursting into tears.

"Yes; you would give her to Him without a word," he said, earnestly, almost reverently; for while he loved his wife for her own sake and for her love to himself, he loved her far more for her whole-souled devotion to Christ.

He went out now to find the doctor and to propose a consultation.

The doctor caught at the suggestion eagerly.

"The case is an obscure one," he said. "The child's debility is very great, but I find no explanation of it unless there is some insidious disease upon the brain."

"So her mother thinks."

"Indeed? I am surprised at that. Yet I ought not to be surprised either, after knowing her all her life. She has her mother's quick intuitions. Well, I will arrange about the consultation, immediately."

"Could not I do that?"

"Why, yes, I will give you the address of the physician I call in for children. You will find him at his office tomorrow morning, at ten."

Mr. Heath was thankful to go. Men are generally as out of place in sick-rooms as steam engines; twenty times he had banged the door and made Mabel cry out, and Belle had shuddered again and again, at the sound of his newspaper, which he could have read just as well in the library.

The word "consultation" sent a chill to Margaret's heart. She rushed away to her own room, locked the door, threw herself on her face across the bed, and cried with that bitter, heart-breaking cry which had won the love and sympathy in which she had been revelling.

"God wouldn't do such a dreadful thing!" she at last said to herself. "Never was a child adored as Mabel is. There is not one among them all, half so sweet. Why should He take her? He won't! I know He won't! What a fool I am for crying so! And there is aunty *slaving* over the twins!"

She flew to the washstand and tried to remove the traces of her tears; then hurried to the nursery, where she found both babies fretting dismally, and Mrs. Grey doing her best to comfort them.

"I have been dreadfully selfish, aunty," she said, taking one of the twins from her. "I must have a very contracted mind, for it can only hold one thing at a time. I am as brimful of Mabel as a nest is full of birds."

"It isn't so much a contracted mind, as an exaggerating heart," was the reply. "You magnify every one you love, and every pursuit you engage in."

The nurses, who had been having their breakfasts, came now to the nursery, and Margaret drew Mrs. Grey away, to see if she could find comfort in her.

"God wouldn't do such a thing as to take away Mabel, would He, aunty?"

"I used to think He *could* not do these agonizing things; but He can, He does, and He knows why I have trembled for Belle when I have seen that steadfast little lover of hers follow her as the needle does the pole. It is Maud and her mother over again—only—"

She broke down now, but only for a moment, and asked Margaret's pardon as meekly as a child.

"Is it wrong, then, to cry?" asked Margaret, bewildered.

"It depends on the time and place, and how old one is. I don't think people of my age ought to indulge themselves by giving way to grief in which the spectator cannot share.

> "'Bury *thy* sorrow, let others be blest,
> Give them the sunshine, tell Jesus the rest.'"[1]

It was now Margaret's turn to feel humbled.

"How could I forget, even for a moment, how you had been afflicted?" she cried, passionately. "But you are so strong, and so patient, and so cheerful, and hide your scars away so carefully, that it is hard to realize that you ever had a sorrow. But, aunty, what will Belle do if she loses Mabel?"

"'She will behave and quiet herself as a child weaned of his mother.'"

Just then the door opened, and Mabel came quietly in. Both

1 *Bury Thy Sorrow* by Mary A. Bachelor.

were startled, for she rarely moved about the house now. She saw that they had been crying, and came and put an arm around each.

"What makes everybody cry?" she asked. "Is anybody dead?"

Even Margaret was astonished at the sunny smile with which Mrs. Grey instantly diverted the child's attention.

"See," she said, opening a drawer, "what I forgot to give you at Christmas."

Mabel looked in and saw a snow-white dove nestled there.

"Oh!" she said, "when I get well I will dance for joy! Grandmamma, I am not so tired today as I was yesterday. May I hold my baby a little while and show him this lovely dove?"

"You may try, darling."

They carried her up to the nursery and put the baby in her arms, but she could not hold him, and burst into tears. They were the last she ever shed.

The doctors came in the course of the day, and examined her from head to foot carefully.

"Does your head ache even a little?" they asked.

"No."

"Where are you sick, then? Put your hand on the place, dear."

"There isn't any place."

"How are her nights?"

"Very restless," said Belle, whose eye was reading every thought of the physicians, as if the faces they fancied so well-trained were open books. "She talks and moans in her sleep, and sometimes has painful dreams."

Mabel, nearly as keen as her mother, though in a different way, detected a tender, almost mournful glance between her physicians, at this answer, and reached out a little hand to each. They had to fight to keep back the tears, as their fingers closed over her wasted ones. All her life the child had had these touching ways which it is not possible to describe; one of the secrets of the peculiar way in which she attracted every one.

After a few more questions the physicians withdrew, promising to return on the following day. Mr. Heath followed them, but learned nothing definite. Mabel had a dreadful night; all the symptoms of water on the brain, hitherto wanting, came on with great force. How they lived through the next harrowing two weeks they hardly knew. Many whom Mrs. Grey had blessed in similar scenes, came now, full of tender sympathy to help support them through the fortnight in which the patient little lamb died daily, so distressing was her exhaustion. They were prayed for by hundreds some of them had never seen; and their faith failed not.

For a week the bright eyes remained open, and there was no sleep. They had ceased asking for her life, but prayed for the mercy of rest.

And at last it came, and the weary eyes were closed. They knelt around the bed and gave thanks. Then came one of those quick decisions on Margaret's part, that dotted her whole life as with stars. She put off her tears, went quietly to her room, and on a wide white ribbon, with teeth set hard together, began to paint. So, when Belle went to take her parting look at her darling before the funeral, there lay upon the coffin, within the ribbon, delicate flowers and green sprays, with the words:

"*Now* I lay me down to sleep."

It was an inexpressible comfort, and Margaret was rewarded by the most loving embrace she had known for years.

"You are entering on mamma's mission of sympathizer very early," said Belle. "God bless you for it. After this you will be associated with every thought of my darling."

"I think God has special love for those He takes so early," said Mrs. Grey. "Dear little Mabel's character was unusually lovely, and now it will never be anything else."

Belle struggled to speak, but could not. At last she said:

"I cut this epitaph from a newspaper when quite a young girl. How little I then thought how it would come home to me!

"'Oh!' said the gardener, as he passed down the garden-walk, 'who plucked that flower? Who gathered that plant?' His fellow-servant answered, 'THE MASTER!' and the gardener held his peace.'"

CHAPTER 24

Mrs. Grey went home with the sorrowing family, taking Margaret with her, but leaving Gabrielle and the two boys at Greylock. They were too inexperienced to understand that a sublime joy is perfectly consistent with deep grief, and shrank from witnessing pain they believed to be without alleviation. The thought of a funeral was very repugnant to them, as was everything connected with the subject of death. They had yet to learn how Christ has conquered that last enemy, and how the soul may be cast down, yet always rejoicing.

It is hard to lay away in the grave a form we have loved, on a smiling, sunny day, under the green grass; but to put it under the snows of winter is harder still. It needs faith and patience of no common sort to tear the nursling from the breast, and leave it out in the cold. But neither Mrs. Grey's nor Belle's was of the common sort, and in the midst of their tears they could look away from the grave and see the "folded lamb" in green pastures and beside still waters, never so full of life as now.

Loving letters came to Belle from every member of the family, which were a great comfort to her; many precious and comforting books were sent her which she was willing to let do their mission to her soul. But the constant, sympathizing presence of Christ was her chief solace. It has been truly said that the best cure for sorrow is an increased, personal love for Him; Mrs. Grey learned this secret long ago, but Belle first learned it now.

Margaret had not their consolations. Every thought of Mabel lacerated her, and her health began to suffer.

"Poor child, it is her nature to take life hard," said Mrs. Grey to Belle, "and her love for Mabel was a passion."

"*Everything* is a passion with her," Belle replied. "If you had not adopted her and toned her down, and she had been left uneducated and unrestrained, she would have rushed headlong to destruction."

"I do not feel sure how she will come out in the end," said Mrs. Grey. "If anything happens to me I shall want you to look after her."

"Anything happen to you, mamma?" cried Belle; "do you think anything *is* going to happen? Why, it isn't living not to have a mother."

"In the nature of things you ought to outlive me, my child. And it is well to familiarize yourself to the thought."

Belle's eyes filled with tears.

"You know what Mabel's death has cost me," she said, "but it is nothing to what yours would."

"Well, my dear," said Mrs. Grey, trying to smile away this almost reproachful tone, "I do not expect to die at present, and may live to be a trial to you all. I hope not, though. I should like to live as long as I can work for Christ; not longer, nevertheless not my will."

"Nor mine!" said Belle. "I spoke in a cowardly moment, dreading any more suffering. It was most ungrateful after all God's goodness to me."

Margaret now came in with a photograph of Mabel she had been coloring.

"Oh, this is a great improvement!" cried Belle. "Thank you, ever so much."

"What a mercy that you had it taken so recently!" said Mrs. Grey.

"Yes; there has been nothing but goodness and mercy from beginning to end."

Poor Margaret could not see it, and her face showed that she could not.

"Things that look like unmitigated evils now will appear differently as you advance into life. You are only on the outskirts now," said Mrs. Grey, kindly. "Belle, my dear, let Margaret read your Mabel-journal."

Belle rose and brought the book. It had been kept from the day of the child's birth till that of her death.

Margaret took it to her room and read it eagerly, and amid a rain of tears. Even she had not realized what a lovely character the little one possessed, and every little detail interested her.

"This book ought to be published!" she said, as she returned it.

"It would not touch the public as it does you," replied Belle.

"It would touch anybody who had a heart," said Mrs. Grey.

Belle caught it nervously, and locked it up. Mrs. Grey smiled, and said she never meant to urge its publication.

At the end of a fortnight she and Margaret returned to Greylock, sent the boys back to Mr. Heath, and everything went on as usual till spring; Mrs. Grey going hither and thither on all sorts of Christian work; Margaret eagerly engaged in painting a portrait of Mabel, partly from a photograph, partly from memory, and busy with her studies also. And now a long-promised visit to Laura was to be made as soon as Gabrielle's vacation should begin, when she was to go home for a visit.

Laura lived on the beautiful banks of the Hudson, and so near to the city that her husband could attend to his business there, and go home every afternoon. Since Mrs. Grey had been there, they had built a new house, and Laura was full of delight in the prospect of exhibiting it to her mother and Margaret. She charged the latter to bring her painting-materials, so as to make sketches of some of the fine views in the neighborhood.

"I don't know about that," said Margaret. "I doubt if I ought to do anything of that sort till Mabel's portrait is done. That will be such a delightful surprise to Belle."

"On the other hand, it would be running some risk to take it with you," Mrs. Grey replied.

"Do you mean from the children?"

"Not exactly. I don't know what I do mean. I only know that I have an impression that it is best to leave it at home. You have put a great deal of work in it, and it would take months to replace it."

"I don't think I could forgive Pug and Trot if they bedaubed this as they did the only other large picture I ever took. I'll leave it."

On a beautiful afternoon in June they met Harry on the steamboat, on their way to his home. He was in splendid health and spirits, and seemed delighted at the prospect of their visit. They sat upon deck, read a little, looked at the blue sky and green banks, and talked when they felt like it.

"We shall soon be there," Harry said, at last. "You'll get a glimpse of the house as we skirt this island. Hollo! what's that?" he cried, starting to his feet and running forward.

"It's fire!" said Margaret, putting out her hand for Mrs. Grey's.

"We are near the shore; there is no danger," said Mrs. Grey.

"Why doesn't Harry come back?" asked Margaret. "He ought not to expose himself for Laura's sake. Oh, aunty, see how the flames are rushing between us and him!"

There was great rushing to and fro, the flames spread rapidly; orders were given in a loud voice, above which could be heard the cries of the terrified passengers.

An attempt was made to make for the shore, but the steamer ran aground. Harry made his way through the flames and came to them now, hardly looking like a human being. His hair was singed, his face black and grimy, and at first they did not recognize him or his voice, as he said, hoarsely:

"There isn't a moment to lose! Jump overboard, both of you! I'm a good swimmer; I can save you!"

"I have a son on board!" replied Mrs. Grey. "I cannot seek my own safety till I am sure of his! But if you will kindly take charge of this young lady—"

"Don't you know me, mother?" cried Harry, impatiently. "I tell you there's not a moment to lose!"

The two women kissed each other.

"Good-bye, darling, darling aunty, if he doesn't save us!"

"Good-bye, my precious child! Good-bye, Harry! Tell Laura—"

He almost pushed them into the water, jumped in himself, bade them hold him fast, and began to strike out for the shore. The distance was greater than he supposed, and his strength began to fail; what should he do? which life should he sacrifice? Margaret's, of course, not that of Laura's mother. But Margaret was so young, it was dreadful to die young; and Mrs. Grey at best could not live many years. The conflict was painful, and so was every stroke of his arms. Neither should die, if it killed him! One more heroic stroke and we are there! No, a wave has beaten us back!

With a groan of anguish he cried, "I cannot save you both! One of you must loose your hold! Which shall it be?"

"Not aunty!" said Margaret, instantly loosing her grasp.

"Not Margaret!" said Mrs. Grey, as instantly relinquishing hers.

Harry uttered a cry of horror, and watched to see them rise; but his over-taxed frame had made its last frantic effort; he felt himself going down, down; there was a faint thought of Laura, waiting for him in her white dress, a faint sense of God waiting for him too, and then he knew no more, till he awoke, and found it was all a dream; Laura was there, very pale, but smiling; the doctor was there, and many others.

"He's all right now," said the doctor, "and as soon as I've set this arm you may take him home."

For reply, Laura, waking also as from a dream, cried, "Where is mamma? Where is Margaret?"

"I did my best," Harry said, faintly. "This arm was broken before we took to the water."

"You don't mean to tell me that you let my mother *drown?*" Laura hissed in his ear.

"Indeed, madam, my patient is in no state to be excited," said the doctor. "Rejoice that Providence has given you back your husband, and only taken your mother."

"*Only* taken!" repeated Laura, almost beside herself. "Only taken my mother! Why, she was one of ten thousand! She was *every*body's mother! And Margaret! That noble girl! And I am to rejoice, am I!"

"There will be little to rejoice over if you go on in this way, madam," said the doctor, pointing to Harry, who had again become insensible.

This silenced her, and she spoke no more, but almost the coldness of death steeled her heart to her husband. She did not realize the self-possession he had displayed, the difficulties in his way; she did not know that if the women she lamented had been less heroic one of them might have been saved; all she knew was, they lay dead in the embrace of the river she had once thought beautiful.

"What news for poor Belle! What a shock to Frank! What consternation among mother's friends!" she thought, and tried to cry, but not a tear would come.

Slowly, when Harry came to himself, and his arm had been set, they drove home. There was the table, set for tea; there was mother's chair; there was the plate of strawberries, and the vase of flowers she had gathered with such delight. She went to the window and threw them out; who cared for fruit and flowers now?

Meanwhile, Harry had been taken upstairs, and laid upon a couch, falling asleep the moment his head touched the pillow. She went and looked at him, and saw how the fire had singed his hair, how deathlike he looked; how blistered were his hands. "But he let my mother drown," she thought.

All night she sat by him, and when he woke and needed attention, she gave it; but that was all. She gave no kiss, no caress, no loving word, but steeled herself with the thought, "He let my mother drown."

Harry was so exhausted that he did not notice this at first; when he did, he was disappointed and grieved, but not surprised. His conscience was clear, and he knew that as soon as he had strength to tell his story, Laura would see her injustice. Then he fell asleep again, and again woke and saw her sitting there, pale, and silent, and stony. He thought she had sat there a week; wondered if she would speak to him again; if she ever ate, or drank, or moved; and then, feeble as a child, he slept again.

CHAPTER 25

It was only one night and part of a day after all, and if Laura neither slept or ate during that time, it was because she had too much else to think of and to do. Vigorous measures must be taken to recover the bodies; that was the first thing. Then to get into communication with her brothers. They would see the news in the daily papers, but that would not be like authentic intelligence from herself. Frank would come to her immediately; she was sure of that; later, if—she could not trust herself even to think there could be an if—they would all be together at Greylock. Dear old Greylock! With mamma and Margaret gone what a mockery it would be!

Messages kept coming in from those who were at work at the scene of the disaster, but they all told of defeat. And so, too, did the constant booming of cannon. In this agony of suspense, she was thankful to have neighboring friends gather around her. She clung to them as the drowning cling to the arm that is trying to rescue them. This was due to her youth. In later years she bore her sorrows unaided by human support. Many of Mrs. Grey's friends came up from the city, full of grief and full of sympathy, and uttering words of hope they hardly felt. Frank was the first of the family to arrive, though he lived farthest off; Mr. Heath and Belle came next, and the group waiting in suspense, grew larger every hour. Belle was a marvel to herself; her treble sorrow, far from crushing her, lifted her up to a calm and dignified height where she had such glimpses of the glory of God that she was almost fain to shut her eyes. They all leaned upon her as upon a rock.

"Why do you stand at the window all the time?" asked Laura.

"To catch the first sight of them when they come," she said, simply.

"Are you still hoping? I have given them up."

"I think God has heard our prayers and that He will grant us the favor of knowing that their precious dust is spared to us. Still, heaven is as easy to reach from the river as from the dry land; we must remember that. Oh, Laura, look!"

A little procession was coming in sight; they bore one body on their shoulders; as they drew near, the sound of heavy boots fell like footsteps on their hearts.

"It is our mother," said Frank, who had been all day by the side of the river. "Look!"

He removed the covering from her face, and there she lay, the last heroic purpose written there, the eyes closed, the attitude one of perfect rest.

"Let us give thanks!" said Cyril Heath.

They knelt around her, but he could not master his voice, and it failed him; Frank tried, and broke down. Then a woman's gentle, calm tones were heard; gentle and calm, but strong and victorious; they almost saw the gates of heaven opened, and the triumphant entrance of a glad and glorified spirit into the presence of Christ.

Laura's tears came now in floods; as they rose from their knees she threw her arms around Belle, and said:

"You are on the wing; we shall lose you next!"

"You are mistaken," Belle said, quietly.

"Poor Margaret!" sighed Laura. "What a short, eventful career!"

"I do not feel sure that Margaret is not living," said Belle. "Mamma was so ripe for heaven that it seemed natural to think of her as being called home without a moment's preparation.

She desired to die suddenly; I have heard her say so, repeatedly. But dear Margaret was full of vitality and very human, and while I think she was nobly 'planned,' I also think the plan was not fully carried out."

"She was one to suffer intensely."

"Yes, and to enjoy intensely."

"But if she is alive, where is she? Why don't we hear from her?"

"I do not know, but God does. I pray for her; and I never knew Him to let me pray for the dead. Again and again I have been restrained from praying for those for whom I was in the habit of praying daily. It was so in the case of Maud. Just before the telegram came, announcing her death, I prayed for all the rest of you, but when it came to her turn I was speechless."

"Dear little Maud! Now she and mamma are together again."

This conversation took place amid many interruptions, while the two sisters prepared their mother's form for the grave with their own hands. She had often alluded to the event of her death, and expressed herself as very weak on the point of being handled by strangers. They nerved themselves, therefore, to render all the last services unaided.

Some one tapped at the door. Laura opened it, and a weeping figure tottered in.

It was old Mary, bent with grief. No one had thought to send her a dispatch, and she was not in the habit of reading the papers. She had heard the disaster spoken of at market, and come away in her working-dress, just as she was, her basket of provisions in her hand.

When her first wild burst of grief was over, Mary said:

"Sure she's got her wish, and died sudden. She was always ready to go, and now she's gone. Often's the time I've heard her talk about dying, and I mind a time when she thought she was going, and there was a light in her eye, and 'What d'ye think of that?' says she. I declare, it was just as she looked when she says to me, 'Mary, I'm going to be married, and what d'ye think of that?' says she. Well, I bursted right out, and says I, 'We won't be long separated,' says I, 'for I've got the brown creeturs, awful,' says I, 'and all I'll ask is to live to nurse you, and lay ye out, and then there won't be no more need o' me in this world,' and the Lord'll say, 'Old Mary, ye'r a poor, ignorant creetur, and you ain't to be trusted without your mistress, and I may as well let you in when I open the gate for her.'"

Indeed, the shattered figure looked as if this blow would be too much for it, as it soon proved to be.

"God has taken her away without pain," said Belle, "and in great mercy. It was quite right in you to come as soon as you heard the news."

"Ye'll let me do her hair with me own hands, Miss Belle," said old Mary. "She always liked me to do her hair. There, now, ain't she a picture?"

She did, indeed, look very beautiful, like one sweetly asleep, not dead. Belle went out to call Frank to see her. He was startled. "Is it not possible that she is living?" he asked.

"Why, Frank! After two days in the water?"

"But she is so like herself, Laura. Harry is very restless; he has asked for you several times."

"I had forgotten there was any Harry!" she said, and moved slowly away.

Harry had slept most of the time during the two days, but was now awake and able to tell his wife all about the fire, and with what difficulty he made his way back to her mother and Margaret. How his arm was broken he did not know, but it was in the struggle to reach them. When he described the moment when they both dropped away from him, she apprehended the whole situation at once, and was down on her knees at his side in a moment.

"And I reproached you!" she cried. "Harry, can you ever forgive me?"

"I knew you would come out all right, at last," he said.

"I did not know you tried to save them, with one arm disabled," she said, very humbly. "Forgive me, Harry."

"There is nothing to forgive, dearie. But there is a great deal I wish I could forget. It was an awful moment when I found I must let one go; but, oh, Laura! when both went! I wonder I did not drop dead."

"You did, nearly, poor boy. But tell me how it was they both dropped?"

"Oh, I was such a fool! Knowing what characters they were, I ought to have known that when I said one must loose her hold, each would resolve to be that one. Margaret was grasping my disabled arm with all her strength, when I spoke; she actually threw it from her, then, as one *disdaining* to purchase her life by another's; your mother's last movement was different: she clasped my hand, kissed me, then dropped it gently, or to express it more truly, *laid* it down, as she would something forever done with; the action symbolized final quiet parting with life. You can't wonder that that awful moment deprived me of my senses."

Some one knocked; it proved to be Frank.

"There is a possibility, a bare possibility, that Margaret is living. There is a rumor that a young woman floated down the river clinging to a board, and was picked up by a fisherman."

"But if it were Margaret she would have sent us some message."

"So it would seem. Still, Cyril is going to see. Belle is very hopeful about it."

"In religion Belle is an enthusiast," was the reply. "Frank, mamma sacrificed her life to Margaret, and Margaret sacrificed hers to mamma. They both had high notions on such points, and I can easily imagine mamma as dying for almost any one she dearly loved; but I did not believe Margaret had such heroism. They died *sublimely!* Better such death than a thousand narrow, selfish lives!"

"Yes, yes, indeed. Shall you be able to leave Harry to go with us tomorrow?"

"Yes; I must. George Van Zandt will stay with him. Poor Harry! I have been so unjust to him! Think of his trying to save mamma and Margaret, with one arm broken!"

"Harry is a noble fellow. There goes Cyril. And Belle with him, I declare! I must see to that."

He ran down and overtook them.

"I looked for you everywhere," she said, "and finally left a message for you. If this proves to be Margaret she is in a disabled condition, or she would have sent a message. She knows how careful we are never to leave each other in needless suspense. So I am going to see."

"Do you think she ought to go, Cyril?"

"Certainly. Let her put on her mother's mantle as soon as she likes. I agree with her that we shall find Margaret, and find her disabled."

Very early the next morning Frank received this dispatch:

"Margaret is living, but insensible."

"Ah, what different news this would be if mamma were alive to hear it!" said Laura. "What a tantalizing telegram! They do not say whether her case is alarming or not."

A little later in the day came another dispatch:

"Cyril will join you at Greylock. I cannot leave Margaret.
                                              BELLA HEATH."

"Belle not at mamma's funeral!" cried Laura, in dismay. "How dreadful! Poor Belle! But she is right; and yet, why could not I go to Margaret and release her? Oh, it would not do to leave Harry. We need another sister."

"Let me go," said Fred's wife. "Belle ought to be at the funeral, and she must."

"Do, Hatty. If Margaret is insensible it cannot matter who takes care of her, if it is only one of the family."

There was no time to lose, and Fred and Hatty hurried off. Fred had only time to land, find the fisherman's cottage where Margaret lay, and almost force Belle away, leaving his wife in her place.

"It was very, very kind in Hatty," Belle said, as the steamer pushed off. "I will relieve her as soon as possible. How often it happens that the tide of grief is partially stayed by a rush of care. I have been so absorbed in Margaret that I have hardly had time to think of myself."

"Can she be made comfortable in that little cottage?"

"They are very kind people who live there; and then as to comfort, she would not know if she was in a palace. The physician who attends her says the brain has received a severe shock and is very doubtful as to what the result will be. But she has a strong constitution, and I think she will live."

"And where?"

Belle turned upon him a look full of astonishment.

"I had not thought of that," she said. "Why, she would come to me, I suppose."

"It would be a great change for her, and interrupt her studies, and put miles between her and any studio," said Fred.

"Yes. It will be time enough to think of that when she recovers."

CHAPTER 26

The funeral was over, and Frank and his brothers examined their mother's papers, to learn, if possible, her last wishes. Everything was in as perfect order as if she had known she was going forth to die. She wished Margaret to remain at Greylock, and that whichever of the family could most conveniently do so, would reside there with her, and keep up the place as of old, until such time as any striking event in the family should make some other plan more desirable.

Nothing, however, could be done at present. Old Mary was left in charge, and the family scattered, gradually, away to their homes. Belle was obliged to go home, on account of her children, and Hatty wanted to go to hers.

"Why couldn't Margaret be brought to me?" asked Laura. "I must be at home, for poor Harry's sake, and Hatty ought to return with Fred. Could we not charter a small steamer, and transport her without danger? What a pity Harry is laid up! He knows every craft on the river."

Frank took the matter in hand. Margaret was their sacred trust now, and must be cared for exactly as if their mother were living. A small steamer was procured, the transportation safely effected, and Laura gave up all other interests in the care of her two patients. In a few days Harry was able to move about the house, and the first time he left his room it was to accompany the physician to Margaret's. She was lying quietly until their entrance, when she aroused, with a more intelligent aspect than she had worn since the disaster. Harry leaned over her and took her hand; she spurned his clasp instantly, with the decided words:

"Not aunty!"

"That is the way she acts to every one who takes her hand," said Laura. "I don't know what it means."

"It means," said Harry, "that she is living over again that awful moment when I asked which should loose her hold on me, herself or mother. It was with precisely that manner that she spurned me, as it were."

"We must avoid taking her hand, if that is the case; and I do not doubt that it is," said the doctor. "What nobility of character she has shown! I never met with so interesting a case. But it is obscure. I should be glad to call in some more experienced man to my aid. Have I your permission to do so?"

"Certainly," said Harry. "Call half a dozen, if necessary. This young lady, to all intents and purposes, gave up a life full of promise to save our mother's; we owe her every tender care, and mean to give it."

"I think she must also have two attendants, so as never to be left alone a moment."

Laura looked at him inquiringly.

"As a precaution," he replied. "There is no knowing what the next phase of the disease may be. She might attempt to injure herself. I should like this pair of scissors removed from the room," he added, taking up a pair that lay within reach.

"How strange and dreadful it all is," said Laura. "If you could have seen her in her days of health, when she never wasted a minute, and contrast it with this listlessness and idleness! O, it all seems so hard! We had been such a happy family; and now everything is changed."

The doctor was silent; he was young and did not know what to say.

After a few moments he said, just touching Margaret's hair:

"I am sorry to say that this must come off."

"She would not care," said Laura. "A more unworldly girl never lived. I believe I was prouder of her than she was of herself."

"I will go to the city this afternoon," said the doctor, "and try to bring one or two of our most eminent men to spend the night; they ought to see our patient's condition at the extremes of the day. Mrs. Worcester, may I trouble you to adjust the thermometer under the arm, as you did yesterday?"

Laura arranged the instrument, and they watched the result in silence. Harry accompanied the doctor downstairs.

"What was the temperature?" he asked.

"100½," was the reply.

"Do you consider that favorable?"

"Yes. I will see the young lady again tonight."

The tramp of four men entering her room together did not arouse Margaret. She lay in an attitude of great exhaustion as the three physicians, accompanied by Harry, came in, and was, evidently, unconscious of their presence.

"I should like to arouse her if it could be done through some pleasant channel. Had she any favorite pursuits?"

"Yes," said Laura, "she painted beautifully, and was full of enthusiasm about it."

"Speak of it, if you please."

"Margaret," said Laura, coaxingly, "you haven't painted at all today. And you paint so beautifully. You'll paint something for me, won't you?"

There was no answer.

"Margaret, dear, you tried to save mamma's life. That was very noble in you. We all thank you so much."

No response.

"Perhaps," very slowly and distinctly, "you think you are lying dead at the bottom of the river, and that God has forgotten your poor soul. But you are not drowned, darling. He could not take you to heaven, because you are alive. Did you fancy, perhaps, that He did not love you, and just left you? Why, He loves you dearly!"

The bewildered brain was reached at last. Like one suddenly awaking from sleep, Margaret looked around upon the group gathered about her. Laura had touched the spring few hands could have reached. It was not the shock of believing herself drowned that had dethroned her reason; it was the horror of being dead and finding her religion a fable. At a signal from the eldest physician all stole quietly away, with the exception of Laura.

Leaning over his patient, he said in kind, fatherly tones:

"You had begun to think there wasn't any God. But there is one. He is here, now. Everything you have ever believed about Him is true. And as it is getting dark, I would say, 'Now I lay me,' and go right to sleep, if I were you."

She looked at him, devouring every word; then, as he gently withdrew out of sight, and Laura did the same, Margaret joined her hands, repeated the prayer, and fell into a sweet, natural sleep.

When the venerable physician rejoined the younger ones, they gathered about him with great reverence.

"I should never have dared to try such an experiment," said one.

"Nor I," said another.

The old man smiled. "I took counsel of One who never errs," he said. "I commend Him to you in all obscure cases. The whole history of my success in my profession lies in this word of Scripture: 'The secret of the Lord is with them that fear Him.'[1] Gentlemen, I think we may return to the city tonight."

"I trust, sir, you will do us the favor to remain, if the others feel inclined to go," said Harry. "It would be a great comfort to my wife, who has been under a great strain. We have long desired to make your acquaintance, and our pure, highland air ought to refresh you."

"I shall have to be off bright and early in the morning, then," was the reply.

The three younger men departed, after a substantial country

1 Psalm 25:14.

supper; and as Margaret continued to sleep, only rousing enough to take nourishment, Harry and Laura had Dr. X. all to themselves. They almost sat at his feet, as he told of case after case, that to him, as a man, was hopeless, which yielded to Divine inspiration when that was resorted to.

"Some laugh at the old man," he continued, "and ask why I study my cases at all, and do not give them all over to Providence. My answer is this: As a man endowed with genius has to toil for success, so a soul endowed with faith is obliged to use all earthly means available to an end; God gives no premium to the idler. As long as I live I hope to dig deep into treasures of wisdom and knowledge; but I expect, also, to put every case that baffles human wisdom right into the Divine hand."

He was a genial old man, and the evening spent with him was something Harry and Laura remembered all their lives. He was up in the morning long before they were, and captivated the children by a joyous frolic with them. This was no small refreshment after so many days of sad faces. He went into see Margaret just before he left. All the soul had come back into her face, but she was still too feeble to speak. She had a wistful look in her bright eyes, but not an anxious one.

"Keep the knowledge of Mrs. Grey's death from her as long as possible," he said to Laura, as he took leave. "Wear a white dress when you go to her room, and assume a cheerful look. Of course, your own physician must watch her with constant care."

Laura had great self-control, and was able to appear as usual when in Margaret's presence. And in a week or two her recovery became very rapid. Now the question was how to break the news to her. Strangely enough she had not asked for Mrs. Grey, or expressed surprise at not seeing her.

"How soon do you think you shall be able to go home?" Laura asked one day.

"I don't know; are you tired of me?"

"No; but when you go we are all going too, and we ought to get away before cold weather."

"That reminds me," said Margaret, starting, "of Mabel's portrait. Did I ever finish it?"

"Not that I know of."

"I ought to go home and finish it. Laura, why didn't aunty come when I did? We were to come together; why didn't we?"

"You forget things, dear. You have been very ill, you know."

"Yes; I suppose she has gone back to Greylock. But why doesn't she write to me? Perhaps I was cross to her when I was sick, and weaned her from me. Was I, Laura?"

"No, indeed."

"I will write to her and tell her how fast I am getting well; then I shall certainly get a letter. Don't you think so?"

Laura was never so tempted to tell a lie. As it was, she answered as carelessly as she could, "It is a long time since I had a letter from her. Are you glad that we are all going to live at Greylock?" asked Laura.

"Oh, are you going there to *live?* Going to leave this beautiful house? Why, Laura!"

"Mamma wished one of her children to go, and it was most convenient for us; in fact, we are the only ones who could."

"It doesn't seem like aunty to want you to leave this house, just as you are so nicely settled in it. Not an atom like her. Something is going wrong; I am sure there is. Has she gone crazy?"

"No, no. Don't worry about it. We are perfectly satisfied to go."

"Doesn't she like this house? Is that the reason?"

"No, that's not the reason. How could she dislike it when she never saw it. Margaret, how you do tease one."

"Do I?" asked Margaret, very humbly. "I don't mean to tease. Only I am puzzled."

"People always are after such illness as yours."

Margaret was silent, and lay back in her chair, to think.

It was going to be pleasant to have Harry and Laura at Greylock. The more she saw of them the more she liked them. Then there were the children. By the way, where were the children.

"Why, Laura," she said reproachfully, "I haven't seen the children since I came."

"You'll see enough of them at Greylock."

"Oh, but I want to see the dear little things now. Bring them to me; do."

Laura went to the nursery, took off the children's black sashes, charged them to say nothing about grandmamma, and led them in. The moment Margaret's eye fell upon their truthful little faces, she looked at them searchingly, and with a startled air that alarmed Laura.

"Harry, who is dead?" she asked.

"Mamma told me not to tell," said the boy, bursting into tears.

"His face has told me, Laura," said Margaret, faintly. "I see it all now. I made Harry save me, and let her drown!"

"It is not true; you did *not* let her drown! You tried to die in order to save her. We all admire and love you for it; we will all do anything and everything for you. Only don't look so; for mercy's sake, don't look as if you were dying. Run, children, and call nurse, and do you stay in the nursery. You've done mischief enough for one day. Margaret, won't you speak to me?"

"She's only fainted, ma'am," said the nurse, a middle-aged, experienced woman. "No fear of her dying. Just help me lay her down flat on her back, and sprinkle her face with water. Or, if you please, a little hartshorn."[1]

Laura had had little to do with sickness, and was now so frightened that she could not remember whether the hartshorn should be diluted or not. She hastily mixed it, half and half, and the nurse poured it down Margaret's throat. It had the effect of bringing her to life again instantly; and there came a time when she and Laura could both laugh at the blunder.

Such is our existence here upon earth. Our hearts break and they are healed. We weep and we smile. We fail, and are disappointed,

1 Hartshorn—the horn of the hart or male deer. The scrapings or raspings of this horn are medicinal.

and we try once more. Nothing had befallen Margaret that has not befallen thousands. Her fate might have been infinitely worse than it was. She might have been left friendless and homeless. But here she was surrounded by loving hearts; her home was secured to her; all her plans of life were to be carried out; had she any right to mourn? Indeed she had. She had lost one of the most magnanimous friends ever given to mortal woman; she had lost the tenderest heart that was beating upon earth for her; she had lost the inspiration of a holy example. Did she well to mourn? Yes, yes. But she bore her grief nobly, and on the very day on which the dreadful truth was revealed to her she wrote in her "book of mercies:"

"I understand, now, how one can be glad to *suffer* God's will when too weak to *do* it. What a mercy!"

CHAPTER 27

Once more the doors of Greylock were opened wide, and children and grandchildren flocked together for the Christmas festival. But it was the last assemblage of the sort. It needed an immense power to call so many, and so widely-scattered households into one; and that power was gone. They loved each other dearly still, but she who held them united was gone; the sacrifice of time, and the thousand discomforts of winter-travel, never thought of during her life, now asserted their rights, and were heard. Now one family dropped off, now another, until at last Laura and her husband and children, with Margaret, held undisputed possession of the house. Yet the strong character of the mother lived still. In every one of the homes this was done, that left undone, to please her. On some of them, it is true, her influence was in the main unconscious, but with most of them she was the constant object of love, study, and imitation. They obeyed her as implicitly as when they were little children, for her laws were those of sound common sense, sanctified by the Word of God and by prayer. Belle wore the mantle of her piety, and her judgment was consulted by them all, in every domestic emergency. Laura went on having Pugs and Trots, whom she never seemed to "manage" at all, but who were delightful creatures; bright, wide-awake, spirited, but in all other points original and dissimilar. She always said she destroyed the pattern by which each child was made, that no other might be made like it, and that if they all had dared to have blue, or all black eyes, she would have put some of them out in order to have variety in the house. But it was enough to her to be a mother, so, though she had one of her quaint babies at all sorts of irregular times, she contrived to bring forth books as well, while developing more and more, not into a second Mrs. Grey, but into a character as pronounced, and as formed to influence her day and generation.

Gabrielle developed very rapidly. At seventeen, she was where many girls are at twenty-five. Her mother thankfully dropped the household reins the moment she saw her ready to take them up, and with grandmamma for her model, she made a well-ordered home for them all.

As to Margaret, there were so many sides to her character that it would be impossible to paint close enough to nature to depict her, without producing an exaggeration. Very few ever did her justice, owing to a modesty of the most deep-seated character. She never did or said anything in order to shine, but when admirers pressed upon her, shrank back, and back, and back, till they wearied of the pursuit and gave her up as a paradox beyond their comprehension. No matter what she acquired or how famous she became, she never seemed to know it, and a little child could always lead her. She knelt to those she loved, even when they were her inferiors; they were not many, but they were a happy few. As Mrs. Grey had predicted, more than one brilliant career lay open to her, but she was too truly a woman, too steadfastly and deeply religious to venture upon either. To follow in the footsteps of that venerated and beloved one, was ambition enough for her; to serve God as she had served Him, to lend herself to every human soul that needed her, as she had done; this was her choice. The humble pathway was little heeded by a world that, struggling for the honors of life, cannot conceive of their being deliberately put by. But it was watched by the eye of God, and how often He met her upon and blessed her in it, is known only to Him.

23490287R00143

Made in the USA
Columbia, SC